Jury Rig

Jury Rig

Korey Kaul

FIVE STAR
A part of Gale, Cengage Learning

Detroit • New York • San Francisco • New Haven, Conn • Waterville, Maine • London

GALE
CENGAGE Learning

Five Star Publishing, a part of Gale, Cengage Learning.

Set in 11 pt. Plantin.

LIBRARY OF CONGRESS CATALOGING-IN-PUBLICATION DATA

Kaul, Korey.
Jury rig / Korey Kaul. — 1st ed.
p. cm.
ISBN 978-1-4328-2586-7 (hardcover) — ISBN 1-4328-2586-0 (hardcover) 1. Jury—Fiction. I. Title.
PS3611.A854J87 2012
813'.6—dc23 2011047023

Published in 2012 in conjunction with Tekno Books and Ed Gorman.

Printed in Mexico
1 2 3 4 5 6 7 16 15 14 13 12

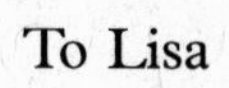
To Lisa

ACKNOWLEDGMENTS

Initially, I want to note that although I consulted several trial consultants in preparation of this book, as I'm sure they've come to expect from an attorney, their advice went largely unheeded. All errors, trial consulting or otherwise, are entirely mine.

My sincere thanks to Bret Dillingham, Ramona DeFelice Long, Laurie Martin-Frydman, Aimee Polson, and Dr. Amy Posey for their invaluable suggestions on the early drafts of this book. I would also like to thank my writing partners Lee Gerhard, Jeanette C. Lytle, and Mary Ann Stewart for their guidance and support. Special thanks to Deni Dietz for seeing something in this book early on and to my editor, Gordon Aalborg, for helping that something become a reality. It is possible this book would have never been published if not for Clay Stafford, the Killer Nashville Conference, and its support staff, and their continued support of new and not-so-new writers. Most of all, I want to thank my wife, Lisa, for her ideas, her humor, and her encouragement.

Chapter 1

People frequently come up to me and tell me how exciting a career in trial consulting must be. In reality, it is almost entirely the dull organization of paper and ideas.

Greene, F. (2003). *The Trial Consultant's Field Manual* (p. 3). New York: Pullman.

Fat, foul-tempered, and from the contorted facial expressions of the two jurors next to her, not without odor, Prospective Juror Eighteen was perfect. Kate Summerlin knew as soon as she saw that angry, stinky woman step into the jury box that the perfect juror had walked right into her life. As Eighteen settled into her chair, elbows taking command of the armrests on either side, she raised her left buttock almost imperceptibly. No juror, except horror-stricken Nineteen, at whom Eighteen had aimed the silent flatulence, saw the sly maneuver. All apparently smelled it. You did not have to be an expert on body language to read those expressions. Oh, yes, Eighteen was the perfect juror.

Kate scanned Eighteen's questionnaire. Thelma Wigginstaff. Fifty-seven years old. Caucasian. Toll booth operator. Kate, glancing over at the tortured faces in the jury box, hoped it was a single-person booth.

Kate wrote a quick note and showed it to the two men flanking her at the large table. Although the men were in their late thirties/early forties and wearing off-the-rack dark blue suits, it was clear which one of them was on trial for his life. The guy on her right had the hang-dog, sad-eyed look of someone whom life had kicked, hard and often. The guy on her left had the bulldog, hard-eyed look of someone who had sued life for kicking the guy on her right and taken life's house and its car, and made it write an apology note to be published in every newspaper in the state of Missouri.

"LEAVE EIGHTEEN ALONE," the note read. "SHE'S THE ONE."

Arnie Montoy, the bulldog, glanced at the note for a brief second and then resumed brushing dust particles off of his pants. The defendant looked at the note and immediately stared at the jury box, his head bobbing slightly as he counted jurors. Kate nudged him before he got to five and, startled into submission, he stared down at the blank table in front of him.

Judge Mervin Mays cleared his throat and the courtroom fell quiet. "Thank you for joining us today. I know you all have things you would rather be doing, but I assure you, we are all very grateful for your service. This case is the State of Missouri versus Richard Wrenshaw. Mr. Wrenshaw is charged with capital murder in the death of Harold Pike. The State intends to ask for the death penalty."

As the judge spoke those last words, Kate focused on the jurors. She was not looking for who reacted, as much as who did not react. Who, upon hearing he may have to sentence a man to death, did not bat an eye? Most of the jurors reacted like Ms. Wigginstaff: quick looks right and left and then back to the judge, a little paler than before. At least no one smiled. Kate had worked a trial in Alabama where half the jurors wanted to pull the switch themselves.

"Counselors, state your appearances."

At the other table, the County Attorney stood up. Her dark brown suit hung loosely off her shoulders and Kate thought she had lost some weight since the last time they had tangled. With a smile that looked as if it had not seen the outside of a courtroom in several years, she said, "I'm Johnson County Attorney Elisabeth Zuckerman and I'm here on behalf of the people of the State of Missourah."

Kate noticed an easy rural twang that had been conspicuously absent during Zuckerman's earlier arguments to the judge.

Pointing at a young man sitting at her table, Zuckerman said, "This is assistant County Attorney Ben Sherwood. He'll be trying this case with me."

Sherwood's hair was cut high and tight and he sat ramrod straight. In his eye, Kate saw an eager glint that said he would have no problem killing anyone in the courtroom, including the judge, if necessary to the pursuit of justice. Kate thought he might salute the jury. Instead, he gave a quick, military nod.

Arnie glanced over at Kate. Because Zuckerman had introduced Sherwood, he would now have to mention Kate. Arnie was not ashamed to have a trial consultant helping him, but he'd found that some people got nervous in front of one, like meeting a psychiatrist at a cocktail party.

Kate put a Post-It note on the table in front of Arnie. "SAY I'M HELPING OUT."

Arnie got up without glancing at the note. "My name is Arnold Montoy. It's my pleasure today to represent Rick Wrenshaw." When Rick raised his hand to wave at the jury pool, a young woman in the front row noticeably flinched. Rick quickly put his hand down. Arnie smiled at Rick and motioned over to Kate. "And this is Kate Summerlin. She'll be helping me out with the jury selection."

Before Judge Mays could begin the preliminary questions, the man next to Ms. Wigginstaff raised his hand. When he spoke, his voice had the hoarseness of someone who talked without breathing. "Judge, I need to step outside for a moment."

"Everyone be back here in fifteen minutes," Judge Mays ordered as he jumped out of his chair, grabbing the jacket handed him by the bailiff as he hurried out the door. The new anti-smoking laws had hit the judge especially hard.

Once the jury pool left, Kate scooted her chair back to form a little triangle with Arnie and Rick. An associate consultant in Kate's firm, Josepherta Harvnor, sat in the front row behind them and leaned forward to hear.

"So, you want the farter, huh?" Arnie asked.

"Hell, yeah," Kate said with a smile. Arnie had fully signed on to her "juror chaos" theory. At first, he had dismissed it. Kate couldn't help but wonder if he would have been more receptive to the idea had it come from a white-haired gentleman rather than a twenty-eight-year-old redhead. Trial consultants were mostly women, but many male attorneys still gave more credence to advice given by men. Eventually, Kate had worn him down.

"The other prospective jurors already hate her," Kate explained. "They'll be lucky if they can stand to be with her through the trial, let alone deliberations. Arnie, if you can get even one of them to vote for life, the killers on the jury won't be able get anyone to stay in the room long enough to argue about it. Chaos. We'll get a hung jury so fast, Mays won't even have time for a cigarette."

From behind, Jo chuckled and then stared down at her shoes. Kate looked over, having forgotten she was in the courtroom. "What do you think, Jo? Will she work?"

Jo glanced over at Arnie and then back at Kate, and nodded. Kate smiled. Any expression of an opinion was a nice step up for Jo. In her last two trials, Kate had brought her along to give her real trial experience. Most new consultants acted like a newborn puppy at trial, jumping around from attorney to attorney and yipping out ill-formed opinions at every chance. Jo faded into the background. Even her brown suit melded into the dark wood pews.

The break in court ended and the bailiff came in and announced, "All rise, the district court of Johnson County is now in session, the Honorable Mervin Mays presiding." Judge Mays climbed up to the bench, looking revived.

"Bring in the jurors," he called with the air of Caesar calling for more Christians.

As the first of the five groups of twenty filed in, Kate slid a note pad and pen over to Rick to allow him to take notes. Mays gave the jurors the standard welcome. After the bailiff swore them in, Mays nodded to the prosecutor to begin the questioning.

Zuckerman limped slowly around the podium as if she'd spent the last week laying tile. The walk, combined with her habit of hooking her thumbs into the belt loops on her slacks, had earned her the nickname "The Duke."

"We appreciate the sacrifice y'all are making here to come and do your patriotic duty as citizens," Zuckerman said. "Now, does anyone here know the defendant?"

A woman in the front row on the right, Karla Blaylock, tentatively raised her hand. Kate glanced over at Rick to see how he reacted. He squinted at the woman in confusion.

Zuckerman took a couple of steps to her right. "Ms. Blaylock, you know the defendant?"

"I guess I don't really know him. But I *know* him," Blaylock declared. Her eyes stayed riveted to Rick as she crossed her arms and sat back heavily in the chair.

The courtroom fell silent. Zuckerman recovered nicely. "I'm not sure I heard you correctly, you say you *do* know Rick Wrenshaw?"

Blaylock inched up to the front of her chair and shifted her gaze over to the prosecutor. "No, I've never met that one. But I know that kind of man. He looks just like my ex-husband, Percy."

Rick immediately grabbed his pencil and began to frantically write "Strike her!" in large block print on the pad in front of him. Kate placed her hand over his to stop the scribbling.

"But, of course, Mr. Wrenshaw isn't your ex-husband, is he?" Zuckerman asked.

"Oh, no," Blaylock said. "But he has that same look about him. Especially around the eyes." As she spoke the last words, she made several small circles with her pointer finger in Rick's direction. Everyone in the jury box turned as one to look at Rick's eyes, which guiltily darted back and forth between the prosecutor and Blaylock.

Zuckerman continued, "But you could still be fair and impartial to Mr. Wrenshaw, despite his resemblance to your ex, couldn't you?" Zuckerman's tone implied only a communist or a moron would answer no.

"I suppose. But after what that man put me through . . ." Blaylock said. Up came the finger. ". . . those eyes." *Circle, circle, circle.*

Kate poked Arnie under the table and he rose up out of his chair. "If we could approach the bench, your honor?" The judge nodded and Arnie and Zuckerman went up to the side of the judge's bench.

A few moments later, the judge said: "Ms. Blaylock, we appreciate your honesty here, but you may be better suited to another case. You are excused. Please see the jury clerk on the way out." Blaylock gave Rick a final dirty look before she slid out of the jury box and left the courtroom.

Zuckerman immediately started back in. "So, does anyone else know the defendant . . . or anyone who looks like the defendant?" Everyone laughed and Zuckerman used the newly found camaraderie to dig into the meat of her questioning.

She had a dogged, straightforward style. If she was not hooking her thumbs into her belt loops, she spoke with her elbows at her side, hands out in front of her, palms up. Kate taught her attorneys the same technique. It gave the jury a feeling of trust and welcoming.

Usually the prospective juror would only have to answer yes or no. In this heavily conservative county, most people favored the death penalty. Local prosecutors did not want to risk exposing an overeager juror.

When Zuckerman came to someone who waffled on whether they could follow the law, she would turn her palm over and pat at the air as she talked. At a subconscious level, the waffler would feel a shift from the welcoming Zuckerman to the officer of the State. Kate thought of it as a kinder, gentler Heil Hitler.

During the questioning, Kate passed notes to Arnie, with questions to ask or topics to follow up on. With some, like Wigginstaff, she did not want him to ask any questions lest the prospective juror say something that would cause Zuckerman to use a strike.

As Fourteen droned on about his relationship with Three (his second ex-wife married her ex-husband's brother), Kate felt a tap on her shoulder. She looked back and Jo handed her a note.

In very neat print it read, "MEET ME AT THE JUNIOR HIGH AT 5:30." Kate turned and looked at Jo, who jerked her thumb toward her left shoulder. In the back of the courtroom, a small, portly old man stared eagerly at Kate. His white hair and beard had a distinct Santa Claus look to it, although Kate noted he needed more belly before it would shake like a bowl full of jelly. Through his white beard he mouthed, "Meet me at the junior high."

"Excuse me, Miss Summerlin." The judge's voice boomed through the courtroom. Kate's head whipped around and she blushed, unable to stop herself. At trial, her goal was to be as invisible as possible. Having the judge call you out was not invisible. "Did you need to speak with that gentleman? Wait. Where'd he go?"

Kate looked back. The man was gone. When she turned toward the judge, he looked disappointed that he was not able to further chastise her. He motioned to Zuckerman to continue.

At four-thirty, Zuckerman finished and Kate felt comfortable that Wigginstaff had flown under the radar. The judge adjourned until Tuesday and hurried out of the courtroom. As they packed up their papers, Arnie turned to Kate. "Say, what was that thing with the judge?"

"I'm so sorry. I don't know. Jo passed me this note." She handed it to Arnie and turned to Jo. "Where'd you get the note?"

"He gave it to me and then pointed at you. He didn't say anything." Jo lowered her voice, although almost everyone had left the courtroom. "Are you going to meet him?"

"Yeah, right. I don't think so." Kate laughed. "I was scared to meet boys behind the junior high when I was *in* junior high. I may be in a little bit of a dating drought right now, but I'm not that lonely. Besides, this is Warrensburg—I don't even know where the junior high school is."

Chapter 2

The two men in the moonlit living room argued quietly. Dr. Walter Townsend stood naked at the crack of the door, peering out at them. With most of his life spent watching people react to unfamiliar situations, he would have bet his professional reputation these two yahoos were swimming in uncharted waters.

He glanced back at the curvy lump of coed sleeping on the bed. When he told this story to the boys at the club, he would describe feeling the courage he never knew he had welling up in his chest as he took any step to protect this gentle maiden from the invading brutes. In fact, had the window not been painted shut, he would be running down the street. Brittany was a resourceful girl. But, unable to leave, he was going to have to take control of the situation, less motivated by courage than by the fear of his live-in girlfriend cutting off his balls if she found out he'd been with another woman.

He stepped out into the living room and whispered loudly, "Excuse me, gentlemen." They turned toward him, wide-eyed. "Could we talk about this in the kitchen? My elderly mother is asleep and I don't want to disturb her." He walked toward the kitchen, motioning the yahoos to follow him.

"Dude, you're naked," the skinny yahoo said. "You sleep naked with your mom?"

Townsend slid behind the center island. "Yes, yes I do." The bigger yahoo glanced over at the other, who shrugged. Each was dressed in identical black jeans and black T-shirt, but the big one wore a white headband. The little one moved toward the door. Without being able to articulate why, Townsend sensed this was the one in charge and turned to stay facing him.

Townsend smiled to try and keep the mood light. "Now then, this is a little better. I think you'll find that I'll be very co-operative." Nothing in the house was worth his life. It was not even his stuff. Just like Greene to go out of town the one night his house gets robbed. And it was Townsend's luck to sneak in with a coed on the same night. "Take what you want. There's quite a bit of electronics in the back room. Very high-end."

"We're not here for stuff, pops," the small one sneered. He sounded much younger than Townsend had thought. Maybe early twenties. "We're here for you. Give me the 'cuffs."

Townsend felt his heart race. Here for him? Who had he pissed off this time? Angry brothers? New boyfriend and pal seeking to avenge a mistreated lover? Why would they handcuff him as opposed to merely pummeling him?

From behind, Townsend heard the big one grunt, then the crinkle of plastic and a soft curse. "Ugh. I can't get them out of the package."

"What?" the small one asked.

"It's this plastic. There's nowhere to tear it. I can't get them out." The voice quavered with frustration and fear, followed by a nervous laugh. "I can't get them out!" The voice leapt a half-octave higher.

The little one reached around and pulled a paring knife out of the butcher block. "Give 'em here."

"I couldn't get it open," the big one mumbled as if to himself.

Townsend saw an opportunity to engage the man. "You'd think they would give you a starter hole or something."

"Yes," the big yahoo repeated enthusiastically, "a starter hole. Or something."

"Shut up, T.J." The small one sliced open the package and

took out the handcuffs. "Turn around."

Townsend felt cold steel close on his wrist. Surprisingly, the small one was careful not to make them too tight. The big one, T.J., looked under the sink and pulled out a grocery sack, which he placed over Townsend's head.

"Where are your car keys?" an angry voice asked, probably the small one.

"I don't know," Townsend said. Technically that was a lie. He knew his keys were in his pants by the fireplace in the living room. He did not know where Greene's keys were, but figured they could be easily found. If something should happen, better it be to Greene's Camry than his BMW. "There's a bowl by the front door. They might be in there."

Footsteps padded off.

He felt a body ease up close to him and then T.J. whispered in his ear. "We're not going to hurt you. We just need to hold you for a while."

"What does that mean? You need to hold me?" That didn't sound like something a yahoo burglar would say.

The body moved away and then the footsteps returned accompanied by a jingle. "Found them. They were in the bedroom. Put these on." Clothes hit Townsend in the chest and fell to the floor.

"I'm still handcuffed," Townsend said. "I'm going to need some help."

A long silence was followed by disembodied voices. Finally, the little one said, "Why don't you, uh, you know. . . ."

The big one's voice shook. "I wouldn't touch that guy with your hands."

Townsend found himself getting annoyed. "Just unlock one of these. I can dress myself." The yahoos seemed relieved and unlocked one of the cuffs.

The little one spoke up as Townsend pulled on his pants.

"You know, I'd say ol' Mother Greene is remarkably well preserved, eh doc?"

So, they'd found Brittany. He could not hear her in the room, so they must have left her sleeping. These guys definitely weren't your run-of-the-mill hoodlums. Wait. Mother Greene? Saints alive, they thought he was Farley.

"Gentlemen," Townsend said from inside his sack, "I think there's been some misunderstanding. You want Farley Greene. I'm Walter Townsend."

There was a brief pause. Although his head was covered, Townsend knew the two were looking at each other for the answer.

After a moment, one said, "This is Farley Greene's house. We double-checked." He sounded defensive. "If you're not Greene, why are you in his house?"

Townsend hesitated. Even if it was only to criminals, he felt ashamed confessing he had snuck into his friend's house to bang a coed behind his girlfriend's back. "I'm house-sitting for him."

"Wait here." T.J. pulled the bag off of Townsend's head.

In a few minutes, the little one returned carrying a framed photograph. "Well, Mr. Townie or whatever, looks like there's pictures of you all over this house." He shoved forward a photo of Townsend and Greene flanking a large fish.

"That's me," he said, gesturing to the right of the photo with his chin. "That's Greene." He nodded his head vigorously to the left. "He'll be back tomorrow night." Townsend winced at his second betrayal, but swore to himself he would call the police and Greene would not be in danger. They put the bag back over his head.

"We were told to pick up some old guy named Greene at this house. You're here, you're old, and you're in the picture, so I guess you'll have to do."

One of them punched him hard in the stomach. Townsend doubled over and dropped to a knee. The small one whispered through the paper sack, "Don't fuck with us."

They walked into the garage and put him in the passenger seat of Greene's Camry. He heard whispering and then the driver's-side door opened and someone got in.

"No talking, okay?" T.J. said, more of a request than a demand. That was not a problem. Townsend was petrified. Inside the house, he'd figured he could give them everything they wanted and the worst that would happen was that Greene got robbed blind. But they hadn't robbed Greene. They hadn't bothered Brittany. They'd taken him. The worst that could happen was now considerably worse.

They drove for a long while before the car stopped and the driver got out. From the lack of turns or stops, Townsend guessed much of the drive had been on Interstate 70, meaning they had left Lawrence and were somewhere in Kansas City.

They walked a short distance on gravel and through a door. Townsend could tell they were inside, but felt a large expansiveness. When they took off the bag, he saw he was in an abandoned warehouse. A single chair sat in front of a table next to a cheap floor lamp. Shadowy figures lurked along the side of the room. After a few minutes of watching the figures remain totally still, Townsend guessed they were statues or mannequins of some sort. A large motor was running somewhere, blocking out any sound that may have slipped in from the outside.

When they stepped fully into the yellow light thrown off by the floor lamp, a pudgy man with white hair and a full white beard came out and stared at Townsend. He looked like a three-quarter-sized Santa Claus dressed in a purple sweat suit, although Townsend had never seen a picture of Santa with a Glock.

"Welcome, Dr. Greene. I'm sorry I can't make you more

comfortable." He motioned toward the table. Townsend now noticed two thick, tan straps nailed to the top of the table. "If you don't mind, Doctor?"

"There's been some sort of mistake. I'm not Farley Greene."

The fat man looked over at the boys. The small one stepped forward. "He's been saying that all night. But we went to the house you said. We saw mail with his name on it. He has pictures of himself all over the house."

The fat man jabbed Townsend in the back with the gun. "Look here, Mr. Mystery Man. Sure sounds like you're Greene. And I hope you are. Because I need Doctor Greene. But if you're not Greene, I don't need you. So, who are you?"

What the hell had Greene gotten himself into? Townsend needed some time to think and figure out what was going on. He bent down and put his hands in the straps. "My friends call me Farley."

Chapter 3

In considering how a particular juror will respond to evidence and, eventually, how they will vote in a case, a consultant must give primary consideration to the juror's family environment.

Greene, F. (2003). *The Trial Consultant's Field Manual* (p. 171). New York: Pullman.

"C'mon, Kate," Bob Summerlin yelled. "The Gildersons will get the good seats."

"Sorry, Dad," Kate cried as she ran past him toward the car. "I'll drive."

"Oh, no." Bob laughed, running after her. "I can't enjoy the good seats if I'm dead."

For Kate, as a child, autumn Saturdays in Lawrence, Kansas, meant football. And football meant drinking: drinking before the game with her father's friends from the Art History department, drinking during the game to distract from the awful play of the home team, and drinking afterward to drown their sorrows at another loss. Saturday afternoons were hard for the University of Kansas football fan. Not as hard, though, as Sunday mornings.

"Hah," Bob said triumphantly, just like he did every Saturday. "Gilderson slept in today." They walked up to their tailgating spot, a tall canopy set on the hill overlooking the stadium. Kick-off was still four hours away. Bob set up his chair in "the good spot," directly facing the tent soon to be occupied by the

Gamma Theta sorority.

Good old Gamma Theta, making girls feel insecure about their bodies since 1897. Every week her father yelled at her for being late, and every week they arrived at least an hour before anyone else. Bob used the "good seat" excuse, but Kate thought he set the time aside so they could talk. When her mother died, their relationship was more professor and student than father and eleven-year-old daughter. But even then, they had the football games. As the years passed, the weekly chats grounded her, through her teen years and—she had to admit—even now.

Bob fired up the generator and plugged in the space heater. "Now that we've taken care of the outside, time to warm up the inside."

Kate laughed at the same joke she had been laughing at for twenty years. Her dad pulled a bottle of Wild Turkey out of its brown paper bag as Kate set out two red plastic cups. He filled the cups half full and handed one to Kate.

"So, is Lloyd coming?" he asked.

Kate took a slug. "No, Lloyd's not going to be coming anymore."

Her father groaned. "Good old Lloyd? Did you scare him off?" he asked with a grin.

"Yeah," Kate said. "I think I scared off 'good old Lloyd' when I walked in on him and a Gamma Delta getting wild in his living room."

"A Gamma Delta?" Bob gasped.

"It may not have been a Gamma Delta. She may have been too young."

"Lloyd," Bob said with disgust. "I never trusted that guy. Can't trust someone that uses the same letter twice in his name."

"What?" Kate laughed. "Your name is Bob. It only took you three letters to use one twice."

"They're not together, though. Like Jimmy Hoffa. Look how

he turned out."

"We're Summerlins."

Bob shook his head. "Not the last name. It's the first name that counts."

"So I have to remove all the Jimmys and Billys and Lloyds from my already shallow dating pool?"

"And the Darrens. They're the worst. Look at *Bewitched.* That guy was nothing but a troublemaker." They both laughed. "I'm sorry, honey. Are you doing okay?"

"Yeah, I'm doing fine. Better to find out now than down the road, I guess. I'm trying to dive into this trial. Keep my mind busy for a week or so."

"Oh, yeah, your big trial. Let's hear it."

"Do you want me to start with the person or the crime?"

"How bad is the crime?"

"It's a death penalty case."

Bob took a sip. "Better start with the person."

"His name is Rick Wrenshaw. To understand Rick, you have to understand he's only about five foot one."

"Little Napoleon?"

"Something like that. But with him, it's even more. I guess he was tall for his age in grade school. He bullied the smaller kids. Rick stopped growing, but the smaller kids didn't. The bully became the bullied."

"Sounds like he got what he had coming to him."

"To a point, I suppose. But kids rarely stop at that point. He got into some trouble in high school and they kicked him out. With no high school diploma and not really big enough to do physical labor"—Kate thought for a moment—"he kind of drifted around."

Bob raised his hand and jabbed his pointer finger repeatedly at Kate. "You looked up and to the right. You just looked up and to the right." Kate leaned her head back. She'd been caught.

"He sold drugs. That's what you were thinking when you said 'drifted around.' "

Because of Kate, Bob was savvier than most Art History professors. Kate studied body movements and their psychological meanings. Early in her studies, she'd learned that when a person looked up and to the right, he was accessing the creative part of the brain—the lying part. If he looked up and to the left, he was accessing his memory. For years, Kate played gotcha with her frequently fibbing family. Eventually, they turned the tables on her.

Kate acknowledged him with her glass and drank. "Yes I did. And yes, he did. And he pimped a little. He got caught with some coke and spent three years in prison in Missouri. When he got out, he sobered up, kept clean, and stayed out of trouble for two years."

"Until . . ." Bob prodded.

"Rick lived next to Harold and Jenny Pike. The Pikes had two girls, nine and twelve."

Bob waved Kate off. "If he touched either of those girls, you can stop right now."

"No. The girls are fine. Well, maybe not fine, but he didn't hurt them. The mother had taken the twelve-year old to dance class and the nine-year old was at home with Harold. Rick says Harold had been drinking since early that morning. It was late June, and Rick was putting out mulch in his rose garden. Harold yelled something about Rick being a garden gnome."

"That didn't go over too well?"

"No, it didn't."

Roger and Sue Gilderson walked into the tent. "Damn you, Summerlin, you got the good seats," Roger said, ogling the two coeds stretching up to hang a Gamma Theta banner on their tent. Sue rolled her eyes and began unloading the food. Roger set up his chair directly between Bob and the Gamma tent.

"The least you can do is give us some of that watered-down cola." Years before, the KU administrators had lifted the ban on alcohol at tailgates, but the lingo from the prohibition days remained.

"So, what happened?" Bob asked Kate as he pulled out a couple more cups. He had a small smile on his lips, knowing Kate was about to shock the Gildersons. Kate understood her role.

"Rick shot him six times."

"Oh, my God." Sue spun around. "Is that one of yours, Kate?" She put her hands on her hips and frowned at Kate with a "what-am-I-going-to-do-with-you?" look.

"Kate's got a death penalty case up in Warrensburg," Bob said. Kate heard a tinge of pride in her father's voice.

Sue's hand went to her mouth and she gasped. "Is that the Urinator trial?"

"Urinator?" Bob and Roger said together.

Sue eyes widened. "That's what the paper is calling him. He commits crimes and then," her voice switched to a conspiratorial whisper, "he pees all over the crime scene. He's been doing it for years."

Kate took a large slug from her cup. "He only did it once before, actually."

Bob laughed. "Once before? How come you didn't include that little fact in your story?"

"I said he got kicked out of high school," she replied, staring at the bottom of her cup.

"That's why he got kicked out of school? For urinating on people? You said he got into a little trouble. A little trouble is fighting. A little trouble is spitting on the principal. That's a little trouble. Urinating on someone. That's something else entirely."

Kate blushed. "He never urinated directly on people. He put

it in jugs and then dumped it on the other kids' cars."

"Ewww," they said in unison.

"It was winter so the urine froze on the door handles."

"Ewww."

Roger rolled his eyes. "Well, as long as it wasn't directly on people."

Sue set up some lunchmeat and bread and then came over and sat down. "So, why did he kill that Pike fellow?"

Bob answered, "Wrenshaw's a little guy. Pike called him a gnome."

"He called him a name?"

"No. Wait. Yes, he called him a name. A gnome."

Sue shook her head. "That seems a little over the top."

"Everything was over the top of this guy. He's five-one," Bob said, slurring.

"No short jokes," Kate said, knowing it was hopeless.

"Kate's right," Roger said. "Any joke we tell would be dwarfed by the magnitude of his crime."

"C'mon guys."

Sue shook her head and drained the last of her cup. "I don't see how you can work with someone who is so—"

"Short on character?" Bob suggested.

"Beneath your dignity?" Roger said.

"—disgusting," Sue said, shooting Roger a dirty look.

Roger held up his glass when Sue went for a refill. "Yeah, it takes a pretty small person to kill over being called a name."

Kate leaned back in her chair. "Something about the whole case doesn't seem right to me. He's supposed to be in this murderous rage about being called a name, but he goes back into the house to get his gun. When he gets to Pike's house, he sends the girl over to a neighbor's to borrow some big trash bags for his yard. Then, after all that, he suddenly goes crazy, shoots Pike, and spreads the urine around. It seems like someone out of control and yet totally *in* control at the same time."

From the food table, Bob looked over his shoulder. "Doesn't that mean it was more likely to be premeditated?"

"Yes."

"And isn't that what the State has to prove to execute him?"

"Exactly," Kate said. "Who needs a refill?"

Chapter 4

"Excuse me," Townsend called to the shadow in the corner. Townsend sat in a chair in the middle of the large room with his hands strapped to the table. Although it was daytime, barely any light crept into the warehouse. The windows, high on the sides, had been painted black and covered. Only a few pin pricks of light on the edges gave a clue the night had passed. In the light from the small lamp beside him, he could make out dark walls about fifty feet from him in all four directions. They did not go all the way to the ceiling, stopping at about ten feet. The ceiling lay in the darkness, far above him.

The little fat man had left several hours earlier. From what Townsend had seen, the boys were acting out of fear rather than a belief in a common purpose. If he could assuage those fears, maybe they would let him go. But they would not talk to him.

"Excuse me, I wonder if I might ask a favor." The shadow shifted slightly but remained quiet. "Honestly, I wouldn't bother you, but I'm afraid I have a bit of a problem. I'm hoping you might be able to assist me."

The shadow stood up. A few minutes earlier, Townsend had thought he had seen the smaller one sneak out the back door. This one, T.J., seemed more sympathetic, or at least less aggressive. "We're not supposed to talk with you," he said.

"I certainly don't want to get you into any trouble," Townsend said. "Fortunately, you don't have to say a thing. You see, I've been sitting here with my hands strapped to this table.

Unfortunately, I happened to think about how awful it would be if I got an itch right in the middle of my back. Of course, as is always the case, my thinking of it caused it to happen. So now I sit here and the more I think about it, the more it itches. And the more it itches, the more I think about it. I think I'll go mad if I can't scratch my back."

The shadow stood and walked over to the outskirts of the lamp's light. "I can't take you out of those straps."

"That, of course, would have been wonderful. But actually, I was hoping you might scratch it for me." The shadow did not move. "Honestly, I wouldn't ask if it wasn't absolutely necessary."

After a moment, the shadow moved forward. In the light, Townsend got a good look at him. Early twenties. Overweight by a nutritionist's book, but pretty solid. Looked to be pretty good looking. Townsend figured he probably did well with the ladies.

Initially, Townsend had made up the back itch thing to start a conversation. But, as in his fake story, thinking about it caused it to happen and his back itched terribly. Now he was in genuine agony, and—worse—he kept hearing the young man's earlier remark back at the house: "I wouldn't touch that guy with your hands."

The boy walked over and vigorously scratched Townsend's back.

"Just a little bit higher, if you don't mind," Townsend grunted out. T.J. made several quick circles and Townsend sighed with pleasure.

"Good?" the boy asked, pulling his arm back.

"Yes. That was better than some sex I've had." Townsend smiled, but the boy turned and started back toward the corner.

"Say, just one more thing." The boy stopped, turned, and glowered at Townsend. "This isn't nearly as important as the back thing, but I'm curious. I thought I saw your cohort had two chicken legs tattooed on the back of his calves." A smile creased the young man's face. "I take it from your expression I am correct. What would cause someone to get a chicken leg tattoo?"

The boy looked behind him and then walked forward. "They're drumsticks. Randy . . ." The boy stopped and winced. "I guess you know his name now," he said. His shoulders sagged.

"It's all right, I knew it anyway. You're T.J., right?" T.J.'s eyes widened. "I heard it back at the house. You were telling me about the chicken legs."

T.J.'s smile returned. "Drumsticks. Randy's a drummer. Or at least he wants to be a drummer. He has trouble staying in bands. Anyway, he wanted to get a tattoo of two drumsticks on each leg, on the calf muscle. You know, like sticks drummers use." He held up two fists and pretended to play air drums.

"So, he hears about this Arab guy who does these cool tattoos, super cheap. The downside is he does it in his basement. But it's supposed to be real sanitary."

Townsend nodded. "Like an operating room, I'm sure."

"We get over to the guy's house and he doesn't speak any English. His roommate came down and translated. Randy told him he wants a pair of drumsticks on his calves. I guess something got lost in the translation because Randy ended up with a couple of chicken legs." T.J. chuckled. "Boy was he pissed. But these guys were some pretty bad dudes, so we bolted." He stood there smiling for a moment and then looked down at Townsend. "It's kind of a sore spot with Randy, so you may not want to mention it to him."

T.J. stood in front of Townsend as he told the story. Townsend tried to remember the verbal and physical tics Kate Summerlin had told him about. Generally, he found it hard to concentrate on what a woman was saying if he had not slept with her yet.

Kate was one of three associates at the firm he had not conquered. While she droned on about reading people's nonverbal skills, he had been imagining her in something soft and skimpy. Although Kate was a little overweight, she was overweight in the right places. But that did not help him figure out whether T.J. was as clueless as he seemed or if it was just an act.

"You said he has trouble staying in bands. Is that because of his temper?"

T.J. shook his head. "No, my brother's got no rhythm. I mean, he can't keep a beat to save his life. When he really gets going, man, you should see him. He looks like he's trying to put out a fire." T.J., eyes glancing up to the left, laughed at the memory. "Man, he's tried everything. Country. Metal. He stuck for a while playing triangle in this girl punk band, the Squirts. He probably played with them for a month. Even had a few gigs. Man, was he happy. He thought he had finally found his place in the rhythm section.

"Then the bassist's boyfriend told him they only liked him because he never hit the triangle on the beat. It was totally random. They thought it gave their sound an edge. He was so pissed." T.J. smiled.

Townsend smiled, too. He didn't know what was going to happen to him, but he wanted to get to know his captors and, more importantly, let them get to know him. Maybe it would be harder for them to kill him.

"Hey, what are you doing?" Randy walked out from the darkness. "He told us not to talk to the old man."

T.J. stood up. "We've got to tell him, Randy."

Townsend said nothing as Randy walked up to his brother, fists balled.

"No, we don't. Our job is to babysit and not talk to the old man."

"He has a right to know who he's dealing with."

The boys stood a foot apart, staring at each other. Townsend felt years of brotherly aggression surge up into the room. He knew if he did not say something, the boys would come to blows or walk away. Either way, they would stop talking to him.

"Who *am* I dealing with?" He ignored Randy for now, looking up T.J.

Randy put his hand out to T.J.'s chest. "Don't."

T.J. looked for a moment at his brother then down to Townsend. "Boris. He's the Devil."

Chapter 5

Ron Tittleton held his breath as he pressed his ear up against the door leading out of his office. Exhaling slowly, he heard nothing and walked back to his desk.

Three stacks of papers sat on the old mahogany partners' desk he'd inherited with the office. Cora Cole, whom he'd also inherited with the office, lurked somewhere on the other side of the door.

The mantle clock on the credenza chimed half past the hour. Four-thirty. On Saturdays Cora usually left by four. Before she left, she always came in and, under the pretense of asking if he needed her to stay late, give him excruciatingly detailed updates of her hillbilly clan's soap opera lives. He had not seen her since two.

Ron had lost track of time prepping for the Stiltson case and panicked when the clock chimed four o'clock, his own personal midnight. Turning to the window, he eyeballed the small ledge just outside. His office sat twenty-six floors above downtown Kansas City. Although he thought of himself as slender, he probably was still too big to inch his way over to Rosenbaum's office. He stood up to open the window and get a better look when the door opened. Cora walked in, carrying a stack of papers.

"Mr. Tonetti had the Stiltson depositions copied." She smiled at him and made a fourth pile on the desk. He smiled back at her and sat down, concentrating intently on the printout of a case that happened to be lying on his desk.

Do not look up, he thought. Cora would sit and talk for hours if he was not busy, but she respected his time when he was working. If he kept staring at this case, she would leave. If he looked up, he would have to talk to her.

Cora bore a situational and physical resemblance to his mother back in Montana. Both in their mid-fifties. Both short and frumpy. Both left alone and pregnant thirty-some years ago.

"Mr. Tittleton?" Cora asked. Ron kept his head down. It would only be for a few more minutes. "I'm afraid I'm going to have to take the next couple days off. I've lined up a temp."

He continued to stare down at the case and said, "That will be fine." If he did not say another word, she would walk out and not come back for two glorious days. Must. Not. Look. Up.

He looked up. He saw it in her eyes. She wanted him to ask. He had to ask.

"Is everything all right?" he asked, hoping against all odds she would say, "Oh, yes, I just need a couple of days."

"Oh, no," she said. "You know my brother Herman, the butcher?"

"Herman, sure," Ron said, perking up a bit. Herman the Butcher's annual hunting/drinking/stripper excursions into western Kansas were the few interesting, if most disturbing, stories Cora shared about her family. He always liked a good Herman story.

"He's got the finger cancer." Cora's shoulders slumped as her head listed over to the left.

"You mean skin cancer?" Ron asked, immediately regretting it.

"No, it's the finger cancer. It runs in our family."

This was the way it always happened. He tried not to get sucked into Cora's world. Then, he would hear a little and the stories became so bizarre he had to hear the whole thing.

"Finger cancer runs in your family?"

"Oh, yeah. My daddy had it and my Uncle Mike." Her face brightened a little. "They caught it early with Herman, though. He's probably just going to lose the two middle fingers on his right hand. It hasn't spread to the thumb yet. That's the real fear with the finger cancer."

Ron, at a loss for words, muttered, "That's great."

"Yeah, but Herman's real upset. Thirty-six years as a butcher and he never lost a finger. He was always real proud of that. He used to say, 'A butcher with all his fingers is a butcher who pays attention to details.' Then he would wiggle all his fingers to show he was a detail person." Cora wiggled the fingers on her right hand. "Now, he thinks everyone will think he's just another butcher who got careless and cut off his fingers." She pulled her middle and ring fingers down to her palm and wiggled the other two.

"We'd even talked about, when he retires in a couple of years, getting a couple of cakes shaped like hands. You know, with all the fingers." Up popped the middle and ring fingers. "But, I guess that's out now."

Ron let the image waft through his mind of Cora's family ceremoniously lopping off Herman's cake fingers. "You just take as much time as you need."

"Oh, I'll be back on Wednesday. I know we've got the Stiltson trial coming up. But I think Herman needs the family there after the surgery. He's going in tomorrow."

"Wish him good luck for me."

"That'll mean a lot to him." Cora nodded her head and closed the door as she walked out.

Ron breathed a sigh and leaned back in his chair. At five minutes, that was a short Cora story. The steering committee had assigned her to him as a joke when he joined the firm four years ago. After a week, they told him Cora had been the secretary for the attorney who had last occupied Ron's office and he could pick his own secretary. He picked Cora.

He could not deny her resemblance to his mother played a role in keeping her. His mother had only been fired from one job—a night cleaning person at a high-rise office building. But her face when she came home early—embarrassed, scared, and somehow still defiant—he never forgot it. He certainly did not want to see it again in Cora's jowly countenance.

Beyond mere sympathy, however, he found her to be a very competent secretary. Most importantly, no one bothered him. Junior associates looking to suck up and senior partners looking to dump projects continually wandered the halls. With Cora sitting out front telling long, inane stories to anyone who would listen, few of the vultures circled his patch of the office.

For Ron, the few minutes spent listening to these stories at the beginning and end of the day were a small price to pay. A full day's work without any interruption was priceless. Especially with the Stiltson case looming.

When the partners first handed him the case, Ron considered it an honor. Maynard Stiltson, founder of Stiltson Mustards, was one of the firm's oldest and most lucrative clients. He felt the Steering Committee must have had a lot of confidence in him to make him lead counsel on such a big case.

Tiffani Artona, another senior associate, set him straight.

"Man, I can't believe the way they screwed you on the mustard case," Artona told him one night over martinis. Seeing his puzzled look, she cackled. "What, you think it's a good thing?"

"I can win that," he said with more confidence than he actually felt. Maynard's daughter, Elsie, had taken a photograph of an undercover cop, Beckwith. When she put the photo in a show without getting permission, his cover got blown and he was shot. It was the lack of a written waiver that was the problem. But if the Steering Committee thought he could win, who was he to doubt them?

Artona stared at him for a minute and then threw her head back and laughed. "Tittleton, Christ, you're such a rube. Of course, you can win. You probably *should* win, which makes it even worse." She leaned forward. "Look, if you win, good for you. You get to shake Tonetti's hand and get a few attaboys. Then it's back to the grind. Nobody is going to remember who saved old man Stiltson's daughter a million bucks.

"But if you lose . . ." She shook her head. "You can be damn sure Daddy is going to remember the lawyer who didn't take care of his little girl. You know why?"

Ron sat there numbly. He felt as if a fog had lifted over a serene country pasture, revealing a minefield.

"Because the little princess is going to be bitching in his ear about how her attorney lost the case. Now, do you think Stiltson is going to give up his law firm to make his daughter happy? Hell no, they'll just get rid of the lousy attorney who lost the case. All risk and no reward, Ronnie boy."

Of course she was right. Why had he not seen it? Now he could not get out even if he wanted to. Not that he wanted to.

Nine months before, when he had first been assigned the case, he had met with Elsie Stiltson. He figured the mustard heiress probably spent more on shoes in a year than he spent on clothes his entire life. When she suggested they meet for lunch at a Davy's Diner in Westport, a bar scene area south of downtown Kansas City, his opinion began to change.

Davy's had been around since the fifties. In its early years, it had catered to the beatnik set and they had never really left. Little Miss Stiltson, if she was a regular at Davy's, would not have spent outrageous sums of money on shoes. Pot, maybe, but not shoes.

Ron had seen her picture in the company file. One nice thing about rich girl divas was they were usually pretty hot. Elsie did not disappoint. The file photo had come from the last Stiltson Family Christmas card. By standing Elsie next to her father, the photographer had captured the entirety of Elsie's long, lean frame. Ron had looked at the photo so he would be able to recognize her at the restaurant. His gaze had lingered below her face, but when he got around to looking up, he thought he saw a bit of melancholy in her eyes. Then again, it was a family portrait. He would probably have some melancholy too if he had to sit for two hours under hot lights with his family.

He saw her immediately when he walked into Davy's. He smiled to himself at her simple sundress and leather sandals. At least those prima donna divas were honest with themselves and the world about who they were and where they came from. What he had here was a wannabe-granola rich girl playing dress-up at being common folk. She undoubtedly considered herself part of the huddled masses yearning to be free. But at the first sign of trouble, like a lawsuit, she ran to Daddy.

"Elsie? I'm Ron Tittleton. Nice to meet you."

"Look," she said, glaring up at him, "I don't like lawyers and I don't like suits. I don't like two-faced bastards who screw people over to make a few extra dollars. You look at me and think I'm some spoiled little rich girl. Right? Well, wrong." Her face flushed with anger and she breathed heavily through her nose.

"The only reason that cop is suing me is because I'm a Stiltson. If I was a Jones or a Smith, he never would have bothered. But because my dad is rich, he thinks he can make a quick score. So, I figure if he wants to screw around with Daddy's girl, then he ought to have to deal with Daddy's lawyers."

Ron stood there, speechless.

"I've been out on my own since I was eighteen," she continued. "I've never asked for dime one from *Daddy.*" She whined out the last word. "So, if you think I'm some bleach blond idiot heiress who's going to do what you tell her and then give you a blowjob when you win the case, you have another think coming. We're going to do this my way or I'll cut off your balls and jam them down your throat. Got it?"

Ron, still standing, stared at her. She glared back up at him from the table. Conversation at the adjoining tables had died.

Turning, Ron walked out the diner door without offering a reply. He leaned against the brick wall and took a deep breath, forcing his mind to dissect the scene he'd just left. Something in Elsie's speech seemed off-kilter. Women who really talked like that were calm. Either you did what they said or you were gone. It was nothing to get worked up about.

Others, nice people trying to act tough, erupted. People like that did not usually make threats or, even more, follow through on those threats. They had to generate some anger just to get the words out.

He turned back around, walked inside and returned to the table. Elsie's face was still red, but confusion had crept in.

"Elsie? I'm Ron Tittleton." In a stage whisper, he added, "Notice I left off the 'nice to meet you.' "

He smiled at her and sat down.

"So, let's see if I understand. I get no blowjob if we win. And if we lose, you cut off my balls and feed them to me. Is that right? Because, and I'll have to check to make sure, I don't think that's our usual client contract." He smiled again and sat back.

The corners of Elsie's mouth crept up.

The waitress came over and slid two menus in front of them. "Hi, Elsie." She gave Ron the once over. "And friend. Welcome to Davy's. What can I get you to drink?"

"She needs some decaf. I need a scotch, but I guess I'll have to settle for a Diet Coke."

Without moving her head, the waitress slid her gaze over to Elsie. "You gonna let this asshole make you drink Jose's decaf?"

"I'll have my usual Diet Coke." Elsie continued to stare at Ron as the waitress walked away. "Okay, so maybe I was a little over the top."

"Yeah, just a smidge. How many times did you practice that in the mirror this morning?"

"Twice. What gave me away?"

"Most of your power bitch set aren't regulars at Davy's Diner." He nodded to the bumper stickers plastered on the wall above each booth. The two angled on the wall over their window read "TAKE THE HIGH ROAD—LEGALIZE HEMP" and "SAVE A BEAVER—KILL A GOLFER."

Elsie laughed. "Yeah, but I meant most of what I said, except the part about cutting off your balls."

"I suppose if I could choose one part for you not to mean, that would be it."

"Look, Dad thinks because he has money he can control everyone. He's what Grandma Portner called 'new money.' He grew up envying the rich. When he married Mom, suddenly he *was* rich and he thought everyone envied him. He expected me to be the debutante daughter, but I split and never looked back. So now some guy comes along and thinks he can make a quick buck just because of my name. If he wants to go up against the name, then he has to go up against *the name,* you know? If he had come to me like a decent person, we might have been able to work something out. Instead, he sues me."

The waitress came back with their drinks. They each ordered a cheeseburger. Elsie smiled when the waitress left. "I figured you to be a sushi eater."

"I like sushi, but not from Davy's Diner."

The smile slid off of her face. "I didn't want you to think I was a typical heiress bimbo."

"Not at all."

As he got to know her in meetings over the next few months, he learned she was not at all typical and certainly not a bimbo. With each meeting Ron became more impressed with her independence. And, having been pretty much on his own from an early age, he was not easily impressed.

His mother had been diagnosed with multiple sclerosis when he was seventeen. With his father long gone, Ron had to get a night job. Driving a forklift on the third shift, Sunday through Thursday, he supported his mother through his senior year in high school and through his time at Montana State University. She died two weeks before he graduated from law school.

He wanted to resent Elsie for having opportunities and shunning them. Instead, he admired her. To have gone through the rough times and not reached out showed a strength of character he knew he lacked. How tough must it have been for her to ask her father for help? If Ron lost this case, she would have to go to Daddy again, hat in hand, begging for the money to pay off the plaintiff. He could not allow that to happen.

CHAPTER 6

T.J. and Randy stood staring at Townsend, apparently waiting for his reaction to hearing that the Prince of Darkness was his captor. When Townsend did not immediately react, Randy began pacing in a wide circle.

At least now Townsend knew the old guy's name was Boris. He said to T.J., "Boris says he's *a* devil or *the* Devil?"

Randy shoved T.J. aside and bent down until he and Townsend were nose-to-nose.

"He is THE Devil. Like Lucifer. Like the Lord of Darkness. Master of Hell. Now do you understand why it might be a bad idea for us to do exactly what he told us *not* to do?" He glared over at T.J. "And he told us not to talk to you."

"Yes, yes, I understand completely."

Randy grunted and went back to pacing. T.J. kept his eyes on Townsend, who pretended not to notice.

"I certainly don't want to get you boys in any more trouble, but I'm kind of an agnostic when it comes to things like God and the Devil and everything. I don't really believe in it, but I'm not sure enough to chuck it all out. Do you think maybe Boris was claiming to be the Devil to scare you into working for him?"

"Yeah," T.J. said, "we thought of that. But he knew stuff and did stuff no regular person could have known or done."

"Like what, for example?"

Randy stopped pacing. After a moment, he threw up his

hands. "I guess if we're going to burn in hell for talking to this old guy, we might as well get our money's worth." He walked over and sat down in front of Townsend. "But I'll tell the story. You tell it wrong." T.J. nodded and sat down next to him.

"A couple of months ago, we were hanging around the playground at the elementary school near our house. It was late and the weed we had absolutely sucked. So, we're sitting in the swings, barely torched, and I was bumming. I was a drummer in this kick-ass band. But they kicked me out. We had a gig that night and I really wanted to be there. Not for the money, but I really get a charge out of making music, you know?"

Townsend nodded. "What was the name of the band?"

"The Four Givens."

"Christian rock?"

"Yeah. You believe that? Fucking Christians kicked me out. Does that sound Christian to you? They're all about forgiveness until you miss a couple of downbeats. Then you're out on your ass. And what are they now, the Three Givens?"

Townsend shrugged. "Doesn't have that same ring to it, does it?"

"Hell, no. Look, I know I'm not Tommy Lee or anything, but Blaine wasn't that good on the guitar." Randy shook his head. "Just because you memorized the whole damned New Testament doesn't mean you can play guitar. Do they kick him out? Hell, no. But I start to thinking, if I was a great drummer, then band politics wouldn't matter. They'd have to keep me. But how do you get to be great?"

At first Townsend thought it was a rhetorical question, but Randy kept looking at him. "Lessons?"

"Ha!" Randy said. "Those morons don't know shit. You can't teach rhythm. Either you have great rhythm or you don't. I'm not bad, but I'm not great. Then I remember this old black guy from Six Lonesome Feet."

Townsend leaned forward and cocked his head. "What's Six Lonesome Feet?"

"It's this blues band I was in," Randy said. "Have you heard of it?"

"No, I'm not much of a blues guy."

"So, I remember Lucius telling me about some old-time black guy who went out to a crossroads, just a regular guy. A year later he came back the greatest guitar player around. People said he had sold his soul to the Devil. So, I thought if it worked for him, it would work for me."

"That's how you met Boris, out at a crossroads?"

T.J. jumped in. "Eventually. At first, we didn't think we would have to drive out to the country. We spent a week or so sitting around the room, listening to Black Sabbath and getting high. Nobody came, though."

Randy picked up the story again. "That's when we decided to go out to the country. We drove around for a while out east of town and got lost. I figured if he was going to show, it would be at midnight.

"So, right when the radio clock turned to midnight, I look up and we're coming up on this intersection. All of a sudden this chill goes over me. I told T.J., 'I think this is it.' "

T.J. jumped in again. "Right when he says that, I look out the window and, swear to God, there's a cemetery right there."

Randy leaned forward. "A cemetery. Right there. At the crossroads."

Townsend found himself getting caught up in the boys' story. "Wasn't there a full moon last Saturday?"

"Yes," Randy said, pointing his finger repeatedly at Townsend. "Full moon. No clouds. There we are, out in the country next to this crazy old cemetery. I know it sounds stupid. That we're waiting for the Devil. But, if you were there, I mean, you would have to be a stone-cold nonbeliever to think anything else.

"We parked back from the intersection in case the Devil arrived in a big ball of fire. It was my mom's car, you know? We waited there, probably twenty minutes. Twenty minutes doesn't sound like a lot, but out there, that night, it was a long time.

"T.J. kept whining, saying we ought to leave," Randy continued. "I was about to give up when a pair of headlights come up over the hill. Straight toward us. This car comes barreling down the road. Then it stopped. Right in the middle of the crossroads."

From the back of the warehouse, they heard a door open and then slam shut.

"Crap," Randy said. The boys jumped up and jogged back to the corner.

From the darkness on the other side, Boris walked in. During the boys' story, Townsend's image of Boris had grown more and more menacing. In person, he was still a short, slightly overweight, albeit crazy, man. Townsend was disappointed.

In one hand, Boris held a gun. His other hand grasped a woman with a bag over her head.

Boris smiled at Townsend, "Dr. Greene, I've brought you a visitor." Boris pulled off the bag, revealing an angry Kate Summerlin.

Townsend hung his head and thought, *Oh, shit.*

Chapter 7

A client's requests are only unreasonable to the consultant with a lack of imagination.

Greene, F. (2003). *The Trial Consultant's Field Manual* (p. 45). New York: Pullman.

Kate had been in a good mood after a surprisingly successful performance by the Jayhawks. Historically dreadful, the team had been steadily improving over the last few years. Although now there was a reason to attend the games other than the drinking, she still appreciated the twenty-minute walk to her father's house to clear her head.

Having done a fair amount of civil litigation, Kate often found herself guessing how much fault a jury would assign in potential accidents. She figured her three beers before the game translated to fifty percent fault if she got into an accident, even if she was rear-ended.

Her dad, having driven back, was already in the house. "You coming in?" he called from the front door.

"No, I need to get down to the office and look at some jurors." She climbed into her lime green Volkswagen Bug and started the engine.

As she glanced in her rearview mirror before backing up, she saw the smiling face of an old man beaming back at her. Screaming, she turned to face him but moved too quickly. The seat belt lock caught and she was thrown back into her seat. As she struggled to undo the belt, she saw the man chuckling at her struggle and a little bit of rage replaced the terror.

"Do you need a hand?" he asked in a soft, sweet voice.

Kate's anger grew. "No, I don't need a God-damn hand." Finally unlocking the seat belt, she turned around, eyes blazing, and screamed, "I need to know what the hell you are doing in my car." He looked vaguely familiar, but Kate's mind, clouded by fear and anger, could not place him.

Neither the tone nor the volume of her voice seemed to have any effect on him. In the same soft voice he said, "I thought we might go for a drive. We have so much to talk about."

"What?" Kate gave a nervous laugh. "A drive? You're out of your mind. I'm not going anywhere with you."

"My, that's quite a shame. I guess it will just be me and Dr. Greene," he said, bringing a gun up from behind the seat. From the gun hand, he dropped a thin necklace with a gold eye attached to it.

When Greene and Townsend got their first retainers for the firm, they had gone to a local jeweler and had a pair of the necklaces made. They said the eye was to remind them of their place as watchers in the legal world. Kate had never seen either man without his. Whoever this man was, he definitely had Dr. Greene.

"Unfortunately, when men get together, it so often turns to violence, doesn't it?" He pursed his lips and looked to the roof of the car in a way that Kate suspected was intended to look thoughtful. It looked more he was sucking on a lemon drop. "Somehow, though, with a woman around, everyone stays on their best behavior." He lowered his gaze and stared right at Kate. "Are you sure you can't join us?"

She put her seat belt back on and drove away, as he directed.

The thought of Dr. Greene—frail, kind, Dr. Greene—held hostage by this lunatic both terrified and infuriated Kate. Dr.

Greene had become something of a mentor to her. When she had first started, he had taken her out on the road with him. The multimillion-dollar lawsuits would drag on for weeks. Each night Kate and Dr. Greene would meet for Manhattans and a dissection of the day's events. Kate would pepper him with questions.

He never raised his voice. He never got angry repeating the same trial truisms over and over. Despite his years of experience, he never treated Kate as anything other than an equal. She had grown to love him as a second father.

Boris directed Kate out to the highway and had her pull over when they reached Kansas City so he could drive the rest of the way. When they got out of the car to switch places, she got a good look at him for the first time. Even though she stood only about five foot five, she nearly looked him straight in the eye. He had maybe fifty pounds on her, but, factoring in his age and her anger, she thought she could take him. Except that would not help Dr. Greene.

"Here," Boris said, shoving a grocery sack at her. "Put this on."

"Are you kidding me?" Kate said. "I'm not putting any sack on my head."

Boris chuckled. "Really? This is where you draw the line? You drive me out to a deserted spot in the country. You agree to switch places with me so I can drive you God knows where. But, hey, a grocery sack on your head? No way." His top lip curled up into a creepy smile. "You're crazy."

Kate didn't say anything. Boris raised up his gun. "Look, if I wanted you dead, you'd be dead. If I wanted to rape you, I'd do it right here and I wouldn't need a bag on your head. Just put it on."

Kate put the sack over her head and Boris drove the rest of the way. The new Bug's clutch bothered him and he frequently ground the gears. After the third time, he gave a high-pitched, flirtatious school girl laugh. "Hee hee, I guess I haven't done this in quite a while." Kate's mood did not improve.

Finally, they stopped and the Bug died when Boris failed to push in the clutch. "We're here," he said. Even with the bag on her head, Kate knew he had that stupid smirk on his face.

They walked inside a building, and then moved through a long series of short hallways. "Dr. Greene, I've brought you a visitor." Boris took off the bag and Kate looked around quickly. She seemed to be in a dimly lit warehouse. Dr. Greene sat on a folding chair next to a lamp, his head hung down. But something was not right. Dr. Greene looked thinner and more pasty than usual. Then she saw his face. Townsend?

As much as Kate revered Dr. Greene, she equally loathed Townsend. Aside from being lazy and condescending, he viewed women as nothing more than sex toys and treated them accordingly. When Kate had first started, Townsend called her into his office ostensibly to ask her about her interest in body language cues. He walked around his desk and, facing her, lightly traced his finger from Kate's neck to the top of her cleavage. He smiled a smarmy smile and said, "I've always been willing to pay attention to body language." Kate had put a hand on each of his shoulders and drove her knee into his groin.

"Yeah? What does that nonverbal cue tell you?"

His response had been verbal, but nonintelligible.

Now, somehow, he had gotten Dr. Greene involved in one of his sicko escapades. Before she could lay into him, he yelled out to her. "Kate, I'm sorry you're involved in this. When Boris said he was bringing someone back, I hoped it would be Dr. Townsend. I know he could get me out of this."

Boris stepped forward. "Wait a minute. I never told you I was bringing someone back. And how do you know my name? What's going on here?"

Kate knew what was going on. The little guy, Boris, thought Townsend was Dr. Greene. Dr. Greene was not in trouble at all. It was that pig Townsend. But if Kate blew the whistle on him, maybe they would go after the real Dr. Greene. On the plus side, if she screwed up and they killed someone, Townsend was as good a choice as anyone. She would play it out until she figured out what was going on.

Kate looked at Boris and then back to Townsend. "What's going on, Dr. Greene? Are you all right?" Townsend smiled just a little. Kate thought she detected an honest look of gratitude. Or he could be picturing her naked. There was really no way of telling.

"Oh, just a night out with the boys," he said as his eyes moved to his right. Kate glanced over and saw two mismatched shadows standing in the background.

Boris stepped forward and laughed. "A night out with the boys? My good doctor, you do Ms. Summerlin a disservice. She's the reason we're all here, after all."

A quick look of betrayal flashed across Townsend's face and quickly vanished. Not quickly enough, though. Kate saw it. The guilt in her rose up, mitigated only by the confusion of how she had caused this to happen.

Boris stood watching the two. He was the only person in the room with a gun, but stood with his left hand clasped over the one with the gun in front of his genitals. The stance indicated a need to protect himself from something. He was scared and trying to hide it, but Kate *knew.*

"You're picking the Beckwith jury in a couple of weeks, yes?" he asked.

Kate blinked at him. Hearing the case name completely out of context threw her off. "Uh, Beckwith. Yeah, Beckwith v. Stiltson. Downtown. I think it's on November 21."

"Right, right," he stuttered, "November 21." He said the date with the awe and anticipation of a child saying Christmas. "You're going to throw the trial."

No one said anything for a moment. Up above a bat fluttered against a window, but no one appeared to notice. "What?" Kate said finally.

"The Beckwith trial," Boris replied. "You're going to rig the jury so the defendant wins."

Kate's confusion overrode her fear. "But I work for Beckwith, the plaintiff. My job is to make sure *he* wins." Which, she reflected, might be an extreme challenge, but was not beyond possibility.

Boris chuckled and rolled his eyes at Townsend with a "get-a-load-of-this-one" look. Townsend returned a "you're-a-freaking-lunatic" look, which Boris ignored.

"I know that," he explained to Kate with no small amount of exasperation. "That's why I chose you."

The two shadows in the back began to whisper to each other and Boris looked angrily over at them. They fell quiet.

"I can't throw a jury trial." Kate said. "I mean . . ." Her words trailed off.

Boris bared his teeth at her in a creepy smile. "Oh, I think you can."

"No, you don't understand. I mean I can't throw a *jury* trial. Especially not a civil one. They don't work that way!"

Townsend nodded his head. Despite being strapped to the table, he tried to cross his legs, a move he regularly made before addressing a confused student in his office. "She's right. She can't throw a trial. She—"

Boris exploded. "You can't?" he yelled. "*You can't?* Little Miss Goody-Two-Shoes is too good to throw a trial? You think this is a game? You think you can fuck with me?" The calm facade was gone. Pure rage burned in his eyes. Facial lines that in normal lighting would have been said to give it character, in the dim lighting, enhanced his demonic look.

"You *will* fix it so the defendant wins the Beckwith case. Or bad things will happen. Dr. Greene, put out your finger." Townsend looked up with a mixture of surprise and horror. The fat man opened a drawer on the other side of the table from Townsend and pulled out a large meat cleaver. "I said, put out a finger."

Townsend's fists involuntarily tightened on the table as Kate tried to break in. "Look, Mister, I'm not saying I can't *do* it . . ."

Boris interrupted her. "No, it's too late for that now. Obviously, you have to be made to understand I am very serious about what I want. A finger, Dr. Greene." He had restored the outer calmness. Under the surface, though, Kate could still sense the raging insanity.

Boris moved around to the side of the table. He spoke slowly and deliberately, "Dr. Greene, you will note your arms are already tied down. I am going to make my point one way or the other. If you do not give me a finger, I will take a hand. I think that would be very unfortunate, and frankly, out of proportion to the example I am trying to make. But you would leave me no choice. Now . . . a finger."

Kate watched the growth of Boris's insanity with a mixture of fear and guilt. He had said she was the reason they were here. If he cut off a finger, she would be at least thirty percent at fault.

Slowly, Townsend slid out the ring finger on his right hand. His eyes were closed. Boris looked over at Kate and she again saw the insanity dancing behind his eyes. He pointed the cleaver at her as he spoke. "You will throw the Beckwith trial." He spun toward Townsend, lifted up the cleaver and swung it down on the extended finger, lopping it off clean at the first knuckle. Townsend let out a low, guttural scream and pulled back at the restraints that bound him to the table. The severed finger jumped around the table as if it too was racked with pain.

Kate stood there, mouth open slightly, not understanding how this had happened in her world. Boris stared without expression as Townsend swayed back and forth and moaned. Kate took a step forward, but Townsend looked up at her, his eyes warning her to stay back.

Boris let the cleaver fall to his side. His lack of emotion during and after the act terrified Kate. He waved over at the shadows and the two guys came out. Blood covered the table and ran onto the floor. Thin streams squirted out of the small stump where Townsend's finger had been.

The boys tied a makeshift string tourniquet around the stump of the ring finger. They would not look at Kate and she sensed they were not as enthralled with the grotesque act as their boss obviously was. As the boys mopped up the blood on the table, Boris gave Kate the Devil's grin.

"So, Ms. Summerlin, do we have an understanding?"

Kate stared down at the table. Her mind tried to find the words. This was not real. It could not be real.

"Good," Boris said. He turned and walked off toward the darkness.

"No, wait," Kate said. "We do not have any kind of understanding. That's what I was trying to tell you." Boris turned, his grip tightening on the cleaver. Kate spoke quickly to prevent him from interrupting her. "I can't throw a jury trial. I don't have that power. I only get to strike three people out of the potential jurors. Whoever is left over, that's who serves. Plus, the attorneys make the strikes, I just recommend. Most of the time, they don't even listen to me."

The last bit was a lie. Although technically the attorneys submitted the strikes to the judge, in almost every case, and certainly with the attorneys in the Beckwith case, Kate would have the final say.

"That's a lie," Boris screamed at her. "I've watched you.

They do what you say."

Kate was taken aback. Had he been stalking her? "Sometimes, sure. But even then, if I kick off someone who is obviously for us, the attorney would veto it and strike who he wants."

"Oh, I'm sure you'll find a way."

Kate pushed her bangs back onto her forehead and held them there. "You don't understand, three strikes aren't enough to stack a jury. I can't do it."

"Perhaps another finger will convince you."

Townsend moaned and pulled back on the straps. He closed his eyes and spoke in a hoarse whisper. "She's right. And if even you could hand-pick the twelve people you think would decide the case against Beckwith, they still might not. The only way to guarantee Beckwith loses is if he doesn't show up for trial at all."

Kate drew back when she saw Boris's eyes look up to the right, accessing the creative part of his brain, undoubtedly hatching a plan to keep Beckwith from showing up to trial. Kate figured that would probably involve the cleaver. "Wait," she said, "maybe that's it. If we can get the parties to settle, then that's a win."

The old man's white, puffy eyebrows furrowed down. "Settle? That sounds like a tie."

"No, no," Kate replied. Excited about her new idea, she took a quick step toward Boris. Boris, startled, took a step back and pulled the cleaver up to his chest, as if he was pledging allegiance to the United States of Cleavers. Kate continued quickly. "Settlement can absolutely be a win. Especially in a case that's a guaranteed loser for the defense, like Beckwith."

When Kate said the case was a guaranteed loser, fear flashed across Boris's face. He quickly returned to his protective stance. Boris was definitely afraid of Stiltson losing the case.

"So, how do we get them to settle the case?" he asked.

"We'll do a mock trial. That's something I can rig so Beckwith loses." Kate realized the irony of the situation. She had often argued with Townsend over what she perceived as his lack of ethics. Now, here she was suggesting they throw a client under the bus to save his hide. But right now, Kate wanted to get out of the room with her and the rest of Townsend's fingers intact. "When Beckwith hears the jurors destroying his case and low-balling the numbers, he'll settle for way less than the case is worth. The defense will count that as a win."

Boris considered this for a moment and then nodded at her.

"Okay, we'll try that. But I want the boys to be there to watch you." Kate nodded. "And no cops. If they see any cops, they'll call me and it's so long Dr. Greene." Boris said the last line slowly and with a menacing tone.

Kate stared at him with a confused look on her face. "Beckwith is a cop. There are cops all over that case. I've got to talk to cops."

Boris stood there for a moment, looking embarrassed. "Okay, *those* cops. You can talk to *those* cops. But not about this. You tell them about this and it's so long Dr. Greene." He said the last line with the same cadence and tone as the first time.

She paused a moment. "How do I know that if Beckwith loses, you'll let Dr. Greene go?"

Boris, now back in full control, replied, "You don't." He smiled, his teeth a yellow spot in his snow-white beard.

Chapter 8

A jury has a personality, as sure as a person. The consultant must craft a jury whose personality best suits the particular case.

Greene, F. (2003). *The Trial Consultant's Field Manual* (p. 231). New York: Pullman.

Kate lay sprawled out in bed, snoring loudly, when a furry paw landed softly on her cheek. The claws did not come out. The paw did not move. It just sat there, resting on her cheek.

Slowly, Kate opened one eye and squinted at the overweight tabby purring on her pillow. Captain Fantabulous had been her 6:00 A.M. wake-up call every morning since she brought him home from the shelter four years earlier. Most Sundays she fed him and then collapsed back in bed for the last four hours of her night. Today, though, she needed to get up.

The Wrenshaw trial team had set a 9:00 A.M. meeting to discuss Friday's jury questioning. She had tried to tell them she needed to go to church, but they had laughed at her. She agreed, figuring she would not need to do any prep for the meeting. But with everything that had happened last night, Friday seemed like a month of Sundays before.

She ate a bowl of oatmeal and tried to forget the image of Townsend's finger bouncing around on the table. She would have to get cooking on the mock trial if she wanted to do it next Saturday, but today she had to concentrate on Rick.

When Kate arrived at Arnie's office in a suburban office park in west Lawrence, she saw Jo get out of her car. Even though nothing of substance would have happened before Kate got there, Jo still lacked the confidence to meet with clients by herself.

Inside the office, Arnie had spread out the questionnaires on a large table. "I really like Sha'niqua Gard," he said with a smile. His bright, white teeth contrasted with his thick, black mustache. Despite being in his mid-fifties, Arnie had a youthful vigor. That energy, combined with his confidence and classic Latin features, made him almost as attractive as he found himself to be. "When I was talking mercy, she was eating it up. We really connected."

Other than the actual jury selection itself, this was Kate's favorite part of the job: sitting with the attorney, debating how the individual characteristics of each juror affected the decision-making process.

"Sha'niqua? Are you kidding me?" Kate shot Arnie a dirty look and took a swig of coffee. Glancing over to see if Jo had caught Arnie's mistake, Kate saw Jo had moved to a small desk, her back facing Kate and Arnie, where she was organizing the questionnaires. It would be helpful later, but Kate knew the real reason she was over there was to avoid this conversation.

"What? You don't like Sha'niqua? She was a four, wasn't she?" Before the trial, Kate scored each juror based on answers to the Court's pretrial juror questionnaire. The scale ran from one, jurors morally opposed to the death penalty, to seven, jurors who would execute a jaywalker. "We need fours with this panel."

"You're right." Kate nodded. "She's a four. And she's professional, she's articulate, and she'd definitely be a leader in the jury room." Kate paused here to make Arnie wait for the *but.*

"But?" he demanded.

"Did you see her belt?"

Arnie snorted. "Her belt? No, I didn't. Not everyone can be as fashionable as you."

Kate hesitated, distracted and surprised that Arnie thought she was fashionable. She made a mental note of Friday's outfit, a black suit that had just moved to the front of her trial-clothing rotation.

Kate glanced up, trying to remember what shoes had completed the outfit, when from behind them, Jo said, "I saw it."

Arnie jumped, apparently having forgotten Jo was in the room. Reflexively, he asked, "What?"

"The belt," Jo replied. She looked nervously over at Kate for confirmation. Kate nodded. "She had notches on her belt."

Arnie's eyebrows shot up. "Notches?" He turned to look at Kate who was leaning back and smiling at him.

"Notches." Kate leaned back to bring Jo into the conversation. "Five cuts along the top of her belt."

Kate sat for a moment to let this new information sink in. Arnie pinched his fingers together rapidly across his thick, black moustache. "Huh. What does that mean?" He looked over at Jo. She shook her head and looked down at her feet.

"It means she's not as big on mercy as her head nods would suggest," Kate said.

"You can tell that just from notches?"

"Not just from the notches. I heard her talking in the bathroom." Early in Kate's career, Dr. Greene would send her into the women's restroom to sit in a stall and listen to prospective jurors' conversations. Through the years, Kate had been amazed at what she had learned. Women bared their souls in bathrooms.

"I heard a woman compliment Sha'niqua on her dress. I tried to peer through the slit to see who it was, but she was out of my line of sight. But she had that squeaky voice, you know."

"She Petty?" Arnie asked.

"Yeah," Kate replied. "She Petty." To help them remember the individual jurors, the trial team came up with nicknames. Prospective Juror Nine, Amy Silter, bore an unfortunate resemblance to rocker Tom Petty. "So She Petty says, 'What an interesting design on your belt.' And Sha'niqua goes, 'Oh, that's not a design. Those are my notches.' And I'm sitting there and it goes totally quiet. I know She Petty is dying to ask about the notches and Sha'niqua is dying to tell her, but they have no idea how to get it started. I thought I was going to have to come out of the stall and ask her myself.

"Finally, Sha'niqua says, 'I teach English over at the high school. Each notch is some hoodlum kid that messed with Sha'niqua and isn't in school anymore to mess with Sha'niqua. People are too soft on kids these days. But everyone at my school knows you don't mess with Sha'niqua.' " Kate looked at Jo and then back at Arnie. "So, I don't think we want to mess with Sha'niqua."

Laughing, Arnie conceded. "All right, all right. What about Harvey Vaughn? Or was there something about his shoes you found troubling?"

Kate laughed and looked over to share the moment with Jo. She had taken a chance and Kate wanted to let her know she had done well. But Jo had already turned back to the questionnaires, shoulders slumped over, hiding as usual in her own world.

Chapter 9

"I hope you like Thai," Boris said, walking out of the darkness with two plastic grocery store sacks. He pulled out two white Styrofoam containers and peered inside. "I've got Pad Thai with Pork and a Chicken Rice thing with curry. It really doesn't matter to me."

"I'll have the Pad Thai," Townsend said. Boris slid the box around to Townsend's side of the table. He reached across and unlatched one of the wrist straps. After retrieving two forks and some napkins from the office, he sat down in the chair opposite Townsend and began eating.

Townsend had been forcing himself to be friendly with Boris. On Saturday night, after Kate had left, Boris had tried to make conversation while he stitched up Townsend's finger.

"I'm not going to lie to you, Doc. This is going to hurt." Boris had given him some aspirin, but truthfulness appeared to be one of his few virtues. "So, how long have you been in the trial consulting field?"

Townsend gritted his teeth as Boris sewed a small piece of cloth onto one side of the wound. When the fire on his finger cooled, Townsend opened his eyes and saw Boris had put some sort of homemade salve on the wound. The pain returned when Boris sewed the cloth to the other side of the finger, closing it over the blunt end.

"Probably not the best time to talk, right now. I've got some

Lortab that should knock you out for tonight. We can talk tomorrow."

When Townsend woke up on Sunday, his finger hurt like hell, but it was not the fiery hot pain from the night before. Since the Lortab had worn off hours earlier, the salve must have worked. With the pain manageable, Townsend was able to think clearly. As much as he loathed and feared Boris, he figured he had to be nice to him. His best chance of getting out of this alive was having Boris and the boys think of him as a person and not an object strapped to the table.

Townsend had never been a hostage before and had guessed that the food would be mostly bread and water. Possibly some gruel. Surprisingly, he was much mistaken. Last night had been a hearty Chicken Tortilla soup. This morning had been Eggs Benedict and fresh fruit. Tonight quality Thai noodles. If the kidnapping lasted more than a week, he was going to have to go on a diet.

Even more strange, though, Boris insisted on dining with him. Every meal, he and Boris sat and made small talk. At first, Townsend struggled to put out of his mind that this man cut off his finger. Fortunately, Boris did most of the talking. Over breakfast Townsend learned Boris had been in the Forestry Service for years.

He talked longingly and lovingly of Yellowstone, the crown jewel posting for Forest Rangers. Although he professed a deep love of the outdoors and the National Park system, he could not help boasting about grifting even in the great outdoors.

"Have you heard of *Boy's Life* magazine?" Boris asked.

"Sure. It's a magazine for Boy Scouts."

"Right. In the back, they have a lot of ads for people selling things the little scouts want. I was sitting out at Yellowstone figuring Boy Scouts had to be the most gullible group on the planet. I mean, when you say someone is extra gullible, what do you call them?"

"A boy scout?" Townsend said, unsure.

"Exactly. So I take out this ad offering to plant a pine tree in remembrance of some poor departed loved one or pet for the low, low price of only fifty dollars."

Townsend nodded. "That sounds nice."

Boris laughed at him. "Were you a Boy Scout by chance? I never planted the trees. Every day, I'd look around and see new trees popping up everywhere. Sometimes I would take a walk and look at all those fifty-dollar bills popping up out of the ground."

"Wouldn't people come to see their trees?"

"Here's where I earned the money. When they first ordered a tree, I would send them out a photograph of the sapling, coordinates to somewhere in the park and a four-digit number. Only two families showed up to look at their tree. I looked at the coordinates and then took them out into the forest. After about ten minutes I would point to a tree."

"How would you know which tree?" Townsend asked.

"I would just point to one. Once, a kid asked me the same thing and I told him, 'That's why I'm a Ranger.' They ate it up. It was easy money."

Townsend was more interested in Boris's present than his past. Halfway through the Thai, he worked up the courage to ask him about the boys who'd captured him on Boris's orders. "You know, I thought I overheard one of the boys say something strange."

Boris bought a little time by shoving a forkful of rice into his mouth. After chewing, he warily asked, "Oh, yeah?"

"Yeah," Townsend said, trying to act nonchalant, "They were over by the office so I couldn't quite make it out, but I got the distinct impression they thought you were the Devil himself."

Boris looked up at him and smiled. "Really? How peculiar."

Townsend did not want to upset his captor, but Boris looked like he was dying to tell him. "Frankly, Boris, you don't look that surprised. Did you tell them you were the Devil?"

"No," Boris said, smirking. He scooted up to the front of his chair. "I didn't have to. Oddly enough, they jumped to that conclusion all by themselves. I never corrected them."

"I find that hard to believe."

"So did I," Boris said letting out a huge laugh. "Here's what happened. I'm coming back from Warrensburg." Townsend lowered his eyebrows. "Yes, I had followed young Ms. Summerlin out there. I had hoped to get incriminating pictures of her with that swarthy attorney she's working with. That never worked out."

Townsend guffawed. "I could have told you that. Believe me, Kate never mixes business and pleasure."

Boris's eyes widened with surprise. "Why Dr. Greene, I would not have expected that of you."

Townsend froze. Of course he would not have expected that of Dr. Greene. No one would expect that of Dr. Greene. Farley did not even like to see his students off-campus lest someone talk. The question was, how much did Boris know about Greene?

Boris smiled at Townsend's scared expression. "Don't worry, your secret's safe with me. But I wish I would have known that before driving all the way out to Warrensburg. But then, I would never have met the boys."

Townsend saw an opportunity to get the other side of the story. "So, how did you meet them?"

"Like I said, I was coming back from Warrensburg. I had gotten off the Interstate to get some gas, and I guess I made a wrong turn because before I knew it I was lost out in the country. After about five minutes I come up to this intersection and see these two guys standing on the side of the road. To tell you the truth, I was kind of scared. I thought they were going to carjack me. I pulled up kind of slowly and then I was going to floor it past them and hope they didn't shoot me.

"When I got closer, I could see their faces in the headlights. It wasn't confidence or anger or attitude. They were scared. I mean, they were almost white. And it wasn't like I caught them at something, it was just . . . strange. You know?"

Townsend knew.

"I did a stretch in the army in the seventies after Vietnam. They always told us, if you stumble upon the enemy, they're going to be as scared as you are. If you bark orders at them and pretend to be in charge, they'll follow. Or shoot you. But most likely follow.

"I roll down the window like I do this every day and yell out 'Howdy, boys.' They just stood there. Didn't say anything. Didn't move. Nothing. So, I honked the horn.

"That got them. Randy shouted 'Jesus Christ.' Then he slapped his hand over his mouth. I didn't get it at the time but, looking back, he had to have thought he said the worst possible thing. T.J. just stood there like a lump. Well, you met him."

Townsend smiled and nodded but thought the boys' silence did not equate to ignorance.

"They were standing there looking at me like they expected me to do something. The smart thing would have been to drive away, but I trust my instincts. And my instincts screamed that these kids would be useful. So, I got out of the car, walked over to them and they each took a couple steps back. That's when I knew I had them." Boris smiled at Townsend. It seemed unnatural, as if someone had pulled the middle of his face apart and stuck a mouthful of yellow teeth in there.

"I asked them 'Is there something I can do for you boys?' Randy looks over at T.J. and then takes this big step forward, like he's stepping out of a line. He says 'I, I'm Randy and I w-w-want to be a world class d-d-drummer.' " Boris used a falsetto voice that made him sound even less like Randy than if he had used his normal voice. "Then he takes this big step back like he's getting back in line.

"Up to this point, I'd been feeling pretty confident and safe, because they seemed so docile. But when he asked me to make him a drummer, I knew they were both higher than kites. What really freaked me out wasn't that he asked, but you could tell he thought I really *could* make him this fantastic drummer."

Boris laughed in amazement and Townsend pretended to join in the joke. All the craziness had left Boris's eyes. To the outside eye this could be a nice dinner conversation between two old friends—if one of the friends had strapped the other to the table and only let him eat with one arm.

"I figured no matter what they were on, they still respected or were afraid of me. I just had to keep the upper hand. So I asked T.J., 'And what is it you have come here looking for?' " Boris had dropped his voice to a James Earl Jones baritone. Townsend had no doubt he used that exact tone out in the country. "T.J. stood there for a moment, looked over at Randy, then back and me and blurted out, 'I'm T.J. and I'm not sure exactly what I want. Sir.' He looked over to Randy for some brotherly support and Randy, I swear to God, looked at him like T.J. had farted in front of the Pope." By now Boris was laughing so hard he could barely finish the story. Townsend continued laughing but found the story more sad than funny.

"T.J. was about in tears at this point. You know he was thinking he had just sold his soul for nothing. Randy leaned over and whispered something in T.J.'s ear. T.J. then said, 'I mean, a girl. I want a girl. You know, to like me.'

"I still had no idea why they were asking me for these things, but at least T.J.'s made sense. I thought I could probably get him a hooker if he wanted one. But I played it cool and told them I would see what I could do."

Townsend interrupted him. "I still don't understand how you figured out they thought you were the Devil."

"I was getting to that. After T.J. asked me for the girl, they still stood there looking at me. I figure, maybe they're supposed to give me something. So, I said, 'I suppose you know what I want?' I gave 'em that smile that I was in on it." Boris flashed the smile, which Townsend thought made him look less like he was in on it, and more like he was alone in the back row of a porno theater.

"Randy takes his big step forward and says, 'Our souls?' " Boris paused and smiled at Townsend. "You know, a lot of thoughts ran through my head trying to guess what they would want from me. Never in my wildest dreams did I think it would be their souls. It took everything I had not to burst out laughing. But I nodded like that was exactly what I thought he'd say.

"I knew that was my clue to get the hell out of there, pardon my pun."

"Wow, that's incredible," Townsend said.

"That's what I thought. I'd been thinking I needed some muscle to grab you. And they just fell into my lap."

"Manna from heaven," Townsend said.

Boris laughed. "Yes. Yes."

"Aren't you worried I'm going to spill the beans on you now?" Townsend asked.

"What, you're going to tell them I'm not the Devil? Go ahead. It won't get you anywhere." Boris walked around the table. They had finished eating and Boris took the bandage off of Townsend's finger and began to reapply the salve. "Oh, I'm sure they have their doubts. Most people of faith do. But they believe." He emphasized the last word.

"Out there at that intersection, those boys had what you might call a religious epiphany. A person goes through that kind of experience," he shook his head, "words and logic can't undo that feeling deep in the gut. So, go ahead, tell them what you want. They'll want to believe you. They may even tell themselves they *do* believe you. But, deep down, they'll know I'm the Devil."

Boris laughed as he walked into the dark skirt of the warehouse. The sound sent a cold chill up Townsend's back. Maybe he had caught a little of that faith too.

CHAPTER 10

Often, when a mock trial is being set up, the attorney-client will attempt to dictate the study's design. The consultant must maintain control of the parameters to ensure the validity of the data.

Greene, F. (2003). *The Trial Consultant's Field Manual* (p. 312). New York: Pullman.

The paw landed lightly on Kate's cheek and gave a gentle squeeze. She kept her eyes closed. The Captain purred a little louder and gave her another squeeze. Kate rolled over and pulled the comforter over her head. As the Captain climbed onto her shoulder to try to find a path under the covers, Kate wondered at the cat's life—everything so routine. Food at six. Nap. Stare out the window and plan escape. Nap. Food at six. Nap. Scratch furniture. Go to bed. No death penalty trials. No crazed kidnappers.

The Captain found an opening and lightly bit Kate's hair. The downside is no control. He needs the food at six, but does not have the ability to do anything about it.

Kate began to wake up and tried to put on a positive attitude. Even if she was not in total control, she at least had some control. She got up, fed the Captain and made herself some coffee.

The Wrenshaw jury selection had been recessed until Tuesday. Judge Mays had attended the annual judges' conference in St.

Louis that weekend. Rumors and innuendoes surrounded the conference. The judges, to their credit, kept the goings-on secret, although prostitution arrests in St. Louis always dropped to an annual low. Whatever happened, most of the judges in Missouri took the following Monday off. Judge Mays was no exception.

In a normal death penalty trial situation, Kate stayed in the town and drove around, evaluating everyone she met as if they were potential jurors for the death penalty case. Cab driver's choice: Killer; waitress: Killer; bartender: possible Lifer, might be sympathetic to alcoholic family background; convenience store clerk: Killer. There were a lot of Killers in western Missouri.

This situation, though, was far from normal. She needed the weekend to plan for the Beckwith mock trial. She sat down at the kitchen table with her date planner. This was Monday and the Beckwith jury selection began a week from Wednesday. The mock would have to be this weekend. First, she had to sell the client on the idea. Second, she had to find a place on such short notice.

She showered, traded her sweats for a pair of jeans and walked out to her car. The trash men were driving by.

"Killer," Kate thought, looking at the young man swinging carelessly around off the back of the truck. His partner, an older man, stood firmly but comfortably on the back bumper. "Possible Lifer."

Kate looked around and saw a gigantic man changing his tire just up the street from her driveway. He looked Hawaiian. After tightening the last bolt, he put the tire iron in the trunk and drove away.

Kate did not think of him in terms of Killer or Lifer. She wondered how such a man would fit into the jury box. And, whatever his vote, you have to think the other jurors would be too scared to disagree with him. She got into the Bug, sniffed the Gerber daisy in the vase and drove to the office.

The main office of Townsend and Greene Consulting took up the fifth floor of the Binghart Building on Massachusetts Street, the main drag in downtown Lawrence. The downtown, mostly buildings from the 1860s (after Quantrill burned it) and the 1950s (after the Kansas River flooded it), maintained a vibrant, small-town charm despite serving an ever-growing community.

Kate's office was on the third floor. As T&G expanded, they rented other offices scattered throughout the building. When Townsend told Kate he had moved her to the third floor, he said she had shown independence to be able to work unsupervised. In fact, she knew the move was a direct result of her continually rolling her eyes whenever Townsend hit on the girls in the office. Once it started affecting his success rate with the new hires, Kate got moved down.

She was trying not to think about Townsend when she walked into the main office. Cyndi, the receptionist, was on the phone and held up a finger at Kate.

"So," she said into the phone, "was that the only thing that was hung this weekend?" She laughed loudly at her own joke. Cyndi's sense of humor ran solely to the sexual. If it was dirty, you could count on her to howl. She now looked up to Kate and rolled her eyes. Having delivered her line, she was ready for the call to end. "Gotta go. Kate's here and I have to find out what happened with the Cuban 'Toy.' " She hung up and trained her eyes on Kate.

"So, how'd it go with Montoy? Is he as good as they say?"

"Arnie hasn't started asking questions yet. We'll probably finish tomorrow." Cyndi made an exaggerated frowny face. Kate waved it off. "How was your weekend?"

"What can I say?" she replied, "They don't call me Cyn for nothing." She cackled but brought her hand up and rubbed her nose. Kate smiled, but knew Cyn was lying. When a person lies, certain physiological changes happen. For example, the nose experiences a slight but noticeable increase in blood circulation. The increased blood flow causes the nose to itch. Cyndi had spent another weekend alone, but was embarrassed. Kate could not say anything without making it worse.

Cyndi made a face, saving Kate from having to come up with something. "Do you know where Townsend is? Maria's been calling all morning. He didn't come home again this weekend. She says she's going to call the cops and report him missing if he doesn't call her so she can bitch him out."

Crap. Townsend had left his fifth wife for Maria a couple of years ago. Having been the other woman, she was constantly thinking that Townsend was cheating on her. More often than not, he was. Sometimes it seemed as if Townsend did not even try to hide it from her. If she was not such a raging bitch, Kate would have felt sorry for her. But it is not like she had no idea what she was getting into. Still, Kate couldn't let her get caught up in this mess.

"Uh, yeah, I saw him in here on Saturday. He said something like he was going to observe a trial in Portland for a couple of weeks. Maybe more."

Cyndi shook her head. "That lying sack of shit. And this time he didn't even bother to make up a lie for Maria. Now I have to deal with her. I'm going stick a poker up his ass the next time I see him."

Kate shuddered. That was an image she definitely did not need right now. "Tell you what, since I talked to Townsend last, if she calls back, send her to me. I'll deal with her. Oh, I'm going to try to put a mock together on Beckwith for Saturday. Do you think Jo is going to be around?"

"This Saturday, like this weekend?" She gave a low guffaw. "Good luck. Jo may be around, but she's been acting all weird and happy. I think she got laid." She laughed again and handed over Maria's messages for Townsend.

Kate's shoulders slumped as she walked down to her office. Even wallflower Jo was getting some? Now Kate was really depressed. Jo had been reluctantly single for the two years she had worked at T&G. She was the girl everyone described as having a pretty face. Her meekness, though, was the biggest hurdle to her romantic happiness.

About a year before, at Kate's urging, Jo began taking self-defense classes. Some men, they had heard, went to the classes believing them to be teeming with single women.

"Oh, there were a few of those guys there," Jo told Kate after she had been taking the classes for a while. "But, after two hours of watching us dropkick Chuck the attack dummy in the walnuts, I don't think they felt like hanging around for a post-class latte. You know?"

"I'm sorry," Kate said. "I thought maybe the guys there might be the shy type. And you guys could, you know, be shy together."

"Who knows? Maybe they were. I guess even shy guys don't like to see a bunch of women practicing groin shots. And some of the women went a little overboard."

"Overboard?"

"We were supposed to pretend Chuck was some unknown assailant out in a parking lot or something." Jo scrunched up her face. "But I think some of the girls pretended it was someone they knew."

"Why do you think that?" Kate asked, although she was thinking of a couple of faces she might be able to superimpose on a dummy.

"They said things. Like Ruthie, she's kind of a heavy-set woman. I was right behind her one time and, right before she went up there, she mumbled, 'So, you think I don't *need* the Baskin-Robbins?' " Jo laughed. "Then she reared back and kicked the hell out of that dummy. I mean, she left her feet. Other women talked about doing things around the house. Football season seemed to be especially violent."

Kate laughed. "Like I said, I'm sorry it didn't work out."

Jo shook her head. "Oh, no. It was great."

"What? Have you been holding out on me?"

"No, not for the guys. For the self-defense stuff. It helped me feel more confident in myself. Did I tell you I'm teaching aerobics now? And, honestly, kicking that dummy was cheap therapy."

Jo had leaned forward and lowered her voice. "And Ruthie's not the only one who pretended the dummy was not a stranger. I put Townsend's face on there a couple times."

Kate had feigned shock. "Why Jo, I didn't know you had it in you."

If Cyndi was right, maybe the classes had given Jo a little confidence. Kate felt guilty that a small part of her hoped Jo had not found a boyfriend. Having a smart assistant who worked well with the hotel staff made mock trials run smoothly. A new fella could jeopardize Jo's availability for the Beckwith mock.

First things first. Kate called Jerry Bingham, Beckwith's lawyer. "Jerry, it's Kate Summerlin, you ready to go?"

"Kate, hon, how's it going?" Jerry always called Kate "hon" or "babe." For the first year or so, she was offended. She felt the diminutives demeaned and singled her out. After working with him on several trials, though, she kept hearing him refer to other men on the trial team as "dude" or "buddy boy." Rather than treating her differently, he was actually treating her the same. She started calling him "bub."

"Babe, I was just thinking of you. How do you feel about Beckwith testifying last? You know, get the story out there and then let him bring it all home? The last thing the jury hears will be his words, the emotion of what this has done to him."

Kate thought about it for a second. "Sure, bub, that'll work as long as your opening is strong on story. The jury needs to know where all the different testimony fits in. But you tell a good story."

"Uh oh, a compliment from Kate Summerlin? Are you greasing me up for something?"

Kate winced. She had not been buttering him up; he was a good storyteller. But she felt slimy enough coaxing him into a mock trial he did not need. His calling her on it made it worse.

"Bub, it's not what you can do for me, it's what I can do for you," she said in her best used car salesman voice. Jerry did not laugh. In her normal voice, she said, "I was thinking about your case last night and it occurred to me you need a mock trial."

Kate paused. When Jerry did not say anything she plowed on. "I know it's late in the game but we don't want to study our strategies so much as try to figure out generally what the case is worth. They're probably going to come at us right after voir dire with a number and we need to know what figures the jury is going to be talking about."

Jerry broke in, his voice wary. "I thought you said these things weren't predictive."

Kate rolled her head back and closed her eyes. She had told him that. She told all her clients that. She told everyone who would listen mock trials were great for seeing how certain arguments played with the locals, for hearing how regular people talked about the case, even for just allowing the attorneys to take a dry run at presenting their arguments. But they were lousy at accurately predicting the number the real jury would come up with.

"I'm not talking about getting a pinpoint number. We want to figure out what the area is. Just to know if their offer is in the ballpark." She squinted and held her breath. That was as far as she could push him.

"I suppose that would be good. It would have been great a month ago. When would we have it? Trial is a week from Wednesday, you know?"

Kate's heart jumped a bit. She was halfway home. "I was thinking on Saturday."

"Oh, Christ, babe, I can't be ready by Saturday."

Kate knew she had him. Excited, she leaned forward in her chair, arms resting on her desk. "Of course you can, bub. It'll be good for you—get the story down early. Can Rich do the defense?"

"Yeah, he's been busting my chops all week." Jerry thought best when he was angry and on the defensive. In the month before trial, all the attorneys in his firm would come by his office to criticize his case. Jerry would get fired up. By the time the trial rolled around, he was battle-tested and loaded for bear. "So, what's it going to cost?"

Now, instead of talking about whether to do the mock trial, they were talking about how to get it done. Kate was home-free. "Probably around ten thousand dollars." Kate had run some preliminary numbers and worked it so she would not make a dime on the deal. She might have to con the client into paying money he should not have to, but that did not mean she had to take any of it for herself.

"Whoa," Jerry said. "Ten grand? I don't know if Beckwith will go for that. Let me call him and see what he says. Everything okay with you? You sound a little edgy."

Kate smiled at his concern. "I'm fine. It's been a long week."

She hung up and crossed her fingers. She felt bad lying to Jerry, although she was not really sure she got away with anything. She knew what the case was worth, but more importantly, Jerry knew that she knew what the case was worth. That he did not ask her what the hell she was talking about bothered her a little.

Cyndi poked her head into Kate's office. "Hey, sorry about this, but Maria is on the phone up there. I told her you would call her back, but she wanted to hold. Can you come up and get it?"

"Sure." Kate had not had time to come up with a plausible excuse for Townsend. There was no way Maria would buy the Portland business. She had to take the call, though. Maria was a bit crazy and would definitely call the police just to spite him.

When they got to Cyndi's desk, Kate kept on walking. "Can you transfer this back to Townsend's office? That way I'm out of your hair." Kate walked all the way to the back of the suite to Townsend's office in the corner. Windows ran from about three feet off the ground all the way to the ceiling. Two blocks away, at the end of the business district, the Kansas River rolled over a small dam. Kate sat back in the tall-back leather chair. A small bar pushed against her lower back, giving it great support. She wondered who would get Townsend's chair if things did not work out. The phone rang.

"Hello, this is Kate."

"Where's Walt, Kate? I want to know where he is and who he's banging."

"I'm sure he's fine, Maria. You know how he is."

"I'm sure he's a hell of a lot finer than he's going to be when I get through with him. Why are you covering for him?" Maria paused for a moment. "Is it you, Kate? Are you fucking Walt?"

Kate shuddered as the image of her and Townsend naked flashed involuntarily through her mind. The image left her speechless.

"Oh, my God, it is you."

Kate saw what she had to do. It solved every problem except that she had to actually say the words. She closed her eyes and leaned her head back. "Yes, Maria, Walt and I are lovers. This weekend we discovered our feelings for each other. I'm asking you to respect our decision and let us have a couple weeks to ourselves." Ugh. Kate wondered if there was any way to give her mind a long, hot shower.

"I don't understand. I thought he hated you. He told me you were fat, overpaid and had hairy legs."

Unbelievable. A girl wears a skirt one time without shaving her legs. One time. Kate cleared her throat. "I guess that's where we get our passion. Please, Maria, let us have our time together." Kate hung up. She walked out to Cyndi's desk and said, "If Maria calls back, tell her I've taken the rest of the week off." The phone rang. Cyndi smiled and raised her eyebrows.

Kate went down to her office and tried to get her mind off of the phone call by rereading the Beckwith file. She heard a clicking sound from out in the hallway. *Snik. Snik.* Kate called out into the hall, "Jo, that you?" Jo bit her nails. Like a cat with a bell around its neck, she could never sneak up on anyone.

Jo stuck her head in the door. "Sorry. Are those the Wrenshaw jurors?"

Kate felt a pang of guilt for not working on Rick's case. "No, this is Beckwith. Do you have a minute?"

Jo walked in and plopped down in the soft chair in front of the desk. Kate thought Cyndi may be right. Normally, Jo would slink in and sit down on the edge of the chair, ready to jump up at the slightest noise. Here she was sitting back, crossed-legged in the chair, seemingly not worried about anything. Kate leaned forward in her chair. "Actually, I'm glad you stopped by. I kind of need a favor."

"Shoot."

"I want to do a mock this Saturday, but nothing's set up. Can you do it?"

Jo smiled back at her. "Are you going to make it worth my while?"

Kate did not know what to say. Jo had always just said yes.

"Uh, sure, I mean, you'll be paid, obviously."

"C'mon Kate, I'm kidding you. Of course I'll do it. What case?"

"Beckwith."

Jo shrugged her shoulders. "I don't think I've done anything with it. Which side are we on?"

"Plaintiff. Beckwith was an undercover cop in Kansas City, Kansas. He's a small-town boy from Edgerton. Still lives there."

Jo frowned. "Edgerton?"

"A half-hour south of Kansas City. About fifteen hundred people. Beckwith had been working in the Mendiro drug family for about six months. According to Jerry, he was getting pretty close to the top."

"Jerry Bingham?" Jo said and made a face. Kate looked back at her quizzically. "He always calls me 'sweets.' What are you supposed to say when a guy calls you sweets? I tell you one of these days I'm going to stick that pen he's always clicking straight in his eyeball."

"He calls me 'babe.' " Kate paused. "I try not to let it bother me."

"If that works for you, great. But one of these days, POW!!" Jo made a back-handed jab in the air. "Right in the ol' eyeball." Kate stared at her, speechless. Jo smiled and said, "So, you said our boy was getting in good with the drug lords?"

"Riiight. Like I said, he'd been out there for six months. Back home, he had a little girl. He got a little homesick. When you're undercover, you can't exactly go home every night to the wife and kids.

"He did all right until his daughter's fourth birthday. Before he took the undercover job, every Saturday, he and the daughter would go to Melvin's Donut Shoppe there in Edgerton and split a bear claw."

Jo leaned in. "Boy, a bear claw sounds good, doesn't it? I'm not usually a dipper, but a bear claw and big glass of milk. Boy that sounds good."

"Focus with me here, Jo."

"Sorry, I missed breakfast this morning. So, cop, birthday girl, bear claw, glass of milk. Got it."

"I'm not sure about the milk, but yeah, he took his daughter out early on a Saturday for her birthday bear claw."

"You don't think they had milk? Who would eat a bear claw without a glass of milk?"

"Jo!" Kate said a little more sharply than she intended. She had never realized how nice it was to tell a case to Jo. Quiet, demure Jo who never interrupted. Who was *this* person?

Jo put her hands up and flopped back in the chair. "Sorry."

"Also in Edgerton that morning is Elsie Stiltson. She is putting together a photography show of rural America."

Jo wrinkled her nose and looked toward the ceiling. "Stiltson. Is that the mustard people?" Kate nodded. "Ah. Helloooooo, deep pockets."

"Right. Elsie Stiltson is the only daughter of Maynard Stiltson, founder and CEO of Stiltson Mustard."

Jo started humming the Stiltson Mustard jingle. "Stiltson. Mustard. Put the Kazaam! on your ham." Kate gave her a tired look. Jo returned a fake, toothy smile. "Sorry, sorry. Okay, princess goes to Edgerton to take some pictures. Why is she taking pictures?"

"That's what she does. She's a professional photographer. Supposed to be pretty good, too. She's had several shows in Kansas City and one in a gallery in Chicago. And she was putting together a series on small-town Americana. So, she's going through Edgerton, taking pictures of the various shops and people walking around the downtown. She clicks through a couple hundred shots and goes back to her studio to see what she has. I don't know the exact details, but the light was funny or she didn't like the angles or something, but anyway, they were pretty much crap. Except one.

"A young guy is sitting across the table from a little girl. The girl has her head tilted back and her mouth wide open. In the air between them is a piece of pastry the guy has lofted toward the girl's mouth. I guess the girl is cute as a button and has this intense look of concentration on the pastry."

"The Beckwiths and the birthday bear claw," Jo said.

"Bingo. Stiltson's torn because it's pretty schmaltzy. But, it's really cute. And cute sells. She thinks she may be able to make a series out of it, if nothing else, to promote her portrait business. So, she goes back to Edgerton to try to figure out who this is. When she shows the donut shop guy the picture, he says that's Mike Beckwith and his daughter, but they don't really come around anymore. He thinks they may have moved and just been in town for the weekend."

"Wait a minute. In that little town? That donut guy would have known they hadn't moved."

"Yeah, he lied to her. He said in his deposition he knew Beckwith was an undercover cop on some sort of assignment. So when this strange woman comes by with a photo of him and the little girl, the baker tried to throw her off track."

"So, he gives her Beckwith's real name and a fake story about where he is?" Jo rolled her eyes. "A foolproof plan."

"Well, it got Stiltson to stop looking for him and she thinks her portrait series is shot. But, she remembered this new gallery, 'Whimsy,' had asked her to submit something funny and light. She sent in the Beckwith photo and they put it in the show. Two weeks later, Azandra Mendiro, wife of drug lord family boss Ulturo Mendiro, took him on their once-a-month 'culture date' to Whimsy."

"Uh oh."

"Yeah, uh oh."

"But that shouldn't be that big of a deal. So, he sees a photo of one his guys with a little girl. So what?"

"Not surprisingly, cocaine dealers, as a whole, are a paranoid lot. I guess Beckwith's cover story was as a loner with no family. Plus, completely unrelated to Beckwith, some mid-level guys were starting to snitch out details of Mendiro's operation to weaken him. Then they would take over. Mendiro saw the Whimsy photo and blamed Beckwith for everything."

"Oh, God. Did they kill him?"

Kate shook her head. "No. Beckwith said he felt some kind of shift in the mood of the guys. Luckily he told his captain and they put a surveillance team on him. A week after Mendiro went to Whimsy he sent Beckwith to a deserted corner downtown to deliver a kilo of cocaine to a local dealer. The surveillance team saw two guys creeping up behind Beckwith and shot at them before they got to him. There was this whole big gun fight. Both the drug guys died. Beckwith got shot in the hip, shattering his pelvis."

Jo grimaced. "Is he all right now?"

"He spent a month in traction in the hospital and another six on his back at home. Our expert says he'll always walk with a limp. He was the real athletic type, you know softball, marathons, all that. He can't do any sports. Except bowling, I guess he can bowl."

"He ought to get an extra million just for that."

Kate stopped and stared at Jo. "Jo, and you can tell me, I won't say anything. Have you been drinking?"

Jo smiled and raised her eyebrows several times. "Nope, sober as a judge. Well, a sober judge anyway."

Kate didn't laugh.

"What happened to Beckwith?" Jo asked.

"He works at a desk. He can't run and if you can't run, you can't be on the street."

"Could he still do undercover work? Like nursing home fraud or something?"

"Maybe, but the shooting made the local news, complete with photo. The newspaper ran the photo too, so now every criminal in the city knows his face. Beckwith sued for using his likeness without a waiver. According to Jerry's complaint, Stiltson's responsible for all damages caused by the publication of the photo: medical, lost wages, and pain and suffering."

"She didn't get any kind of waiver?"

"No. Stiltson claims she has every right to use a picture taken on the street, even without a waiver. And even if she is somehow liable for damages caused by the picture, her damages should be limited to the profit she received for using the photo, which is nothing, not any damages caused by the criminal acts of a drug dealer who happened to see it."

Jo got up and walked around the desk. "So, you say this guy is athletic? You have a picture?"

Kate pulled out Beckwith's academy graduation photo.

"Hubba, hubba. That's some nice-looking cop candy right there."

"Jo," Kate said, "he's married, remember."

"Hey, if I go to a restaurant, I can look at what someone else ordered. Doesn't mean I'm going to eat off her plate."

Kate took the picture back, slid it into the file and closed it. She looked up at Jo, "Okay, give."

Jo walked back around the desk and smiled. "What?"

"Ever since you walked in, you've been acting, well, you haven't been acting like yourself."

"You mean I haven't been schlumping around the office with my eyes on my shoes?"

Kate did not want to hurt her feelings, but that was exactly it. "Yeah, kind of. You're acting weird."

"You want to know why I haven't been acting like myself?" Jo smiled and her eyes widened.

"Yes, yes, I want to know why."

"Because I'm not myself. I'm someone else."

Chapter 11

"Okay, I've got a shrimp etouffee, a gumbo and two jambalayas. Is that right?" Boris looked up from his notepad and scanned the room.

T.J. raised his hand. "Could I get some extra cornbread?"

"Oh, yeah," Boris said, leaning over the table and scribbling. "We've got to have lots of cornbread. All right, I'll be back in a bit."

Whatever doubts T.J. had about Boris, they did not extend to the man's choice of food. That old guy was crazy but he knew how to eat. It was the crazy part bothering T.J. now. He heard the car pull away, and then turned to Randy. "This is bullshit, man. What are we doing here?"

"Shhh," Randy said in a loud whisper, "not in front of the vic."

"Vic? Vic? What the fuck are we doing with a vic? This whole thing is getting way out of hand." T.J. looked over at Townsend, who immediately stared down at the table. But T.J. had seen the fear in the old man's eyes. It had been there since they took him.

T.J. felt bad for him. *Old guy like that lives his whole life working for the day he can take it easy. Then, no sooner than he gets there, Randy and T.J. come along and bring him into Boris's world.*

"What are we doing? We're breaking into warehouses, we're grabbing people out of their houses, we're cutting off fingers? Did you see him cut off that guy's finger? Christ on a cracker, I didn't sign on for this shit."

Randy looked quizzically at his brother. "Did you just say 'Christ on a cracker'?" He shook his head and refocused. "Look, man, you sold your soul to the Devil. Didn't you think there would be some *shit* that went along with that?"

"Honestly," T.J. replied, "I never thought there would be a Devil. I thought we would get high and eventually you would forget about it."

"That's not the song you were singing out at the crossroads."

"I know, I know. The cemetery, meeting him out there, right when you said the Devil was coming, I just got caught up in it. Now, I'm not sure he's really *the* Devil. I mean, come on. Why would the Devil dick around with us?"

Townsend saw an opening. "He's not the Devil. He's just some guy who's using you."

Randy turned toward Townsend. "Look, Dr. Greene, you weren't there. You don't understand."

"Maybe he's right, Randy. Maybe we wanted it to be him. Then he happens to show up, tells us what we want to hear and brings us here."

Townsend interrupted. "Where is *here,* by the way? I mean . . . where, exactly, are we?"

The boys hesitated for a moment. Then T.J. said, "The Tomb of Doom. It's a haunted house during the season." The old man shook his head. "Back in the seventies, someone bought up all these abandoned warehouses down here in the rail yards. They decorated them up with a bunch of scary stuff. I think this used to be Warmer Brothers' Coffee."

"This one is pretty tame," Randy said. "It's more of a date house. There's a maze over there and a mummy room and, I think, a vampire room." He gestured toward the back of the warehouse.

"What's a 'date house'?"

"There are enough scares to get the girls close to you, but not so scary to get them out of the mood, if you know what I mean." He looked over at T.J. "Of course, T.J. doesn't know what I mean." T.J. hit him hard in the arm.

Townsend tried to cross his legs under the table and looked at T.J. "So, you think Boris brought you here to use the decorations to reinforce his persona as the Devil?"

"Maybe." He turned to Randy. "You have to admit, when that woman was here you had your doubts." Randy did not say anything. "Even before then, when Boris was strapping the doc to the table, you shot me a look."

Randy smiled. "Yeah, I was thinking if he pulls that old man's pants down, we're out of here."

T.J. did not laugh. "If he's the Devil, how come he needs that woman to fix a trial? Why can't he fix it himself? And why did he need to get Greene here to get her to do what he wanted? Couldn't he, like, make himself all Devil-like and scare the hell out of her or something? And what about that finger thing. Why would the Devil need to use a meat cleaver to cut off that guy's finger? What if this is just some fat, twisted dude?"

Randy paused. "What about the crossroads? What about that whole conversation? How did he know all that if he's not the Devil?"

Townsend kept quiet. Randy was wavering and he did not want to push the kid.

"I don't know. Maybe he guessed?" T.J. replied.

"He guessed? He comes across two guys standing by their car out in the middle of nowhere and he doesn't think, 'Oh, I bet those guys' car broke down,' or 'Hey, I caught a couple of fags getting it off.' No, because that wouldn't make any sense. He thinks, 'I bet these two losers are waiting here to sell their souls to the Devil. And, what do you know, I happen to be cooking up an evil scheme that needs two guys to run it. I'll tell them

I'm the Devil and away we'll go.' That's how you see it?"

"I don't know. I don't get why he's always here at the Tomb. Other than when he goes out for food, he's here the whole time. Shouldn't he be out doing Devil's stuff somewhere? He just sits back there in the office and plays solitaire on the computer. That doesn't seem very Devil-like. One time he saw me coming and toggled onto his background. Like I wouldn't know he was playing solitaire." T.J. paced back and forth for a moment. "So, you really think he's the Devil?"

"I don't know." Randy sighed. "He's pretty whiny for the Prince of Darkness. And this place seems like kind of a shit hole for a hangout. If I was going to pick a haunted house, I'd go for the Main Street Morgue. That place kicks ass. So, yeah, I guess I'm maybe starting to wonder a bit, too."

The old man looked up at T.J. "So, what are you going to do?"

"We make him prove it."

"And if he can't?"

Randy stood next to his brother and looked down at Townsend. "Then we kick his ass."

Thirty minutes later Boris came back with the food. "They were out of jambalaya, if you can believe that. They had some sort of other spicy rice thing. Looks like jambalaya to me." He pulled the food out of the bags and was beginning to open the boxes when he looked up. Randy and T.J. stood side-by-side glaring at him. He glanced between the two and then down at Townsend. "Did I miss something?"

"We need to talk," Randy said. If Boris was concerned, it did not show.

"About what, my children?" He sat down in a chair and smiled up at them.

"We're holding up our end of the deal here, pretty good. By my count we've committed like six different felonies so far for you, and you haven't really done anything for us. So, we think it's time for a little advance on your end of the deal."

"I'm sorry, it doesn't work that way," Boris replied, his expression unchanged. "You've made what might be called 'all-or-nothing' requests. I mean, a little bit of rhythm is really no rhythm at all. Either you have it or you don't."

Randy winced at this very personal truism.

"Once I give it to you, it becomes a part of you. I can't take it back. I've learned the hard way it's best to wait until the job is complete before doling any rewards." He smiled.

Randy sighed. "The truth is, we're not sure you're really the Devil. Can you prove it?"

Boris laughed. "It's not like I've got a driver's license with Beelzebub on it."

The boys did not laugh. "You better come up with something or we're going to beat your ass. And if we can beat your ass, then you're not the Devil."

The smile fell off Boris's face and his expression grew grim. The change was quick and startling. "Trust me, you don't want to do that. But, I understand." He thought for a moment. "This one time, if you need a miracle to reconfirm your faith, I'll give you a miracle. Meet me at St. Christopher's Cathedral over on Elm. Six o'clock tomorrow night. Don't be early. Don't be late. Six o'clock."

Randy looked over at T.J. and the boys nodded.

CHAPTER 12

Everyone has one true self amid several facades they present to the world. During jury selection, the consultant must see through the facades to the juror's true self.

Greene, F. (2003). *The Trial Consultant's Field Manual* (p. 175). New York: Pullman.

"What do you mean, you're someone else?" Kate asked.

Jo paused for dramatic effect. "I'm Jo," she said as she broke into a broad grin.

Kate stared at her. "You're Jo?" Jo nodded. "Haven't you always been Jo?" Jo shook her head. "Okay. Who were you before?"

Jo spit out, "Josepherta."

"Yeah," Kate said, shrugging her shoulders, "that's your real name, right?"

"No," Jo said sharply. "It's not my real name. That's the point. I'm not a Josepherta."

"I'm pretty sure that's what you had on your resumé. I think the main reason we brought you in was to see what a 'Josepherta' looked like."

"Hey, if it got me this job, it's the only good thing it ever did for me. Back when I was a kid, whenever I got in trouble, my mom would always yell, 'Josepherta Bean Harvnor.' I always thought I was Josepherta and Jo was a nickname."

"Your middle name is Bean?"

Jo waved her off. "I'm immune to middle name smack. When you think your first name is Josepherta, it really doesn't matter much what your middle name is." Her eyes lit up as she pulled herself to the front of the chair. "So, last night, I'm digging around for my birth certificate. I'm going to the Fitness and Relaxation Training Conference in Toronto next summer and I need to get a passport."

"The Canadians are holding a FART Conference?"

Jo frowned at her. "It's the FRTC, thank you very much. Nobody uses the A. Except the Fonz."

Kate squinted at her, not understanding.

Jo gave her two thumbs-up and said, "AAAAAAAA"

Kate rolled her eyes. "Easy, Josepherta. You were saying you needed a passport to get to your FART conference."

"Right, with the FRTC being held in Toronto, I needed a passport. I go over to my parents and I'm in the basement digging around in this old trunk. Finally, I find this old birth certificate for Jo Bean Harvnor. I couldn't believe it. The date matched. The parents matched, the hospital matched. It was mine." She stopped and looked at Kate, mouth slightly agape, expecting confirmation of this miraculous finding.

"Maybe there were twins and your parents thought you were going to be the evil twin. So, they named you Josepherta. The other one, the good twin, they named Jo." She smiled at Jo. "Have you seen any of your baby pictures? Were you an evil-looking baby?"

Jo ignored her. "So, I take it up to my mom and I ask her, 'Is this mine?' And she said 'Of course, dear. Who else's would it be?' I couldn't believe it." Jo leaned forward and spoke in a loud whisper. "I kind of yelled at her. 'Maybe it belongs to some girl named Jo and not Josepherta.' " Jo giggled and nodded her head slightly, obviously pleased with herself. "So, you would think having her only daughter rage at her would shame her into confessing why I spent my whole life thinking my name was Josepherta.

"But she starts laughing. She said, 'Josepherta? Boy I haven't heard that one since you were a kid.'

"I said, 'Exactly. You told me my name was Josepherta. And it's really Jo?' She looked at me as if I was crazy." Kate sympathized with Mother Harvnor on that one. "She kept laughing. 'You really thought your name was Josepherta? I made that up for when you acted out. I thought Jo Bean was too cute to use when you were bad. And Josepherta, it just sounds like a bad girl's name.' That's what she said. 'Josepherta is a bad girl's name.' Can you believe that?"

Kate tried to suppress a smile. "So, you really thought your name was Josepherta all this time?"

"Yes, can you imagine that? My whole life, I've been walking around thinking I was a Josepherta." Jo's eyes narrowed. "That can take a toll on a person, you know?

"I used to lie in bed in night praying God would change my name to Jo. Short, strong, it was like some cruel joke that I got to use this great name, but secretly, I knew I was really Josepherta. A name, a person's real name, is very important. Anytime I thought I could really do something great, a voice in my head told me I couldn't. Josepherta's voice. You know there hasn't been one famous person named Josepherta? Not ever! I Googled it."

Kate raised a finger. "To be fair, that's probably a pretty small pool of people to be working with."

"Still, you think there would be at least one. Somebody. But Jo." Her eyes lit up. "There have been tons of famous people named Jo. When I was a girl I read *Little Women* over and over. Jo was a heroine to me. Now, I feel like this huge weight has been lifted off my shoulders." She fell back into the chair, her arms flopping over the sides.

While Jo had been telling her story, Kate had forgotten about Boris and Townsend—forgotten the whole mess. Jo's enthusiasm had wiped it all away. But once she mentioned the weight, it all came crashing back. Kate burst into tears.

"No, Kate," Jo said, misunderstanding, "it's all good now. The weight has been lifted." Jo pulled both hands up from her shoulders to demonstrate the lifting.

Kate shook her head. "It's not that. I'm sorry. Really, I'm very happy you're Jo. I've just got a lot on my mind."

Jo threw back her shoulders and cocked her head. "Lay it on me, sister. I'm Jo. I'll kick whatever or whoever's bothering you straight in da *aaaass.*"

Kate did not want to tell her. She did not want to ruin the good mood by dragging Jo into the mess. But, she could not help it.

"Townsend's been kidnapped by a couple of kids and some guy named Boris. I have to throw the Beckwith trial or they'll kill him."

"What?" Jo asked as her mouth dropped open.

"This Boris guy is really scary. He cut off one of Townsend's fingers. I don't know what I'm going to do."

"He did what?" Jo asked, looking around the room for a possible hidden camera.

Kate told Jo the whole story. When she finished Jo shook her head. "Sounds like you've really got Townsend by the balls," she said with an expression of almost vicious glee.

"I'm serious. I don't like Townsend either, but you should have seen him. They had him strapped down to this table and . . ." Her voice trailed off. "He always had that bravado, that arrogance that he was the best or, of course, you were going to sleep with him. As much of an asshole as he was, he always seemed so big, you know?"

Jo nodded. "When you say big asshole, I think of Townsend."

"But in that building, he seemed so small. I've got to help him."

Jo stood there quiet for a minute. Then she smiled and said, "Well then, I guess we'll have to kick ol' Boris straight in da ass." Jo sat down in the chair in front of Kate's desk.

Kate cut her off. "Hold on. There's no 'we' here. I shouldn't have told you any of this. You can't get involved."

Jo shook her head. "Like hell. What did the police say?"

Kate looked down at her hands and did not say anything. Jo's mouth dropped. "What?! You didn't call the police? You could call Beckwith. He's a cop. You have to call someone."

"I can't call Beckwith *because* he's a cop." She waited for Jo to understand. Jo just stared at her. "If I go to Beckwith and tell him someone is trying to rig the case, he'll tell Jerry and Jerry will tell the judge. They'll put the trial on hold until this whole thing is over.

"And what exactly am I going to tell them? They're keeping Townsend in some creepy warehouse. That narrows it down to about ninety percent of the warehouses in Kansas City. Boris will kill him. I'm sure of it. We've got to do this." She stopped and corrected herself. "*I've* got to do this."

Jo smiled. "How do *we* do that?" Kate started to protest but Jo interrupted her. "Look, we're just sitting in your office, talking. It's not like I'm going to go on some black op commando mission. It's not dangerous to talk. And if it is . . ."

Kate interrupted her in a deadpan voice: "You're Jo and you'll kick it straight in da ass."

Jo curled her lip then grabbed a pad of paper and a pen off Kate's desk. "So, how do we rig the jury?"

"We can't. But we can rig a mock trial." Kate looked up guiltily at Jo.

Jo picked up the file. "So, do you think Boris is working for the Stiltsons?"

"I don't think so. Jury tampering is a pretty serious crime. Stiltson is worth billions. He may not want to lose a million or two because of the daughter, but in the big picture, it's chump change. Plus, after that rat hair thing last year, I don't think Stiltson Mustard wants any more bad publicity."

"I thought that turned out to be a hoax."

"Yeah, but they had those pictures on the Internet. That image kind of sticks with you." They both sat quiet for a moment until Kate shook off the image. "You know, one weird thing about Boris, he never talked about the money. You know those defense guys, they're all bean counters. It's all about the money. Boris kept talking about Beckwith. As if it was personal or something."

"The Mendiros? Getting even for betraying their trust."

Kate shook her head. "I don't think so. Sabotaging a personal injury lawsuit is a little subtle for a drug lord. The way I understand it, they're a little more direct."

They bounced ideas around for most of the day. Just before six, Jerry called back. "Babe, it's a go. Beckwith said okay and I got it all set up. You just have to show up Saturday morning at ten."

Kate was dumbfounded. It was unheard of for a client to make any arrangements, let alone all of them. "What do you mean all set up? What's all set up?"

"The mock trial, it's all a go for Saturday."

"Oh, bub, I don't know about that. You know I kind of like to set up my own gigs." What Kate meant was she needed to control the set-up so she could rig the mock trial. But she could not exactly tell Jerry that.

"Look, babe, I'm not even sure we need to do this. I've got a pretty good idea of the number we can expect from a jury and I doubt Tittleton's going to offer us that. But, hey, if Kate Summerlin says I need a mock trial, then I'm going to do a mock trial." A pang of guilt shot through her. "But I'll be damned if I'm going to pay any ten thousand dollars. I've got it all set up in a way that we can afford it. If you don't want to do it that way, we don't have to do it at all. What's it going to be?"

She could feel him smiling his big, toothy grin on the other end. "Okay," she said warily. "Where's it going to be?"

"At Big Mamma's."

"Big Mamma's?" She couldn't believe it. "The casino? You can't put my mock in the middle of a casino."

"Can and did, hon. Plus, it's not like they're going to be deliberating around a craps table. We're in the Henry the Eighth room."

"Oh, the Henry the Eighth room," Kate said sarcastically, "that's fine then."

"Great," Jerry said, "see you at ten." He hung up before Kate could yell at him.

She immediately dialed his number. Jo looked on, wide-eyed. Jerry's secretary answered. "Becky, let me talk to Jerry."

Becky did not hesitate. "I'm sorry, Kate, Jerry's gone for the day." Kate started to yell, but stopped herself. She knew Becky was lying and Becky knew that Kate knew she was lying. Letting it pass, though, would win her some points. Lord knows she needed some points with somebody.

"Oh, okay. Tell him to call me as soon as he comes in tomorrow."

"Sure will. Thanks, Kate."

Kate slumped down in her chair until her chin was on her chest and her eyes were level with her desk. "We're having the mock at Big Mamma's casino."

"That'll be a first."

"And last." Kate sighed. "I was going to set the thing up for Jerry to lose. Then Jerry goes and does all the set-up."

"Maybe the jurors will be big mustard fans."

"Maybe. We're going to have to hope they hate Beckwith." For some reason, she thought she would have a better chance at the roulette wheel.

Chapter 13

Jury selection is less like a salad bar than it is like watching television. You do not get to pick what you want and discard the rest. Rather, you get rid of that which you do not want and whatever is left is what you have.

Greene, F. (2003). *The Trial Consultant's Field Manual* (p. 159). New York: Pullman.

The alarm clock's shrill cry startled Kate. She sat straight up in bed, trying to figure out why she was in a strange room. She quickly recognized the Warrensburg motel room, slapped the alarm for a ten-minute snooze, and collapsed back onto the bed. Her racing heart kept her from relaxing. She realized she'd been spoiled by the Captain's gentle nudging and purring. While the rest of the world started the day with the harsh ring of an artificial alarm, she was normally awakened by love. She made a mental note to give the Captain a special treat when she got home that night.

When the buzzing repeated, she got up and jumped in the shower. She slipped into her lemon suit and paired it with a black blouse. By six-thirty, she was ready to walk out the door. She did not need to be in court until eight but liked to drive around the town prior to jury selection. It gave her a feel for the people—how they lived and worked and played.

At least that was what she told people. In fact, she was extremely superstitious and horrible with directions. The year before, on the morning she picked a jury in Birmingham, Alabama, she got lost on the way to the courthouse. She drove hopelessly in circles for an hour until she finally got her bearings. During that hour she went through half a five-pound bag of Red Hot candies listening to an Erin McKeowan CD. The jury ultimately convicted, but did not give the death penalty. Kate considered that a win and attributed it, in large part, to the combination of spicy treats and the funky, upbeat stylings of Ms. McKeowan.

In every trial since, she superstitiously drove around the town every morning before court, popping Red Hots and dancing in her seat to McKeowan. It gave her an edge, a confidence to take into court.

Before she began the drive around Warrensburg, though, she had to clean the room. She picked up the clothes she had thrown down the night before and stuffed them in her suitcase. She pulled the blanket up onto the bed, threw an empty water bottle away, and straightened the papers sitting on the desk. In short, she did everything but vacuum.

The cleaning stemmed not from any freakish sense of order; Kate would be the first to say she was a bit of a slob. Rather, when she was in her impressionable teens, her Uncle Brian, a bit of a joker, had passed on an urban legend. According to the ill-informed uncle, some hotel maids, already dissatisfied with their jobs, would become outraged at slovenly guests. In retaliation, the maid would stick the offending guest's toothbrush up her ass and then put it back where the guest had left it, no one the wiser.

This story haunted Kate. She knew it was an unreasonable fear and laughed at herself as she wiped up the water circles on the night table where her cup had sat. She knew 99.9% of all maids were good people who would never even consider punishing a guest for being messy, let alone do something as vile as the "toothbrush violation." But there was still that 0.1% she could not get out of her mind.

To avoid incurring the wrath of the maid's ass, Kate did everything possible to make the room as clean as when she first walked in, if not cleaner. Others had suggested she merely take her toothbrush with her. But she could not take all of her belongings, and heaven knows what might make it up into the hypothetical maid's voracious rectum.

Kate inspected the room one last time, left a five-dollar tip on the bed to atone for any mess she may have missed and left for her hour-long commute to the Courthouse, three blocks away.

When Kate finally walked into the courtroom, she saw Arnie's eyes twinkle. "You look like a banana," he laughed. "A big bruised banana."

Kate gave him a sharp look but was secretly pleased. That morning in her hotel room, she had bent over to pick up some potato chips she had dropped the night before and seen herself in the full-length mirror. Sitting back on her legs, the yellow suit covered her completely and she thought she looked like a round, plump lemon. At least bananas were long and lean. Either way, she certainly was not giving up her lucky yellow suit.

The day went by quickly. Kate and Arnie had worked together several times and he had a good feel for what type of information she wanted. Mostly though, he had to engage the middle of the road jurors so Kate could read how they answered the questions.

Going into the day, Kate had pretty much determined eight of their nine strikes. For the last strike, there were three prime candidates. She could not decide who would be the worst juror. At around four, with the questioning over, Kate, Jo, Arnie, and Rick sat around the table to discuss their strategy.

"It comes down to the Preacher, She Petty, and the Bug Guy," Kate said.

Jo looked down at her score sheet. "Charles Billings, the Preacher, is a five."

"He's also a minister at the First United Methodist Church. Do we know if he's an Old Testament or a New Testament kind of minister?" Everyone just stared at her. "You know, fire and brimstone versus turn the other cheek?"

Jo raised her hand. "I drove by his church last night. This Sunday's sermon is 'Come in and give yourself a Faith lift.' " Everyone groaned. "I'm not really sure where that puts us."

"Before I heard that, I liked him," Arnie joked. "Seriously though, I think he really sympathized with Rick."

Kate shrugged. "Of course he sympathized with Rick. He's a minister, he's going to sympathize with everyone. Including Pike. And he's really smooth, too. If he goes against us, he could easily take the rest of the jury with him. Since our whole strategy is based on getting a fractured jury, this guy could be really bad news."

Arnie shook his head. "I don't think we'll lose him. Who else you got?"

"Troy Whaley, the Bug Guy. He's an exterminator. His downside, of course, is he kills for a living. Talk about not wanting killers on the jury. Whaley is, literally, a killer. He's a five, though."

"People are different than bugs," Arnie said. He, Kate and Jo all turned and looked at Rick. Rick's eyes darted back and forth between them.

"Sure," Kate said quickly. "Of course. Uh, last we have Amy Silter, She Petty."

Arnie looked through his notes. "I don't remember her. Who is she?"

"She didn't say much. On her questionnaire, she says 'Prisons are too easy' and she thinks, even with life without parole, Rick could get out again. She's a six." Kate looked around the table. "So, we've got a guy who if he goes against us, could take the whole jury; a killer; and someone who probably doesn't think life is enough of a punishment."

Kate turned to Rick. "What do you think? It's your jury. Which one would you strike?"

Rick sat back in his chair and ran his fingers through his hair. "I don't like the preacher. He kept giving me these looks, like he was giving me last rites or something. That's a weird feeling." He stopped for a moment and no one looked at him. "Plus, if we're doing this crazy juror thing, he could screw it up. Everyone's on their best behavior when there's a preacher in the room."

Jo jumped in. "Look, we went through all the trouble of classifying each of these people on the scale. We've got two fives and one six. We should strike the six. She Petty."

Kate looked at Arnie and raised her eyebrows. "Counselor?"

"I guess I'll take door number three. You can't change who you are and Bug Guy, in his heart, is a killer. His whole livelihood is based on the philosophy that if something is bad and you don't want it around, you kill it. That's not going to change once he gets in the jury room."

Kate nodded her head, more to acknowledge the problem than to agree with what anyone had said. She turned and stared out the window. They were all right. Those were the same arguments she had been debating all last night.

It had not been an easy night. Even when she had dozed off for a couple of hours, she had a nightmare. Boris was in the jury box, dressed like Santa Claus and smoking a thin pipe. Kate knew he was a killer, the worst killer on the panel. Kate kept screaming to strike him, but Arnie could not hear her. Then, they were out of strikes. She stared in horror at the fat man as Rick turned to her pleading, "Why did you leave him on? I'm on the bad boy list for sure." She barely slept the rest of the night.

As Jo and Arnie argued about the last strike, Kate saw the bailiff walk in, a signal the judge would soon follow. In that moment, she made up her mind. The Preacher. It was too big of a risk having such a charismatic leader in the jury room. Plus, Rick was right—people are less likely to act like an ass around the clergy.

Mays had a long torso and short stubby legs so he was at his most imposing behind the large bench. Attorneys were used to him practically sprinting from the side door to the bench, about fifteen feet away. He quickly glanced down around the courtroom. Zuckerman, having been tipped off by the bailiff the judge was returning, slipped in just before he reappeared. Mays banged his gavel. "Ms. Zuckerman, are you ready to present your strikes?"

Zuckerman rose from her chair, walked up to the bench and handed the paper up to the judge. Most judges let the parties exchange strikes during a recess. The end result could be handed to the judge when court started up again. Judge Mays, though, viewed jury selection as a game and he liked to play along. He made two lists of jurors he would strike, one for each side. Because his defense picks were determined, in part, by the State picks, he always looked at the State's list before he made his final defense cuts.

After scratching out the appropriate names, he said, "Very good. You may hand that to Mr. Montoy." Zuckerman walked over and handed the paper to Kate. The three of them, Kate, Arnie and Rick, all huddled around the sheet. Kate had guessed almost all of them, but there was one surprise. Zuckerman had struck She Petty.

"Whoa," Rick said. "I thought we were going to strike her?"

Kate turned and looked at him. "Zuckerman was afraid of the same things we were, the unknown. She was a six on her questionnaire, but much softer in court. Without knowing which one would show up in the jury room, Betsy decided to play it safe."

Arnie took the list up to the judge, who snatched it and immediately began comparing it to his own. When he was done, he looked back at Kate with a slightly puzzled look on his face. It quickly passed, and he stood up and looked down at his calendar. "Very well, we'll start up at nine sharp tomorrow morning. Anything else?"

Neither Arnie nor Zuckerman said anything. The judge banged his gavel and hurried out. Zuckerman quickly packed up, leaving only the Wrenshaw team in the courtroom.

Kate blew a sigh of relief when the door closed behind Zuckerman. "She didn't strike the Farter," Kate said to no one in particular.

"So, the Farter sits?" Arnie asked with a smile. "What about the other two?"

In addition to Wigginstaff, Kate thought two jurors would help the "chaos theory" along. One, Steve Rusa, they had nicknamed Squeaky. Rusa had lost his arm to frostbite up to his elbow in an Alaskan kayaking accident several years earlier. Cheap by nature, he bought a used prosthetic replacement that squeaked, just slightly, when Rusa manually turned the hand back and forth. Rusa turned the hand whenever he got nervous. Courtrooms apparently made him very nervous because he twisted and turned the thing all day.

The Grammar Lady rounded out the trio. Holly Pennwell, a housewife and mother of three, had a perfectly coifed helmet of yellow-blond hair. She had frequently, and almost always erroneously, corrected the attorneys' grammar during voir dire. "It's 'would you agree with the prosecutor and *I*' not 'the prosecutor and *me,*' " she had chastised Arnie. Also, judging from her cough, she smoked at least three packs a day.

Kate smiled at Rick. "They all sit. It's our perfect chaos jury. Between the Farter's hygiene, Squeaky's arm and the Grammar Lady coughing a lung up on the jury room table, they should deliberate about five minutes."

Kate smiled at Arnie, then looked down at the list of the final twelve jurors and sighed.

Arnie looked over at her. "What's wrong? We got the three crazies. They won't be able to agree on which chairs to sit in, let alone agree on death. You did it."

"Yeah," Kate lied, "I'm just worried about Bug Guy. Him being a killer, you know."

"What's done is done, Red. You did good. Enjoy it."

She had done well. She had devised the plan to get the jury to hang as quickly as possible and gotten the exact jurors she needed. But was that the right plan? The more she talked to Rick and the more she learned about the case, the more she thought there was something else there—something under the surface that needed to be studied and analyzed to be seen. So, was it really a good idea to pick a jury that would get in and out of the jury room as quickly as possible?

CHAPTER 14

Boris stood in the doorway of St. Christopher's Cathedral, staring out into the rain-soaked street. He glanced at his watch. Six o'clock. At least the boys were not early. Although, what was the worst that could happen? They would find out he was a fraud and beat him up? He had been beaten up before. They might go to the police, but he doubted it. They were in it as deep as he was. With or without them, the plan would go forward. That was the important thing.

But it certainly would be easier with them on board. As long as the priest did his job, it should hold them a couple of weeks. That was all he needed

Earlier that day he had made an appointment at the Cathedral. Twenty years ago, when they had finished the church, this had not been a bad part of town. It still was not that bad, but the creeping blight was getting closer block by block. The head priest came to the door wearing one of those funny collars. This surprised Boris. He knew the nuns had stopped wearing black and white and figured it was all across the board. Although now a confirmed atheist, he had been raised Catholic. Deceiving a priest, especially one wearing the funny collar, bothered him more than he cared to admit.

Fortunately, Father Brad was not a traditional, old-school priest. First, his name was Father Brad, rather than some ominous, judgmental name like Joseph or Bartholomew. More importantly, though, he was young and had soft, trusting eyes.

Boris had been expecting one of the cynical old codgers he had confessed to as a youth. Ol' Father Bartholomew knew you were lying before the lie was born in your mouth. This guy, if Boris had said he had left a baptismal font around here somewhere, would have loaded the thing into the truck himself.

"My name is Steven Stevenson," Boris said, shocking himself by using such a moronic name. He had been waffling between Steven Richardson and Richard Stevenson but, in the moment, panicked. Father Brad smiled back at him trustingly.

"Nice to meet you, Mr. Stevenson. What can we do for you?" Boris was surprised by the young priest's voice. Moderately deep and rich, it had that disassociated quality of a radio announcer, as if the voice was actually coming out of someone else. He also had a trace of the mid-Atlantic in there, probably rural Pennsylvania.

"I'm with a local film production company and we're shooting a movie about a young girl growing up in Kansas City. Part of the film needs to be shot in a church and we're scouting locations. Frankly, I think your sanctuary would be perfect. The big space, the lighting. It's perfect." Although Boris had described almost every church in the Kansas City metropolitan area, Father Brad readily accepted the compliment. Boris put out the bait. "Of course, we would pay you to have the space available to us for forty days." Boris smiled at his cleverness in choosing the Biblical number.

Father Brad's eyes lit up. One thing about priests, be they young and gullible or old and cynical, they all needed more money for the parish. Boris set the hook a little deeper. "I thought it would be best to speak directly with you rather than going through the diocese. Or do I need to start downtown?"

"Oh, no," the priest blurted out, his eyes darting involuntarily toward a large picture of a dour man in a miter hat. Turning back toward Boris, Father Brad said, "No, I think we can handle this just fine between us. I assume there would be no interruption of the services?" The young priest may have been gullible, but he understood how not to share the pie. If someone complained to the bishop that services had been cancelled, there would be questions that could only be answered with money.

Boris smiled as he reeled him in, "No, no, we don't want to interrupt anything. You just need to make sure we have a schedule so we can have enough time to shut down."

"Of course, of course. You said you needed forty days?" the priest asked hopefully.

"Right. I don't know how much these things cost, but we figured a wedding probably takes a half a day. We want it to be available for the full forty-day shoot. So I would guess eighty times what you charge for a wedding for someone not in your congregation." From the look on his face, the priest was good at math. "But first we have to make sure it's the right church."

Father Brad's face fell as he saw his fat payday slipping away. "Oh, I'm sure you'll be very pleased. Our sanctuary is consistently rated as the most beautiful in Kansas City."

Boris nodded in agreement. "Oh, yes, everyone told us we needed to come here first. If it were up to me, we would sign it right now. But the producers are a couple of young guys. It's really their call. They want to come by during an evening mass and get a feel for the church during a service."

Father Brad scooted forward in his chair. "We have a mass tonight at six. It won't be a full house like on Sunday, but, being a Friday, I bet we'll fill up a third of the sanctuary." He was excited now and the mid-Atlantic lilt gave way to an Appalachian twang. Boris smiled. Father Brad might be shrewder than he first appeared. Greedy and shrewd is often easier to con than honest and trusting.

"Tonight would be perfect. Let me tell you what they'll be

looking for. They want to check out the acoustics and how people react to the noises. It's absolutely critical the parishioners not react to us at all. They need to pay attention to you as if we weren't there. In addition to the sanctuary, we may need some extras for the church scenes. The boys will need to know they won't mug for the camera. Will you be able to get your people to ignore us completely?"

Father Brad nodded vigorously. "That shouldn't be a problem. From what I hear in confession, they ignore everything said in church anyway." He laughed nervously at his own joke. Then his face darkened. "Except the children. You know how hard it is to control children." His left hand came up to cradle his face and he quickly squeezed his cheeks together several times.

"Oh, that's not a problem, it's really the adults they'll be looking at." The priest dropped his hand and smiled. Boris stood up. "We'll probably slip in during the service and then slip out again. It shouldn't take more than ten minutes. I will call you next week either way."

"Next week?" the priest asked as his smile disappeared. "You won't know anything sooner?"

"No," Boris said. "But I'm sure the boys are going to have an unforgettable experience." Boris smiled as he left, pleased at his cleverness in finally saying something actually true.

At 6:05 Boris was starting to get a little worried. He walked around the side of the church to see if the boys were at the wrong door. When he came back around to the front, he saw T.J. opening the door to the church.

"Wait!" he screamed. The boys had apparently walked around the entire church looking for the front. They both spun around, eyes wide. Boris smiled. They were scared and edgy. If they had

even a little faith left, the next ten minutes would bring them back.

"Before we go in, I want to explain what is going on. You needed proof I'm the Devil. Frankly, if you had asked for that at the crossroads, I would have struck you down.

"But since you're more than half the way toward completing your end of the bargain, I thought I'd put your minds at ease." Upon hearing they were halfway home, Randy looked over to T.J. and smiled.

"I don't want there to be any more doubts in the future, so I brought you here to the Lord's house. Here, His power is the strongest and I am at my weakest. Still, during the mass that is going on inside, I will make us invisible to them. We will walk among them, talk among them and they will never even notice us. We will, in fact, still be there, so you can't touch anyone or anything. Also, children are the innocents and I have little power over them. So, a child may look at you or react to you. But to the adults, you will pass among them like the wind."

The boys giggled.

"What?" Boris asked sharply. They should not be laughing right now. Was he losing them?

"Will they be able to smell us passing like the wind?" Randy asked.

Boris still did not understand. "I suppose not. It's never really come up. I'd say no. They won't be able to smell you." Boris looked at his watch. The service would be over while they argued about air quality. "They can't see you, hear you, or smell you. If I can do that, in the House of God, will you believe I am the Devil?"

The boys looked at each other and, for a few moments, some unspoken conversation was held. Finally, Randy said, "Yeah. If it's like you say."

"Let's go." Boris said as he walked in the doors.

The sanctuary had two large sections of pews on either side of a wide center aisle. Father Brad stood behind an ornate lectern in front of the section on the audience's left. Boris knew the first part would be the hardest. He had no doubt the priest had properly instructed the congregation that it was critically important to the financial stability of the church that they ignore the three strangers who would soon be walking around during mass. Nonetheless, all it took was one person, turning at the movement in their peripheral vision, and the gig was up.

Boris stayed back and surveyed the crowd. It was closer to a quarter full than the third the priest had promised. Good. The fewer people, the less of a chance for error. Father Brad seemed to be beginning his sermon. When Boris stepped forward, there was no physical change in the priest, but Boris noticed the re-emergence of the twang.

Not wanting to startle anyone by sneaking up, Boris spoke in a loud, but not booming voice. "See, just like I told you. No problems. No problems at all."

Randy and T.J. walked together down the aisle, shoulder to shoulder like a father and a bride. Boris, ahead by several paces, had been facing forward to make sure nobody had moved or given them away. Satisfied everything was okay, he turned and began walking backwards.

"What do you say, boys? Do you have any questions, now?"

T.J. stopped walking even with the front pew. "C-can we talk?" As he spoke he looked around at the people sitting in the pews. Everyone was staring with rapt attention at the priest. Boris became a little concerned, having never seen any congregation so enthralled with a sermon. It was decidedly unnatural. The boys, however, seemed to be buying it.

"Sure, noise was one of the things we talked about before we came in. I want you to have all your questions answered before we leave here."

Randy turned and looked directly into the side of the face of an elderly man sitting at the end of a pew. *"Can. You. Hear. Me?"* Randy yelled into the man's ear. Spittle flew from his lips onto the old man's face. Bending down, he looked for the slightest reaction. *"I. Said. Can. You. Hear. Me?"* The old man held strong, continuing to listen intently to Father Brad's every word. Boris smiled and mumbled, "This old place must be broke."

He began walking the boys back out of the church. Everything had gone perfectly and that could not last. "Satisfied?"

The boys looked at each other and nodded. Boris could see it in their eyes. They believed. "Let's get back to work."

CHAPTER 15

Rick sat down in the metal chair and waited for Kate. He ran his finger along the gray metal table and thought that people on the outside do not appreciate the softness of wood. On the inside, everything is metal or concrete. The doors, the floors, the trim, tables, chairs, bed—not a scrap of wood to be found. He chuckled to himself. Every time he went back in, he realized one more thing they take from you on the inside. Wood. Who would have guessed he would miss the feel of wood?

Down the hall, he heard a metal door clang against its metal jamb. Two more clangs and Kate would be in the room. He looked down at his shirt and pressed it with his hand. It was not as if he was going to try to pick her up or anything. But she was the only woman he regularly saw.

He stared at a dimple in the table until she was a few steps into the room and then he looked up to see it. The smile. That was something he realized early on they take from you: seeing people smile. Inmates do not smile because, well, they are inmates. Guards do not smile because they do not want to be seen as soft. Visitors do not smile because the person they are visiting is inside. So, nobody smiles. Except Kate. She had a great smile.

He smiled back at her and stood to greet her. She was about 5'2″, so he was able to look down at her. The guards would not let them touch, but that was just as well. He did not want Kate to get the wrong idea and stop coming. He just wanted to be around a woman every once in a while.

"Hey Rick, what do the stars tell you?" Kate said, winking at him.

"Jupiter's rising into Mercury. I think it was a good day to pick a jury," he said. The banter was solely for the benefit of the guard. At least six foot three, he towered over both of them. Neither Kate nor Rick cared much about astronomy, although Rick loved to look out at the night sky. He had told Kate and she had snuck in some small glow-in-the-dark circles he had stuck on his ceiling. Every night before he closed his eyes, he stared at his ceiling and pretended he was on a beach, looking up at the sky. Kate regularly asked about the stars to make sure they had not been confiscated.

She nodded at the guard who left the room and took up his post on the other side of the door, staring in through the glass window. "Yeah," Kate said, "it was a great day to pick a jury." She pulled a piece of paper out of her jacket and raised it up for the guard to see. He nodded and she put it down on the table sideways so Rick could read it from across the table.

"You know how we wanted the three crazies to hang up the panel?" Kate asked. Rick nodded. "I think it may be better than we thought. When I first got the list, I focused on the three we wanted. But as I was waiting out there, I looked at the whole list and there are some more oddballs on here. Not full-blown crazies, but enough that it may help cause a little chaos in the jury room."

"Who do you mean?" Rick asked.

"Do you remember Ebeneezer?"

Rick nodded. "The guy with the British accent who wasn't British?" Ebeneezer, about five foot ten, was the star of the Community Theater's presentation of "A Christmas Carol" and did not want to lose his accent. "He seemed like a pretty decent guy."

"Sure," Kate said, "he's fine. Until he calls someone 'Gov'na' for the thirtieth time. Then they'll want to kill him." They both laughed.

"The whole panel's like that. Just a bit off. You've got Travolta and Miss Cocoa Butter. They're not going to get along. We've got Valley Girl, who is going to drive the Grammar Lady up a wall. And Zuckerman also left on the Magic 8-Ball. That's a pretty whacked-out jury."

Rick ran through the list in his head.

"What's wrong?" Kate asked. "That's a pretty good panel."

"That's only eight? Who are the other four?"

Kate winced. "There's the Bug Guy. I still don't know if leaving him on was the right thing to do."

"Don't worry about it," Rick said. "It's done."

"Thanks," Kate said and gave him the smile. "So, there's him and then 'Spring Break.' She could be trouble. The middle school pays her as long as she serves, so she may want the trial to last a long time. Then there was Charlie Brown and the guy that owned the university coffee shop. Really, that's the best we could have hoped for."

"It's all because of you," Rick said. "I like Arnie and everything, but I really appreciate everything you did for me."

Kate stared down at the table and then looked Rick in the eye. "Look, I'm done now so I won't be coming around anymore. Hopefully I can come back for closings, but this is kind of a crazy time for me right now, so I may not make it back." She paused for a moment. "You don't have to tell me if you don't want to, but, honestly, I've got to ask."

"You want to know why I do the urine thing."

Kate nodded.

"Everyone asks. You know, I only did it twice. It's not like I'm peeing all over Warrensburg."

"Oh, I understand that. But still, it's kind of a strange thing to do even once, you know?"

"Yeah, I know. But I was like sixteen. You know how stupid you are when you're sixteen? There was this girl, Cheryl Sabler."

Kate laughed. "There's always a girl in there somewhere, isn't there?"

"Yeah, it seems that way. Cheryl was really something. We had gone steady when we were in sixth grade for a couple of months. Even though I stopped growing, she was always really nice to me. So, I asked her to the Christmas dance our junior year. She told me she would have gone with me, but she was grounded. It's funny, but even though she turned me down, I felt great. She would have gone with me. If you could have seen her you would understand."

"I understand," Kate said. "Mine was Danny White."

Rick nodded. "I guess everyone has a Cheryl Sabler. So, anyway, a couple days after I ask her, I hear that she's going with Derrick Kozwalz, this tall, jock douche bag. I couldn't believe it. She wasn't grounded. She just didn't want to go with me. I was so pissed off. I don't know where I heard it first, but that dumb saying was going around back then: 'It's better to be pissed off than pissed on.' I was pissed off, so I decided to piss on them."

"What happened with Pike?" Kate asked. "Why the relapse?"

Rick paused for a moment. He had hoped she would have forgotten the Pike incident. Most of the time he told the story, people focused on the grossness of the first time. He did not like lying to Kate. "I just lost control and, I guess, reverted back to what I did before."

Kate frowned at him. "Rick, I've got to tell you, that doesn't jive with me. You say you lost control and shot Pike, but everything you did right before then was very orderly, very well thought out."

Rick stared back at her blankly.

"It doesn't make sense. And the one thing about juries, crazy or not, like water moves downhill, they move toward what makes sense. If it doesn't make sense, they'll think you're lying. And if they think you're lying to them, they will find you guilty and they will kill you. Can you clear it up for me? What were you thinking then, how did it all happen?"

Rick thought about telling her the truth. When she said that the jury would think he was lying, he knew she meant that *she* thought he was lying. If this was the last time he saw her, could he live with her thinking that he had shot down Pike for no better reason than being called a name? He shook his head, moved his chair back, and called out to the guard.

"Larry, I need to go back to my cell."

Chapter 16

Ron took several deep breaths in the elevator. He kept telling himself screaming at Tonetti would not help Elsie's case. He was an advocate. He had to advocate.

"Hi, Veronica," Ron said to the shapely brunette secretary. "Is Mr. Tonetti available?" She got up slowly and walked into Tonetti's office. She could have called in, but then Ron would not have been able to watch her walk back to the corner office. Just before she opened the door, she looked back and caught him staring. She smiled and opened the door, leaning in.

"Mr. Tittleton wants to know if you have a minute."

From inside, Ron heard Tonetti say, "Is he standing out there?"

Veronica looked back and gave Ron a sultry stare. "Yes."

Ron heard some mumbling and then Tonetti pushed through the door. Gino Tonetti had been the firm's managing partner for the past fifteen years. He had been a cross-country runner in college and ran with a group of associates at lunch every day. Everyone who had been a part of his running club had made partner within five years. Everyone who had joined the club and quit had left the firm within two. Ron was not a runner.

Tonetti strode past his secretary's desk and shook Ron's hand. "Ron, good to see you. I'm glad you came up. Spradlin has been raving about you lately." They walked into his office and Tonetti sat behind his desk. Behind him, a glass window faced north, looking down on a lazy bend in the Missouri River.

The thirty-first-floor view extended for miles over the downtown and industrial areas to the farmland in the distance. Ron always felt small and insignificant facing Tonetti in front of this panorama.

Tonetti sat for a moment, letting the view work its magic. "Ron, how long have you been with us?"

"Just over four years, sir."

"You should be coming up for partner soon. Very soon. I don't imagine there should be any trouble. As long as you don't sleep with Spradlin's wife." Tonetti laughed at his own joke and Ron joined him, mostly out of discomfort.

"Thank you, sir. I'm actually here to talk to you about the Stiltson case?"

The smile faded from Tonetti's face. "There are a lot of Stiltson cases, Tittleton. Which one are you talking about?" Ron guessed from the change in tone that not only did Tonetti know which case, he knew exactly why Ron was in his office wanting to talk about it.

"A police officer named Beckwith is suing Elsie Stiltson for publicly displaying his image without getting his permission." Ron paused, waiting for Tonetti to acknowledge the case. Tonetti sat still at his desk, hunched forward with his hands steepled together. "In order to prove Elsie did not need his permission to use the photograph in her show, I need an expert witness to come in and testify she had no legal duty. I just got off the phone with my expert. He says you called him and told him we would not pay for his deposition time or trial time."

Tonetti leaned back and spread out his hands. "Ron, I know this is your first big trial and you want to make sure you leave no stone unturned. I respect that. That's what we want in our young lawyers. But these experts cost a lot of money. The reality of litigation is we cannot afford to bring in an expert on every little point in the trial."

Ron's face flushed. "This isn't a little point, *sir.*" The last word came out more harshly than Ron had meant it. Tonetti's eyes narrowed. Ron suppressed his anger. "What I mean is, the whole trial boils down to whether she had to get his permission. The plaintiff is bringing a photography professor who's going to say the first words out of his mouth in every introduction to photography class he ever took or taught are, 'Get a release before you use someone in a photograph.' We need our own photography professor to say that's a bunch of crap. The bottom line is that if our expert does not testify, we lose the case."

Tonetti pursed his lips and brought his hands together. "Ron, did you know I personally assigned you to this case?"

Ron was not sure where Tonetti was going so he treaded carefully. "No, sir. I certainly appreciate the opportunity. I think we can win, but we have to have that expert."

Tonetti continued as if Ron had not spoken. "I have known Maynard Stiltson for thirty years. I personally oversee all of the Stiltson files that come through this office. There are two things Maynard loves more than life itself: mustard and his daughter, Elsie.

"Mustard has been good to him. Elsie, not so much. The last ten years or so, she's drifted away from him. Now she's going through this photography phase. God knows he's tried. Did you know he set up a studio in their house? Two hundred and fifty thousand dollars he spent and she's never set foot in it.

"Fifty years ago, Maynard wasn't even ten years old when his parents divorced." Tonetti shook his head sadly. "Maynard's mother took his only brother and went down south. He never saw either of them again. When his father died several years ago, Elsie was all he had left." Tonetti met Ron's eyes. "All he wants is a relationship with his daughter."

Ron began to see where Tonetti was headed, but needed the old man to say it aloud. "What are you saying?"

"I am saying your future here at Clark and Tonetti will not be adversely affected if you do not happen to win this case. We all know Jerry Bingham is a fine attorney and, frankly, Elsie should have gotten the officer's permission. If you should happen to lose, no one would think the less of you. Better yet, if you feel this case needs to settle, even for a fairly sizable sum, Mr. Stiltson is willing to cover those costs."

Ron shook his head. "But Elsie would have to go to him and beg him for the money."

"That would not be our concern."

Ron hesitated and then played his ace card. "I don't think Elsie will want to settle." Ethically, Elsie, as the client, made the decisions of whether to settle the case—not the person paying the bills.

Tonetti could not order Ron to settle the case against the client's wishes. "Maybe she doesn't fully appreciate the slim chance she has of winning." Tonetti waited for Ron to speak. Ron stayed quiet. If he said anything now, it would get him fired and possibly arrested. After a moment, Tonetti sighed. "Mr. Tittleton, we have not been authorized to pay for any experts. You will need to prepare for trial accordingly. I expect daily reports on your progress."

Ron thanked him for his time and left the office. In the elevator he let out a long breath. Not only had he not gotten funding for the expert, now Tonetti would be lurking over his shoulder watching for other ways to sabotage the case.

First though, he had to find an expert. He had not exaggerated the importance of having an expert testify. If the jurors did not hear someone say Elsie had no duty to get a release, they would almost surely find her liable. Liability meant damages. Damages meant begging for money.

If he could not pay for an expert, maybe he could find someone to do it for free. A photography expert would have been perfect, but all he really needed was a legal expert. One of his friends from law school could do that.

He turned the corner to his office as Cora looked up. She was on the phone, saying "Olive, I really don't want to talk about it anymore."

Ron caught her eye as he walked back into his office. "Come in and see me when you're through."

As he walked into his office he heard Cora say, "Yes, that was him, but I'm not going to ask him." Ron closed the door but stayed to eavesdrop on the rest of Cora's conversation. "I just can't, Olive. It's too . . . disturbing. Well, he wants to see me. Yeah, bye."

Ron scurried back around his desk and picked up a file. He pretended to read it as Cora walked in. "You wanted to see me, Mr. Tittleton?"

"Yeah, sit down, Cora. I need you to go through that law school directory they send me every year and look for anyone working in trademarks or art law. I don't think you'll find anyone in art, but trademark or even regular commercial law will work."

"I could talk to some of the girls in our commercial section. They may know someone."

"No!" Ron shouted. Cora jumped. "Sorry. Let's keep this between you and me, okay?"

Cora nodded but did not say anything. As she got up to leave, Ron stopped her.

"Cora, I'm sorry I couldn't help but overhear you on the phone. Was there something you wanted to ask me?"

Cora stared down at her shoes. "Oh, no. Thank you very much, but it's just some stupid question my sister was asking me."

"There are no stupid questions, Cora." In fact, Ron believed there were lots of stupid questions, many of which Cora herself had asked him, but now he was intrigued. What question could be so stupid even Cora recognized it?

"It's my nephew, Hugoton, Olive's boy." She paused, still looking down. "He wanted to know whether you use people years or animal years to figure the age of consent for an animal."

Ron was at a loss for words. All he could manage was "What?"

"See, I told you it was stupid. Just forget it." She turned and started to leave.

"No, Cora. Come back. I wasn't saying it was stupid. I'm not sure I understood what you meant." He understood exactly what she meant. He just could not believe it.

"You know, they say if a dog is two, that's really fourteen years old in dog years. So one people year equals seven dog years. I would guess the numbers are different for every animal." She looked at Ron for confirmation. He did not know. "So, if the age of consent is twelve, then would a dog have to be twelve in dog years or twelve in people years?"

"Is the age of consent twelve? That doesn't seem right." Ron was impressed he was able to single out one thing in this conversation that did not seem right.

"I don't know," Cora said quickly, "I'm just repeating what I've been told."

"Oh, okay." Ron sat for a minute. "And when you're talking about age of consent, you mean . . ." He could not finish it.

Cora again stared down at her shoes. "Consent to have sex."

Wow, Ron thought, Cora did not disappoint. When she says she has a stupid question, you can bet she has a doozy. He tried to keep a straight face. "I don't remember that coming up in law school. I suppose I could do some research."

"No," Cora said quickly. "Let's just drop it. And I'll see if I can find an art attorney."

"Thanks, Cora."

As she walked out, he tried to collect his thoughts and get up the nerve to call Elsie.

Chapter 17

Generally speaking, a woman's personality is formed in tandem with and in opposition to her father; a man's to his mother.

Greene, F. (2003). *The Trial Consultant's Field Manual* (p. 284). New York: Pullman.

Early one bright May morning, a doctor walked out of the delivery room and told Kate's grandfather, Jim Summerlin, that his wife had just given birth to a boy. To his wife and the rest of the outside world, and perhaps even to himself, Jim had repeatedly said it did not matter whether the child was a boy or a girl. A healthy baby was all he cared about.

If Robert had been Roberta, Jim may have believed that for the rest of his life. But, when the doctor said "It's a boy," he knew the truth. He wanted a son. Jim had been a star football player in high school. No girl, however much Jim loved her and whatever she might accomplish in life, could fill a former football player with fatherly pride like a son playing the game.

As Bob grew older, however, it became apparent that he took after his slender mother more than his burly father. In pee-wee football games, Bob ran with reckless abandon and got crushed by his bigger, faster classmates. Jim coached the team and heaped praise upon his son for his effort and resiliency. Even at ten, though, Bob could sense his father's underlying disappointment.

In junior high school, Bob discovered wrestling. Finally, against opponents his own size, Bob's aggression and determination won out. He would later say that, despite graduating as valedictorian, obtaining a doctorate degree, and becoming a father of his own, the only time he ever saw true pride glitter in his father's eye was after he won the seventh-grade city championship.

A good junior high wrestler, Bob was average in high school and not nearly good enough for college. After high school, he tried to satisfy his fix by watching professional wrestling on television. Although entertaining in a violent, soap opera-ish way, it was not wrestling. Boxing was certainly real enough, but it lacked the constant action of a good wrestling match. During the high school wrestling season, Bob went to the local meets. The rest of the year, his wrestling itch went unscratched.

In the mid-nineties, however, Bob discovered mixed martial arts, MMA to devotees. A combination of boxing, wrestling, and various martial arts, fights were designed to determine the best overall fighters in the world. After seeing his first match on cable, Bob was hooked.

His enthusiasm spread throughout the athletically challenged Art History department. Now, on the second Friday of every month, Bob hosted a watch party for the MMA Friday Night Fights on pay-per-view. To take a break from the Beckwith situation, Kate came over to help her father with his latest party. Too often he would get caught up in the fights and forget to put out more chips. Bob also acted as bookie for the light betting that took place on each fight.

"Turgemenov is built like Michelangelo's Moses," Professor Melissa Whitly said. She had been one of the first to join Bob's fight circle and was the most vocal of the group. In her early forties, she had toned up her naturally curvy body after her husband left her for a younger woman. Her "cougar hunts" through the college bars were notorious fodder for the Art History department rumor mill. As often as not, she brought some young conquest to the Friday Fights. Tonight she was alone.

"You Renaissance goobs are always talking up Michelangelo," said Professor Elkharte, wagging a finger at Whitly. "How about a Bernini once in a while, huh, or a Rodin?"

"Ooooh," everyone in the room roared.

"What happened?" Elkharte cried, turning toward the television. "What'd I miss?"

"Submission hold. Turgemenov hooked his elbow and Gregor tapped out," Whitly replied. Elkharte shrugged. At least he had not missed anything good like a knockout or a dislocated shoulder.

With a break in the action, the Modern and East Asian professors went outside for a smoke, while the European section filed into the kitchen to refill their plates and cups. Whitly called over her shoulder, "So you think I should compare them to Balzac? That fat pig? Moses would have kicked his ass."

"Not Balzac, necessarily," Elkharte said, following her. "What about the Thinker? That guy was ripped. And smart probably, too." Their voices trailed off as they went into the kitchen. Bob walked halfway up the stairs and motioned with his head for Kate to follow. She saw him duck into her old room.

Everything was exactly as she'd left it when she graduated from high school. More out of laziness than nostalgia, Bob had never redecorated. Still, the familiarity made Kate feel comfortable here. Looking around, she was glad she had not been like so many of her friends who hung posters of then-teen idols. Old Cary Grant movie posters lined the walls. *My Favorite Wife* and *North by Northwest* were timeless.

Bob sat on the bed and patted it next to him. Kate sat down and leaned her head on his shoulder.

"I'm worried about you, kid. You look tired."

"It's just been a long week."

"Did you finish up that urinating trial?"

Kate laughed and straightened up. "Yes, Dad, I finished the urinating trial."

"I hope you're going to take some time off now. I don't think you should do those any more. They take a toll. You don't notice when you're young, like you. But when you get older, you look around and think, 'How did this happen?' and then you remember."

"Actually, I have a mock trial tomorrow and a jury selection next week. But I should get some time off after that."

"Tomorrow?" Bob said. "Well, if you need to leave early, everyone will understand. You know how these parties can get."

Kate knew. Around eleven, everyone would start praying for a knockout so they could go home and go to bed. "It's all right. I'll stay and help you clean up. I don't have to be there until ten."

"Your choice," he said, getting up. "Now I'm going to see what Gilderson is up to."

"Wait a minute," Kate said as he hurried out the door. "Gilderson's a smoker. Are you smoking again?"

"Only one or two during the fight parties," he said. He was down the stairs and out of the door before Kate could harass him anymore. She had nagged him since she was a preteen to quit smoking. Finally, three years ago, he had smoked his last. Or so she thought. Next weekend she would have to talk to him.

She heard the bell ring on the television. They were announcing the next fighters. She went downstairs, grabbed a beer and sat down on the sofa. Normally, she would save Bob a seat. This time, he was on his own.

About a minute into the first round, Sue Gilderson rushed into the room. "Call 911. Bob's been hurt."

Kate ran outside. A small gathering of people stood in an oval at the end of their neighbor's driveway. Someone knelt at one end. Kate ran over and saw her father lying on the ground. His pants were torn at the knees, but his face had suffered the most damage. Blood trickled out of his mouth. A large red welt covered most of his forehead and his right cheek was beginning to swell. Fortunately, his eyes were open.

"Did someone get the number of that truck?" he asked and then chuckled. Blood gurgled out of his mouth and splattered on his shirt. "I always wanted to be able to say that."

"What happened?" Kate asked.

"It was the darndest thing," Roger Gilderson replied. "We were all standing out here," he took a quick look at Kate, "talking."

Kate interrupted. "I know he was smoking, Dr. Gilderson, just tell me what happened."

"Okay, we were all out here when this big truck pulled up. It looked like that Escalade Whitly just got, only a dark color. Some guy inside called out, 'Hey Bob, come here for a minute.' When Bob gets over there, this arm reaches out and grabs him by the back of the neck, as if he was picking up a cat. All of the sudden, the guy guns the engine and the truck takes off with Bob just kind of, uh, dangling there. Only they don't pull away from the curb, so Bob goes head first into that mailbox." Everyone looked over at the black metal mailbox lying in the middle of the street. "Then they drop him and drive off. It's like they were playing mailbox baseball, but with Bob's head instead of a bat."

"Glad the Mulroneys didn't get that brick mailbox they were talking about," Bob joked. He tried to sit up, but Roger put his hand on his chest.

"Did anyone see who it was?" Kate tried to act as if she didn't know exactly who it was. First Townsend and now her dad.

Maybe it was unrelated. Yeah, right.

"We were all standing over there. Bob?"

"I couldn't really tell you. It was dark and then when I got closer, he grabbed me and turned me around. Maybe it was a disgruntled student. I gave a lot of Ds this term."

Kate stayed with her father until the ambulance came, then went to the hospital while the Gildersons locked up the house. The fights were the last thing on people's minds. Except Kate. The next time she saw Boris, it would make those MMA guys look like they were playing patty-cake.

CHAPTER 18

A well-planned mock trial is a well-run mock trial.

Greene, F. (2003). *The Trial Consultant's Field Manual* (p. 181). New York: Pullman.

"Thank you for coming in, Ms. Summerlin. Britinni will be right with you. Please help yourself to a cool towel." Kate sat down in the chair and draped the towel over her head.

Last night in the emergency room, the doctors had found a small fracture in Bob's cheek. He was scheduled for surgery at one that afternoon. The surgeon had said it was a simple procedure. Kate still wanted to be there, but could not put the task of rigging the mock trial on Jo's shoulders. Bob was sleeping when she left the hospital at eight-thirty.

She hadn't slept. Getting her father admitted took half the night and then she sat with him, even though he had been out cold from the drugs. She had to get focused. Nothing quite settles the mind like a good massage and a manicure. Unfortunately, she couldn't afford a good massage or manicure.

Fortunately, a local cosmetology school in North Kansas City offered discount prices. If she had to put up with some sloppy polish or a spaghetti-armed masseuse, it was a small price to pay. Plus, the school was on the way to the casino.

"Hello Kate, welcome back." Kate took the towel off her head and saw Britinni smiling at her. One of the drawbacks to using the cosmetology school was the constant turnover. The school courses ran six months and then, Kate assumed, everyone graduated. Britinni, however, looked familiar even though Kate had not been there for almost a year. She felt alarm bells going off, but she could not remember why.

"What are we going to be doing for you today?"

Hearing her voice again solidified Kate's feeling that something was about to go horribly wrong. Figuring she could always wipe off misapplied nail polish but an overaggressive massage could leave her wounded, Kate said, "I think I'll start with a manicure. I can't really decide on which color though. Do you have several I could look at?"

"Sure. Thish Tulsha Twilight should go sho good with your shuit." Britinni said. Ah yes, there it was. Now Kate remembered. Britinni had a small gap between her two front teeth. Her breath whistled through the gap when she said the letter s. Kate had never realized how many words use the letter s.

"Actually, I think I want something sort of fun. Do you have any fruity-type colors?" Kate thought maybe a nice peach or mango would brighten her up.

"Shure. We've got lotsh of fruitsh. And even shome vegetablesh."

"No," Kate said quickly. "Just the fruits." Logically, Kate knew there probably was not much of a difference in nail polish world between orange and carrot. But one felt very fun and the other felt nutritious. No one wants nutritious nails. Except maybe Jo.

"I'll shee what we have." Britinni walked over to a large cabinet and Kate closed her eyes to rest for a moment.

Kate woke up and looked around, disoriented. Looking down at her watch, she yelped. Late. More stress. "What happened?" Kate screamed to no one in particular.

From behind her she heard, "You shlipped off to shleep. It

wash sho peashful, we deshided to let you shleep. And now your nailsh are dry." Kate's eyes slid over from her watch to her fingers. She let out a small whimper.

"What color is this?" Kate asked. Her nails glowed in a bluish-purple.

"You said you wanted fruity. So, I mixed a blackberry and blueberry to give you shomething shpecial."

Kate splayed her fingers out in front of her and took another look. The bluish-purple hue had a distinct bruise quality to it. Black-and-blueberry sounded about right. She looked as if she had slammed both hands in a drawer. Looking up at the hopeful eyes of Britinni, Kate could not break her heart.

"Looks great," she said as she gathered up her stuff. Britinni beamed.

Kate checked the backseat before she got in the Bug and then sped off. The mock did not start until noon, but she always had the attorneys show up two hours early. A quick glance at her watch showed 10:05. Even the way she drove, the casino was twenty minutes away. She punched in Jerry's number on her cell phone.

When he answered, she began talking before he could yell at her. "Hey Jerry, I got caught up on a conference call this morning and couldn't get away. I'll be there in 15 minutes."

"Don't worry about it, babe. Everything is running perfectly. Matelyn has everything set up and we're ready to go. Just come back to the Henry the Eighth Ballroom." Kate searched his voice for some level of agitation, but found none.

"Great, I'll be right there. Wait. Who's Matelyn?"

A new fear gripped Kate. Was this a new consultant? Is that who set this mock up? Had Jerry already been planning a mock with this Matelyn bitch before Kate had even suggested it? If she lost Jerry as a client, word would get out. She could lose all of her Kansas City clientele.

"Matelyn is the casino projects manager. She's fantastic. You'll see when you get here. I gotta go." He clicked off.

"The casino projects manager," Kate repeated with disdain. She took a deep breath, tried to remember the feeling under the cool towel and pressed down harder on the accelerator.

Fifteen minutes later, Kate walked in the casino and stopped. For the most part, the main room looked like it would in any other casino. Lots of slots, a couple rows of blackjack and craps tables and miles of gold-flecked red carpet. And like many casinos, it had a theme. The theme, however, was not some old European city or a tropical paradise. The theme at Big Mama's Casino and Love Palace was large people.

As Kate walked down the row of blackjack tables, she tried not to stare at the dealers. All were at least two-hundred and fifty pounds. The pit bosses prowling behind the tables were even larger. Kate walked by an old couple staring straight up. Looking skyward, she saw a reproduction of Michelangelo's Creation of Adam, with both God and Adam repainted as huge, rosy-fleshed gods. Professor Whitly would have a heart attack. The only nonobese employees Kate could see were the waiters and waitresses: stick-figures in shorts and tight shirts.

One particularly bony waiter flashed by and gave Kate a sly wink. She followed him down the row until he disappeared behind a large, beige slot machine. Kate stood still for a moment, alone with her thoughts. Suddenly, the beige blob Kate thought was a slot machine got up and waddled over to another machine, bringing Kate out of her reverie.

The "machine" was actually a large Hawaiian man in a beige coat. Kate laughed at herself and thought it was the largest man she had seen since, well, wait a minute. Since yesterday. Wasn't there a large Hawaiian man changing his tire down the street? She followed him and tried to get a look at his face.

She stared at him for a full minute, trying to get him to look at her. If he was following her, he sure was not paying much attention to her. Maybe it was a coincidence. Just because a guy was in Lawrence yesterday and at the casino today, did not necessarily mean he was following her. A guy that large, if he wants to gamble on a Saturday morning, he is probably going to come to Big Mama's. Although, even by Big Mama standards, he was a big one. This Boris thing was making her paranoid.

She tried to put it out of her mind as she walked toward a sign that said *Ballrooms.* On a gold tripod just to the side of the main floor exit, a sign read: RAFFLE WINNERS—HENRY THE EIGHTH BALLROOM.

She stepped in a long hallway and saw Jerry walking toward her.

"Hey babe, you made it."

"Good to see you, Jerry. Look, the casino messed up." *Ha. Screw you, Matelyn!!* "The sign out here says there's some sort of raffle going on in our ballroom. We can't have them interrupting our mock."

"Oh, no," Jerry said. "That's us." Kate's brows furrowed and she pursed her lips. Jerry looked like a kid with a surprise present for his mother. "That's how we got our mock jurors. The casino held a raffle."

Kate stared at him in disbelief. "We won our jurors in a raffle?" she deadpanned.

"We didn't win them. They're the winners. People join these Gold Card clubs where the casino gives them points for every dollar they bet. So, Matelyn came up with the idea that they could bet their points. Each of them put up 200 points to be in a raffle and the winners got to be in our mock trial."

Kate stared at him in disbelief. "People would do that?"

"Oh, sure. At the end of the day, there's another drawing and the winner gets 5,000 points and two free nights at the Big Mama's mother ship casino in Vegas. It's all crap to the casino.

But for these gamblers, it was the best bet they've seen in weeks."

Kate could not believe what she was hearing. Any valid social study required the participants be randomly selected. She tried to ignore the little voice reminding her that valid social studies don't have the outcome rigged by the social scientist. "C'mon bub, we've talked about this before, the jury has to be random."

Jerry's eyes suddenly grew large. "Oh, my God," he cried. "What the hell happened to your hands? No wonder you're so bitchy."

Kate looked down at her fingers. They looked awful. "It's nothing. And I'm not being bitchy. There's a right way to do these things and choosing jurors by raffle is not the right way."

Jerry stopped and turned toward her. "On two days' notice it's the best we could do." Kate felt her face flush. "Plus, you said it would cost ten grand. The casino had the ballrooms open and they figured they could use the promotion to get more people in here, so they gave us the rooms. They gave us the prizes for the raffle. They even let us tap into their security cameras for the live jury cam. I think Matelyn did us right." Now it was Kate's turn to pout.

They walked into the Henry the Eighth Ballroom and Kate surveyed the set-up. The room was a standard hotel ballroom space. Twelve tables were lined up in six rows, a center aisle running down the middle. At the front of the room, two tables for the attorneys angled slightly toward each other.

Everything was exactly as she would have designed it, which she did not like at all. She felt unnecessary. "Looks like everything's good here. Where's the attorneys' room?"

"We're down the hall in the Rubens room," Jerry said as he walked out the door.

Kate rolled her eyes as she followed him. "Of course we are."

The smell of caramelizing onions wafted out into the hall just before they entered the room. Clearly the casino recognized who the clients were. In the mock courtroom, for the mock jurors, they had set out a simple selection of Danishes and muffins, along with carafes of tea and coffee. In the private attorney room, the spread included a full breakfast buffet and an omelet station, where a thin, olive-skinned man folded three eggs into a skillet for Mark, Jerry's partner. Kate realized for the first time that she had not eaten yet today.

A well-dressed woman in her early thirties sat at one of the tables scribbling on a pad. Women did not last too long in Jerry's testosterone-driven firm so Kate doubted she was an associate. That would make her Matelyn. Kate eyeballed her warily.

Jerry saw the concern in her face. "Is something wrong? I tried to set it up exactly like last time."

"Everything's fine," she said. Jerry *had* paid attention. The room looked just like the last job. That is, if the last job had taken place in a NASA lab. Kate had very nice, very expensive equipment. But it was two soup cans and a string compared to this stuff. The pictures on the televisions were so clear, they looked like windows into the other room. At a control panel the size of an old church organ sat a huge man with intricate tattoos on his telephone pole–sized arms.

"Who's that?" Kate whispered.

Jerry did not even look over at the man. Staring straight ahead, he said, "That's Butch. He's the video guy. Since we're getting our jury cam feed through the casino's security system, nobody touches any of the wires or any of the video stuff except Butch." Knowing Kate did not respond well to being told she could not do something, he gave her an imploring look.

"Don't worry," she said.

Matelyn looked up and, seeing Jerry with Kate, walked over. "Kate," she said with a smile as she extended her hand, "it's so nice to meet you. We are so excited to do this for you. When

Jerry called, my mind started spinning with all the possibilities. We want to be the first place you turn when you have mock trials."

Kate stared at her for a moment. "Yeah."

Mark, sitting at a table wolfing down his omelet, waved them over. "You guys have to try an omelet. Armando is a genius." He gave the cook a salute with his fork and Armando smiled back. Kate looked over at the station. Open flame and oil in a hot pan. It could easily tip over and burn one of the attorneys. Thirty percent fault to Armando. Forty percent to Matelyn for a poor set-up.

Mark stood up, still holding his fork in his hand. "Kate, I don't know why you haven't done this . . . Good God, what happened to your hands?"

Matelyn looked down and her eyes widened. She quickly looked up at Kate, speechless.

"Nothing," Kate said, dropping her hands to her side and making fists. "When are the people going to show up?"

Jerry looked at his watch. "10:45. We told them 11:45 so we could start at noon, but you know someone is going to show up any minute." No matter when people were told to be at an event, someone, usually an old man wearing plaid, showed up an hour early.

"This is a special crowd. And they have to walk through the casino to get here. That should slow them down," Kate said.

"Not this time," a voice behind them said. Butch pointed to a monitor where a white-haired man walked up to the sign-in table outside the Henry the Eighth Ballroom.

Kate smiled. "I guess I'm on." She started to turn around when something on the monitor caught her eye. Her heart stopped as she recognized the two boys walking up behind the white-haired man. Boris's spies. Kate feared for a moment they were going to stab the old guy. She watched for a minute, but they only seemed to be asking him a question.

Butch picked up on Kate's distress. "Is there a problem with those two?" Kate took a step back when he reached into his coat pocket. He pulled out a walkie-talkie and Kate breathed. "No, it's just usually the young guys are the last in. It kind of surprised me." Butch gave her a dead stare. Despite much practice, she was not a good liar.

Kate scurried out of the room. If the security got there before she did, she did not want to think about what would happen to Townsend.

Chapter 19

Randy stared at the large mole on the back of the neck of the old man standing in front of him in line. Three straggling hairs sprouted out in a small tuft from the side of the growth. Randy looked over at T.J. and moved his eyes over toward the mole and grimaced. T.J. ignored him.

This could be a problem. T.J. rarely missed the opportunity to chuckle at the physical oddities of other people, especially old people. The funk around him had been growing ever since the night at the crossroads. Even after the miracle at the church the day before, T.J. had expressed his doubts.

They had left the church and driven down to the river to get high. The air down by the river was cool and crisp. Although the moon was only half full, its light filled the small clearing and reflected up off the barely moving water. Neither had spoken on the drive and the heavy silence continued until each had taken a toke on the joint.

"Maybe he's a hypnotist," T.J. had said. "Maybe it was some kind of trick. Or maybe they're all in on it together."

Randy, for once, had been the relative voice of reason. "If he was a hypnotist, then he could just hypnotize us. He wouldn't have to prove anything. And why would a whole church want to kidnap an old dude?"

"It's not about the old dude, it's about that trial," T.J. had replied. "Look, I don't know how he did it, but I don't think that proves he's the Devil. We need to get out of this before we get in some real trouble."

"We're already in it, T.J. Are you sure he's not the Devil? Can you look me in the eye and tell me he's not? Because if he is and we screw him over, it's over for us. And I think he already has our souls. So we spend the rest of eternity in hell with the Devil pissed at us. He doesn't strike me as the real forgiving type. You know? So, unless you're sure, we see it through."

In his own mind, Randy also had his doubts. He looked over at his brother. Smoke curled into T.J.'s eyes and he squinted to keep out the tears.

"But I know what you mean. Something wasn't right about that whole thing. It felt like a magic trick. You know, like when you're sitting there and some guy makes an elephant disappear. You know it's fake, but you don't know where the elephant went."

T.J. nodded and took a deep breath. "Yeah. Nobody looked at us, or moved or anything like that. Even when you yelled at that old guy, everything went perfect. But it felt like they knew we were there."

Randy exhaled and took the joint from T.J. "But are you sure? We can't get out, man."

T.J. reluctantly agreed. "We keep our eyes open, though. He's going to mess up. Then we beat his ass."

Boris had said he could not be seen at the casino, so the boys were on high alert as they stood in line. They were supposed to come to this meeting and then report back on what had happened.

Randy smiled. "He said we wouldn't have any problem getting into this thing and we haven't. Pretty strange coincidence."

So they stood there in line, T.J. pouting and Randy staring at the old man's mole. At the table in front of them, Jo took the old man's driver's license.

"Good morning, Mr. Jones, how are you this morning?" she asked.

The old man hitched up his jeans. "Feeling pretty good today." He reached his hand around and fingered the mole like a lucky talisman.

Jo looked up and smiled at him. "Good to hear. Do you have your winner's certificate?" The boys shot each other a panicked look as Mr. Jones pulled out a gold-edged piece of paper and laid it down on the table.

Jo checked the name on the certificate and moved it over to the side. "You're here a little early so you have your choice of seats. There's food and coffee over there. Just help yourself." As the man shuffled off into the room, Jo looked up at the boys.

"Hi," she said. "Are you here for the study?"

When the Moleman walked into the room, Randy had to step behind T.J. to let him pass by. Jo looked up at T.J. expectantly. T.J. stood silent, staring at Jo. Randy waited for a minute to let his brother answer, then poked his head around. "Yes. We're here for the mock trial thing."

"Okay. I need your driver's license and winner's certificates."

The boys stood there silent, unsure of what to do. Boris had not given them any certificates.

"They probably haven't got their certificates yet, Jo." The voice came from behind the table. The boys looked up and saw Kate walking quickly toward them. She gave them a warning look. "These were the last two winners this morning. The casino just called down. You guys can go ahead and go in and find your seats. We should be starting in about an hour."

"Oh, thanks Kate," Jo said, giving her an annoyed look. "Are there any more people not on the list?"

"No, that should be it," Kate said. Jo turned back around and handed the boys two blank name tags. She pointed to a coffee cup containing magic markers. "Just put your name in here and fill out these questionnaires. There's some food in there, be sure to help yourself."

T.J. stood still, looking at Jo and holding his name tag with both hands. Randy bent over, wrote his name and slapped it on the left side of his chest. He looked up at T.J. and said, "Do you want me to fill that out for you, dear brother?"

T.J. came out of his trance and wrote "Thelonious" on his tag.

"People call me T.J.," he said. Randy glared at him.

"Well, T.J.," Jo said, "if you want to put that on your tag, we're pretty informal here." Randy's scowl became darker. T.J. grabbed another name tag and filled it out. "It was very nice to meet you, ma'am."

They walked into the main room and picked out a couple of muffins and some coffee. "You kind of liked her, didn't you?" Randy asked.

"Who?" T.J. replied, pulling off the top of his muffin.

"That mousey girl out front." Randy did not often get to tease his brother about girls and he relished the opportunity.

"Shut up, I don't like her. I don't know what you're talking about," T.J. said, slapping his brother across the arm.

"Maybe I'll ask her out after we're done," Randy said, facing straight forward, but watching his brother out of the corner of his eye. "I thought she was kind of cute, in that pent-up librarian sort of way."

"No," T.J. said, a little too loudly. The old man two tables up turned around and glared at them. T.J. lowered his voice to a whisper. "I mean, we shouldn't get involved with anyone on the job. Someone, you know, working for the other side."

Randy smiled. "Yeah, you're probably right. But man, sure hate to give that up. Those librarian types, they're tigers in bed." T.J. said nothing, but the tension had left the air.

Randy began reading his questionnaire. The first few questions asked how he felt about litigation in general. Randy thought it was just people getting over on other people. It seemed to be a pretty good racket for the lawyers, but most of it was someone trying to get rich off someone else. And more power to them.

The next question asked whether he had any feelings one way or the other about police officers. Randy wrote in all caps. COPS SUCK.

T.J. glanced over and nudged his brother on his arm. "You can't put that in there. You can't say you hate cops. This place is probably stacked with cops. You have to say you appreciate the sacrifice they make and all that."

Randy began to scratch out the answer with his pen. T.J. grabbed his wrist. "You can't do that. You need a new one. I'll go get it." Before Randy could say anything, T.J. jumped up.

Ten minutes later he walked back into the room, smiling. Randy raised his eyebrows, smirking as he took the new questionnaire from T.J. "Everything go all right out there? Seemed to be gone a long time." T.J. ignored him and went back to filling out his own sheet.

They were about finished when a cop walked into the room. Six foot even, 180 pounds, he was dressed in street clothes but everything about him screamed cop. He stood at the back for a moment before walking up the left side. He stopped at the front of the room and gave it a cop onceover. When he saw the boys, his eyes narrowed and he gave them his best cop stare. They put their heads down, but could feel the heat of his gaze.

He walked over to them and stood in between them, leaning forward to read what was on the paper. "You boys supposed to be in here?"

Randy did not even try to keep the disdain out of his voice when he replied. "Yes sir. The lady out front told us to fill out these papers. So that's what we're doing."

The cop opened his mouth to say something when the back door flew open. By then, the room was about half full. All heads turned as Kate rushed into the room.

"Carl!" she screamed. Seeing everyone looking at her, she took a breath, smiled at the cop and said, "Carl, I, uh, I need to talk with you outside about something, uh, very important."

Carl looked down at the boys as if he didn't want to end the conversation before he had exerted total control. Kate repeated, "Carl?" and the cop walked around the table and out the door. Neither boy watched him leave, but each could feel his absence when he walked out.

The boys watched as the other people filed in the room. After a half-hour, about fifteen people sat around the room. No one sat at the table with the boys. Randy whispered over to T.J., "They're all old people. And not like forty-year-old old people. Old, old people."

Although not all of the others were white haired or bald, most were. A morbidly obese man in tent-sized overalls and a tall, shaky guy were the only others under thirty. Six people rushed in at the last minute, but still only two-thirds of the room was filled when Kate walked to the front of the room.

"While y'all are getting food, I'll get started with the preliminary stuff." The latecomers stood at the back of the room, filling their plates. "I know some of you are finished with your questionnaires and Jo and Carl are going to be collecting those when you're done. Just hold them up, they'll come and get them.

"I'm Kate Summerlin and I want to thank you all for coming today. I understand you are the lucky ones. And you may get even luckier." The audience tittered and gave each other knowing glances. "But first, we're going to make you earn that chance. Today we're going to be asking your opinions about a lawsuit. This is a real case and these are real attorneys. This is

Jerry Bingham. He is representing the plaintiff Michael Beckwith. Over here we have Mark Carver. He is representing the defendant, Elsie Stiltson. They're going to be talking to you about this case. You have some paper and a pen if you need to take notes. If you'll look to the back, that's Carl and Jo, they'll be the room monitors. Raise your hands, guys." Jo raised her hand. Carl shot Randy a look that said he would be frisking him later on. Kate continued on. "If you need anything, just flag one of them down."

The Moleman looked back at Carl and then at the Randy. He laughed and said, "Friend of yours?" Randy rolled his eyes.

Kate quickly said, "Mr. Bingham, they're all yours."

She started to walk away when a hand shot up from the left side of the room. A fifty-something woman with an auburn beehive hairdo asked, "Are you going to have smaller raffles during the breaks?" Everyone turned to look at Kate expectantly.

Kate's jaw stiffened and she forced a smile. "No, Betty. On the breaks we'll want you to go to the bathroom or smoke a cigarette and get back as quickly as you can. We've got a lot work to do today and we don't want to hold you past six o'clock. Are there any other questions?"

The lack of intermediate raffles seemed to deflate the group and no one else raised a hand. The boys listened over the next hour as first Jerry, then Mark, explained the case. Depending on who you believed, the case was either about (1) a careless trust-fund baby who had intentionally embarrassed and very nearly killed a local hero; or (2) a greedy, risk-taking renegade who was trying to cover up his own ineptitude as an undercover cop.

After the initial presentation, Jo and Carl handed out pink questionnaires asking how the people felt about the case so far. Randy filled in about half of the questions and got up and retrieved another strawberry yogurt from a bowl of ice on the food table. He had first tried it that morning and had been delighted to find fruit at the bottom of the cup.

When he came back to his seat, he saw T.J. had written long paragraphs on each question. "Jeez, ya brown-noser, what are you doing? We're just here to watch, we don't have to actually do this stuff."

T.J. leaned over and whispered, "Maybe we can get this thing over with. Remember at the warehouse, Boris kept saying he wanted to 'win the Beckwith case'?"

Randy tried to remember back. T.J. always had the better memory. "Sure, I think so."

"Okay then, what if we can win it right here. If we give Beckwith a whole bunch of money, then he wins, right?"

"I don't know, T.J. If Boris wanted us to do that he would have told us."

T.J. shook his head, "He couldn't trust us with that important of a job. He's counting on that Kate to fix it. But we're on the inside. We can help her. The sooner this is over, the better."

Randy thought about it. "Okay, I guess, what's the worst that can happen? We give this Beckwith a big pile and, if it's not enough, they still go on like before."

T.J. smiled. "Right. So we'll drive up the price as high as we can."

Randy agreed. He waved his hand at Jo. "I need another one."

Jo smiled at him as she handed him another questionnaire. "Maybe I should have given you two at the beginning," she joked and winked at T.J. He blushed and jerked his head down toward his paper.

After Carl and Jo picked up the remaining questionnaires, Kate came back in.

"Next up we are going to watch a couple of videos from

expert witnesses from both sides. Each expert should run about thirty minutes and then we'll take a break. Any questions?" No one raised a hand. "Alrighty then, the plaintiff's expert will go first."

Having decided to take a more active role in the process, the boys listened with a heightened interest, especially to the plaintiff's expert. They wanted to be able to repeat what he said to the other people in their group.

After the video, Carl and Jo passed out bright yellowy-green questionnaires. T.J. finished first and looked around for Jo to take it. As he turned in his seat, the two double doors in the back of the room flew open. The loud bang drew all eyes in the room toward the back as an old woman, dressed in oversized overalls and a dark red plaid shirt, stood square in the doorway. Her hands at her hips, she eyeballed the room, as if daring anyone to speak. She took in everyone in the room, until she got to T.J.

Her eyes widened. She raised a bony finger and pointed it at him. In a thin, scratchy voice she screamed, "The Devil is within you." A man in a gray suit came up from behind her, looped his arms around her chest and dragged her out of the room as the doors slammed shut.

CHAPTER 20

A consultant cannot be secluded in an ivory tower. In order to understand the wide range of people serving in juries, the consultant must regularly interact with diverse groups.

Greene, F. (2003). *The Trial Consultant's Field Manual* (p. 154). New York: Pullman.

"Thanks, Armando," Kate said, waving her fork in the air. Mark was right. The omelet bar was a must for the attorneys' room. She sat down in a folding chair that felt more comfortable than it should. For the next fifteen, maybe even thirty minutes, she could relax.

"Who is that?" she heard Butch say. She looked at the monitor and saw a wild-eyed, shabbily dressed woman standing in the doorway like Charlton Heston parting the Red Sea. Kate knew she should get in the other room, but she was mesmerized by the woman's intensity.

Suddenly, the woman raised her finger and pointed at T.J. and shouted, "The Devil is within you." That broke Kate's spell. Good-bye sweet, sweet omelet. Kate stood up as Butch rumbled by her toward the door.

"Butch," she yelled, "stay with the equipment." Butch turned and gave the equipment a dirty look. He seemed to be balancing his need for a steady job with the opportunity to bust heads. Practicality won out and he grumbled as he walked back to the sound board.

"Should I call security?" Matelyn asked. She was clutching her clipboard and Kate enjoyed her discomfort.

"No," Kate replied, "I'll take care of it. I think I know who they are." Kate had no idea who they were. But the last thing this mock needed was more security.

She rushed out of the attorneys' room door just in time to see Bernie Timlin pulling the woman out of the presentation room.

"Esmeralda! Esmeralda!" he screamed. "Indoor behavior. I need your indoor behavior." The woman seemed to calm down. Kate noticed others in the pack around Bernie come over to comfort her. Four other people, similarly dressed in oversized, under-cleaned clothes, had a nervous energy palpable even from down the hall.

"Bernie?" Kate asked as she approached. "What are you doing?"

Known throughout the streets and alleys of Kansas City as the homeless man's attorney, Bernie made a meager living fighting for the rights of the homeless and downtrodden—usually for being trodden down in the streets and alleys of Kansas City. Kate had worked with him on several cases at a third of her normal rate. At the start of the case, she felt good helping those who could not afford her regular fees. By the end of every case she swore she would never do it again.

"Oh, Kate. Hey. Great to see you." His eyes flicked down to her hands. She stared him down, daring him to mention it. He did not. "Look, I'm real sorry about Esmeralda, she does that from time to time." He smiled with a what-are-you-going-to-do shrug.

"Does what? Say people are possessed by the Devil?" As if on cue, Esmeralda pointed a finger at Kate and screamed, "The Devil is within you!" Kate stared back at her. She was not in the mood for any shit this morning.

"No, no, Esmeralda," Bernie said patiently. "Kate is an angel, sent to help us fight against Bronson Te." At the mention of Te's name, a low grumble came from the group and the tension in the hall grew noticeably.

Kate herded the group into the William Taft Room across the hall from the ballroom. Over the din of the chattering mob, she turned on Bernie. "What the hell are you doing here?"

The room fell silent. The group had never seen their champion dressed down. They stared, waiting for his response. Bernie smiled. "I called your office yesterday afternoon. They said you had left but you would be here today."

Kate's face grew red.

"Don't get mad at Cyndi. I told her it was an emergency." Bernie's face turned grave. "And it is an emergency. We need you Kate. They need you. This could be the big one." The group turned as one to Kate.

"This really isn't a good time." She paused, something Bernie had said finally sinking in. "Did you say Bronson Te?" Like anyone associated with litigation, Kate had a keen ear for the deep pockets. And pockets did not get much deeper than Bronson Te. Only twenty-seven years old, Te already had reached legendary status among the party crowds in Kansas City. His father, a real estate developer in Hong Kong, died when Bronson was twenty-three. The younger Te had always dreamed of coming to America and threw a dart at his future adopted country to decide where to settle. An expert dartsman, he hit the bull's eye and came to Kansas City.

Te had voracious appetites and the money to satisfy them. He frequently rented out a warehouse on a random weeknight. Six fully stocked bar stations and two loaded appetizer tables provided free food and drink to anyone hip or good-looking enough to make it past the bouncers. His parties raged until the sun came up. He would never advertise them. Word would spread like wildfire through the city. When he was not drinking the night away, he was expanding his father's real estate empire, although rumor had it that he also had a sizeable cocaine distribution business. In both endeavors, like the elder Te, he had the Midas touch.

"I said Bronson Te," Bernie announced. At that, a small man wearing torn, light blue pajamas with the feet attached mumbled, "Asshole." Kate had never seen adult-size pajamas with the feet attached. Bernie's eyes slid over for a moment then returned to Kate. He never stopped talking.

"At one of Te's parties, he and a few buddies thought it would be funny to give a homeless guy a million dollars and then see what happened."

Pajama Man again mumbled, "Assholes."

Bernie ignored him. "He gave the money to Reggie the Mumbler. Did you know Reggie?"

Kate looked at Pajama Man and guessed that, notwithstanding his current speaking style, his mumbling was not enough to earn him a permanent moniker. Plus, he did not look like someone who had a million dollars. "No, I don't think I did."

A small circle had formed with Bernie, Kate, Esmerelda and Pajama Man. A very large black woman stuck her head in next to Kate and said, "Salt of the earth," and pulled it back. The smell of cooked celery lingered in the air. Kate found it disorienting and stepped back to allow her into the circle. Esmerelda stepped over quickly to close the gap. Celery Woman did not seem to mind.

"Well," Bernie continued, "you give an addict like Reggie a bunch of money and he's going to go on a spree."

Celery Woman stuck in her head in again. "As sure as day follows night." Kate turned to face her, but she had already pulled back. A new smell of bananas mixed in with the celery.

Bernie's shoulders slumped. "Poor Reggie didn't make it a

week. So we're suing the bastard."

"Huzzah!" came the cry from the youngest member of the group. Probably in his early twenties, he had long black hair and a beard only three or four days from being neatly trimmed. Standing next to the cheerer and probably a few years older, a thin, black man filled out the group. Both men stood behind Bernie so Kate could not tell what, if anything, they smelled like.

Bernie was on a roll now. "Indeed. Anyone knows you give a million dollars to a homeless drug addict, he's going to die of an overdose. Te killed him as sure as if he held a gun to his head and pulled the trigger."

A thought began to bubble in Kate's brain. "How much are you asking for, Bernie?"

His shoulders straightened as he said, "Five million dollars. A million for each of Reggie's family, his real family, which now has to carry on. All because of the intentional and malicious acts of Bronson Te."

"Hear hear," said the young one.

"So, you're going to ask a jury to award each of these homeless people a million dollars because it's intentionally malicious to give a homeless person a million dollars?"

"Drug addict," Bernie corrected. "Giving a homeless *drug addict* a million dollars is malicious. None of my guys do drugs."

Kate looked around at the group. There weren't too many positives she could think of about their appearances, but they did all look sober.

She sighed. "You know I would love to help you, Bernie. I really would. But this is really a bad time. I've got the Wrenshaw trial, and this week I'm getting ready for Beckwith. I just don't have the time."

"That's fine. That's perfectly understandable." Bernie laughed nervously. "Uh, just so you know, though, I kind of already told the other side you were working with us." He gave her a toothy grin and lowered his neck into his shoulders.

"What?" Kate cried.

"I know, I know, I shouldn't have. And certainly you are under no obligation to do anything. I thought if they knew there was a big-time trial consultant on the other side, they might be more willing to settle. But that in no way obligates you. To be fair to you, though, I wanted to make sure you knew in case you heard something from someone." He paused and then made one last pitch. "All we need is a little witness prep. A couple of hours, max."

Kate looked around at the group. Pajama Man had his finger in his nose up to the second knuckle and Esmerelda mumbled under her breath. Kate heard "succubus" and something that sounded like "man hole cover."

She looked back at Bernie's hopeful face with disbelief. "A couple of hours? Are you kidding me? I couldn't get this group ready for a deposition in a couple of weeks."

A heavy silence filled the room.

"Bitch," Pajama Man muttered.

Bernie raised up a hand. "No, no, Larry. That's not right. We barged in here on Ms. Summerlin's job and, well, let's be honest. You all are a bit much the first time."

They all chuckled and nodded their heads. "Sorry," Pajama Man said, looking down at his pajama feet.

Jo stuck her head in the door. Her eyes darted around the group, but she did not comment on the unusual menagerie.

"Kate," she said in a loud whisper. "Mark just started his closing. We're going to need this room for jury deliberations."

Kate turned back to Bernie. "Look, I've got to go." Bernie nodded and turned to talk with the young one. Kate raised her voice. "You're going to have leave, Bernie. I need this room." Seeing the hurt look in his eyes she composed herself. "When are the depositions?"

"They're supposed to be this week, but Dander hasn't been able to hit any of them with a subpoena yet." The group chuckled at this.

"Morons," Pajama Man said.

Kate smiled. "Okay. You guys stay out of sight and we can meet in Bernie's office tomorrow night at six."

Celery Woman stuck her head in the circle. "I'll have to check my calendar." The group erupted in laughter and Kate joined them. It felt good.

"That's great, Kate. Honestly, it's not as bad as it looks," Bernie said with a smile. Kate looked around the circle as the group put on their best faces.

She said, "Let's hope not. Now, get out of my room." As Kate stepped out of the room, she saw Matelyn peering around the corner. "Say Bernie, wait a minute." She turned and waved at Matelyn. "Hey, Matelyn, could you come here for a second?" She glanced over at Bernie with a look that said play along.

Matelyn gingerly walked up to Kate. "Is everything all right?" she whispered.

"Oh, yes." Pointing to Bernie she said, "This is Bernard Timlin." She leaned in and whispered, "Very VIP. Very." Matelyn nodded. "I would consider it a personal favor if you could take Mr. Timlin and his associates upstairs and make sure they're taken care of."

Matelyn eyeballed the group and then looked back at Kate. "Of course," she said, although a hint of hesitation lingered in her voice. The group swarmed around her and moved her down the hall. As Matelyn looked back pleadingly at Kate, Pajama Man said, "Nice ass, Matty."

Heh, heh. That should take care of her for the rest of the day. Kate chuckled to herself and turned to walk back to the attorneys' room. Down the hall, T.J. stood spread eagled against the wall,

Carl's hand in the small of the boy's back as he frisked his leg.

"Christ," Kate sighed as she ran down the hall.

Chapter 21

"How do you like your steaks, Doc?" Boris called out. He rubbed olive oil on a T-bone and sprinkled it with salt and pepper.

"Medium rare, if you can manage it. Probably prefer you err on the side of medium though."

"Oh, I can manage medium rare," Boris said, laughing. "When I was up in Yellowstone, let me tell you, those people know how to cook. Say, when do you think the boys will be back?"

Townsend looked down at his watch. Six o'clock. "Kate's mock trials usually run about six hours. We usually finish up around six, so the rest is just driving time."

Boris did some calculations in his head. "We'll wait a little while." He stirred the coals in the Weber kettle drum grill he had brought in. It was costing him a fortune bringing in the take-out food for everyone. Yesterday, he had broken down and gotten a Weber. Nobody had been complaining about his grilling.

He walked over to Townsend's table and pulled up a chair. "We'll give them another half-hour or so. How do you think our girl is doing?"

Townsend tried to lean back and cross his legs but the straps stopped him. Instead, he readjusted himself in his chair. "Boy, I'm sort of out of the loop on that. Kate's very good at what she does. If there's a way to lowball the verdict, she'll find it."

"How long have you known her?"

Townsend paused. "I met Kate when she was an undergrad. She was dating this guy who was all upset about companies using animals for research. Kate got caught up in it. What bothered her the most, apparently, was the cosmetic industry using monkeys to test the irritability of their skin products. She felt it was barbaric.

"One of the big problems, she found out, was even if the companies stopped, nobody knew what to do with all the monkeys. They had been bred in captivity for research purposes. If they were dropped back into the jungle, they'd starve. So Kate came up with the idea that advertising companies could use the monkeys in small group research."

"Advertising companies?" Boris asked.

"Yeah. What Kate got right was the idea that a lot of advertising is subliminal. She figured if companies wanted to know how people would react at a primal level, they should ask primates existing at the primal level. She figured it would be much cheaper to use chimpanzees because they only required bananas and some water."

Boris nodded. "Sounds reasonable enough."

"No," Townsend said, shaking his head, "it's not reasonable at all. Kate was right that advertisers want to reach consumers on a primal level. The problem with using primates is not only do they feel at a primal level, they express themselves at a primal level. So, if a chimp throws his shit at a whiteboard presentation, there's no way to know whether it is a comment on the content or the monkey felt like throwing some shit."

"But you hired her anyway."

"Oh, yes. The thing about Kate is, she's so passionate about everything she does. You know they talk about 'fiery redheads'? That's Kate, except it's not her temper, but her drive and determination."

"You sound like a proud father," Boris said with a smile.

"I suppose that's right," Townsend said.

A cloud fell over Boris's face. "Do you have any children?"

"None that I know of," Townsend joked.

Boris erupted. "That's not funny, Dr. Greene. Family is the most important thing we have in our lives. A whole family. Mother, father, children. Do you have any idea how hard it is for a young man to grow up without a father? Do you know the statistics comparing men who grew up with a father to men who did not? Do you?"

"Yes," Townsend answered slowly. "I know it's certainly advantageous to have a father."

"Advantageous?" Boris screamed. His eyes flashed. "Yes, Dr. Greene, you could say it is 'advantageous' to have a father growing up." Boris paced around the room, mumbling to himself. Before Townsend could say anything else, they heard a large bang from the back of the warehouse. The boys walked in, laughing, as they came into the light.

"It's about time," Boris growled, meeting them in front of Townsend. The boys stopped laughing. "Did everything go all right?"

Randy relaxed. "Went great, good guys won. Everything was perfect right up until T.J. got arrested." He shot a smile at his brother who looked over at him in horror.

"I didn't get arrested," T.J. said, his hands coming up defensively in front of him. "Some cop thought he smelled pot on me."

"It's those freaky cigarettes. Smells like shit," Randy said, crinkling his nose.

"They're cloves, man," T.J. said, dropping his hands and turning to Randy. "Perfectly legal. That cop wouldn't know marijuana if it bit him in the ass." Townsend looked up at the odd phrase, but no one else seemed to notice.

"So, you got arrested?" Boris asked. He had anticipated, even accepted, the boys would probably turn him in once the trial ended. After all, he had no way to grant their absurd requests. He had hoped to be long gone by the time they figured out they had been tricked. He had not considered they might get arrested before the trial and flip on him early.

"No, that Kate woman stepped in while he was frisking me. She was pretty pissed. Right in front of everybody, she tore him a new one. I didn't see him the rest of the day." T.J. turned to Boris, narrowing his eyes, "You didn't tell us we'd be working for a cop."

Boris smirked at the boy. "Actually, you're working against a cop. You didn't think I'd be on the side of the law, did you?" He sat back down and leaned back in the chair. "It did go well? Yes?"

The boys looked at Boris, confused. Townsend immediately looked up at the boys then over to Boris.

Randy shook his head. "Beckwith's the cop, and we're working for Beckwith, right?"

Townsend looked at Boris for a long moment and then hung his head.

Boris blinked at the boys. "You mean the photographer didn't win?" His face began to turn red.

T.J. pointed his finger at Boris. "You said you wanted Beckwith to win. When you were talking to the woman. You said Beckwith should win." He kept repeating it, trying to convince himself as much as Boris.

Boris stepped up and slapped T.J. hard across the face. "You idiots! I said nothing of the sort. I don't want Beckwith to win. That would ruin everything."

T.J. glared at Boris but did not move. Randy moved just in front of his brother.

Without raising his head, Townsend interrupted. In a calm,

even voice, he said, "You and Kate only referred to it as the Beckwith case. And you said you had to win. It was reasonable for the boys to think you wanted Beckwith to win." Turning to the boys, he asked them, "How much did you give him?"

Randy looked down at his shoes, "Fifty million dollars," he said in a quiet voice. "Honest to God, we thought we were working for the cop."

Boris began pacing back and forth in front of Townsend's table. Pointedly ignoring the boys who stared at him with wide eyes, he sat down at the table. "So, is it over? Has the Stiltson side lost?" The redness had faded from his face. His shoulders slumped and the ends of his mouth sagged down like a sad clown.

Townsend paused for a moment to study Boris's changed demeanor. "No, it's not over. This was make-believe; a way to pressure Beckwith into settling the case for less than it's worth." Townsend gave him a wry smile. "Of course, that's out the window. And probably any settlement is out the window since Beckwith isn't going to want to settle for anything the defense offers. He thinks his case is worth fifty million dollars. It's probably worth a tenth of that, if anything." He turned to the boys. "Is that about what the juries were talking about before you stepped it up? Five or six million?"

Randy stood silent, staring at a spot far behind Townsend's head. T.J. softly said, "Actually, they weren't sure whether to give any money at all. Then this old black guy and I started talking to them and, before I knew it, we were at seventy-five million."

Boris jumped out of his chair, his face again bright red. "Seventy-five million? You said fifty."

Townsend tried to get up but was pulled down by the restraints on the table. After taking a moment to recover, he said "It doesn't matter. Fifty, seventy-five or five hundred million. Anything over two million and Beckwith would have taken his chances with a jury. So, really, we're right back where we were a couple of days ago: waiting for the trial."

The boys looked over at Boris, waiting to see if he would explode again. He slowly nodded his head. "So it's on Ms. Summerlin then, huh? Can she do it?"

Townsend did not say anything. Boris turned to the boys and said, "You better hope she can," and stormed off into the office.

Boris plopped down in a chair and stared at the phone. They could not lose the trial. If he missed this opportunity, it could be years before he got another one. And, even then, it would never be this good.

He repeated Townsend's words aloud. "We're in the same position we were yesterday." Okay. Going to trial was the original plan. He had the jury consultant on board. Really, everything was going just as he planned. A possible shortcut had not worked out, but that was okay. It was worth a shot. The plan was still solid.

He picked up the phone and dialed Kate's cell number. Now that the plan rested in her hands, he wanted to remind her of what was at stake—get her focused for the week ahead.

When she answered, he said, "Kate? It's Boris." Silence filled the line.

"So," he said with a lilt in his voice, "how'd it go today?"

Kate exploded on the other end. "How'd it go?" she shouted. "How'd it go? Are you kidding me? I had everything all set up. We could have won that, you know? Then you send those two yahoos in here and submarine the whole thing? If you didn't want to do the mock, then you could have just told me. Jerry only asked for ten million. Your boys gave him fifty."

Boris smiled. He liked Kate upset. It meant she was off-balance. She was easier to control that way. "Yeah, sorry about that. We had a little miscommunication. *Que sera.* So we're still on schedule for the trial next week?"

Kate remained silent for a few moments. "Yeah, we're on schedule for next week. But I promise you this. If you hurt my father again, not only will I pick a jury that will break the Stiltson bank, I will hunt you down and I will hurt you. I will hurt you where you live."

Boris was nonplussed at her outburst. "Hurt your father? Who's your father?"

"You didn't attack my dad last night?" Kate asked, her voice weak.

"I was here all night playing cribbage with Dr. Greene. And frankly, he put the hurt on me. Honestly, I didn't know you had a father. I wonder, if you care this much about him, maybe I should have grabbed him instead of Dr. Greene." Boris paused. "But, having grabbed Dr. Greene, I assumed you were sufficiently motivated to throw the Beckwith trial. In any event, if I did need to hurt your father to motivate you, I wouldn't have waited until the night before the big mock trial to do it."

Kate did not respond. Boris did not mind. He could wait her out. After a moment she spoke in a quivering voice, "But if you didn't hurt Dad, then who did?"

Boris shrugged his shoulders, although he was talking on the phone. "I don't know and I don't care. It wasn't me and it wasn't my boys. Maybe your dad is screwing some broad and her husband got upset."

"I don't think so."

"Whatever. Kate, listen, you need to focus. I don't care if your dad is in a coma. You need to focus on getting me a good jury. If you get distracted by this, Dr. Greene is going to die, understand?"

"I'll be fine," Kate said with little conviction in her voice.

"For your sake, and Dr. Greene's, I hope you are."

Boris hung up and leaned back in his chair. That wasn't good.

He only had one shot at this thing and Kate seemed unstable. If only he could bring Dr. Greene in, maybe he could get Kate back in the game. That guy got his finger chopped off less than a week ago and still took him for twenty bucks last night. That's focus right there.

Obviously, he couldn't take Dr. Greene to court. Or could he? If he couldn't take Muhammad to the mountain, maybe he could take Muhammad's writings.

Boris sat up to the computer and brought up his Google home page. He typed in a search for Dr. Greene and jury selection. Sixty-six thousand results popped up. Boris clicked on the first linked titled "Greene—The Trial Consultant's Field Manual." That sounded promising.

Boris stared at the screen, confused. There was Dr. Greene's name and a link to buy the book. Next to the picture of the book was a small photo of a cheery, old man that was not Dr. Greene. Seemed like an odd mistake to make on his own website. Boris went back to his search results and clicked on a link for a conference in Toronto. The conference dates were this week and Dr. Greene was listed as a presenter. Boris quickly scrolled down to the presenter biography section. The face from the book's website smiled back at him.

He printed off the page and stormed out into the main room. "Dr. Greene?" he called.

"Yes?" The old man said it as if he were answering a question he didn't know. Something in Boris's voice had tipped him off.

"You're not Dr. Greene." Boris shoved the paper in front of the imposter. "This is Dr. Greene."

"Yes, we've met. To be fair, I tried to tell you I was not Greene when you first brought me here. I'm Walter Townsend, Farley Greene's partner."

Hmmm. This Townsend fellow was still Kate's boss. Plus, she appeared to be doing everything she could to help him. Maybe it was a good thing his bozos snatched this guy.

"Does Kate like you as much as she does Dr. Greene?" Boris asked.

Townsend paused. "Well, uh, you know, Farley's a very likable guy. And I'm, well, I'm more of a hard-liner at the office."

"So, no, she doesn't like you as much as Greene?"

"No, she doesn't. But she's very professional and when she agrees to do a job, she does it all out."

"Even when the job is throwing the case against the client," Boris asked. "That doesn't sound too professional."

"If she said she'd do it, she'll do it." Townsend nodded curtly, as if that settled the matter.

"For your sake, Dr. Townsend, I hope she does."

Chapter 22

A consultant must always be on guard. Hidden dangers lurk in the dark corners of every case.

Greene, F. (2003). *The Trial Consultant's Field Manual* (p. 22). New York: Pullman.

Kate parked the Bug a block away from her office and slumped over with her head in her hands. "Fifty million," she said out loud. She pulled her head up just as a forty-something woman walked by and glanced into the car.

"Fifty million!" Kate screamed at her. The woman jumped and scurried off. Just then, Kate began to think the woman looked familiar. One of those people she saw shopping every week or so at the grocery store. That little outburst should preempt any annoying little Aisle Five conversations.

Kate's phone rang. "Kate? Jerry."

"Hey, Jerry. Congratulations."

"Oh, yeah," he said sarcastically, "I'm thrilled. I just got off the phone with Beckwith and told him the results. He's ecstatic. It's not every day you hear you're going to win fifty million dollars in your lawsuit. Especially when your lawyer told you the top end on the case was probably five million."

"I'm sorry, Jerry. Sometimes those things can go a little haywire, you know? Can you get Beckwith back under control?"

"I'm kidding, he's fine. He's a cop so he kind of expects the worst to begin with. I told him beforehand the numbers were unreliable, so he was ready for it. But fifty million really perked his ears up. I just wanted to give you a little trouble."

"Thanks bub. After the week I've had, I certainly needed some more trouble."

"Well, rest up. I need you at your best to get me that fifty mil you promised."

Kate hung up and, although it hardly seemed possible, felt worse than before. She had blown her one chance to get Beckwith to settle low enough for it to be a win for Stiltson. The case was absolutely going to trial now.

She got out of the Bug and walked toward the office. Dr. Greene kept a shelf of jury selection strategy books in his office. There probably was not a chapter on picking jurors for the other side, but maybe something would trigger an answer in her brain.

Darkness had set in and the weekend shoppers had started to give way to the college partiers. Kate's mind drifted over to Boris. He had seemed genuinely surprised to hear about her father. More importantly, he was right that it was distracting more than motivating her. Plus, he didn't need to give her more motivation. He had Townsend.

Standing in front of the building, she was glad to be back at the office. She loved this old building. The warm wood trim up against the plaster walls, windows that actually opened in the summer. Perhaps it was sad, but she felt most comfortable in this friendly old building.

Townsend was always threatening to move. They constantly needed more space. Worse, the building manager, Stanley, was getting up there in years and could not keep up with the maintenance. They joked that the heater must have come from Australia because it only worked during July.

As far as Kate was concerned, as long as Stanley kept the elevator in top shape, she could live with the rest. A caged door relic from the thirties, the elevator was Kate's favorite part of the building. A large window on the outer door let her see the floors pass by as she went up. It gave her a feel for the space of the building, rather than being magically transported from one floor to the other.

She got into the elevator and pushed five for the main office. Through the glass, Kate saw light under Dr. Buckney's door on the second floor. At least someone else was working late on a Saturday night. The second floor disappeared and the third floor slid into view. A dim, red exit sign barely illuminated the lobby.

Instinctively, Kate glanced over at her office door as the elevator passed her floor. Something moved. She leaned forward toward the glass, peering at the large fake plant outside her office door. From behind it, the big Hawaiian jumped out and charged the elevator door. Kate thought he was going to come right through it. By the time he reached the door, the elevator had pulled her up to the fourth floor. The Hawaiian had looked right at her. It was not a nice look.

She had to hide. No, she had to call the police. This they could help with.

"911. Please state your emergency."

"A large Hawaiian man is chasing me," she yelled into the phone. "I need the police over here right away." Maybe if he heard her, he would go away.

"What is your location?"

Kate blanked out on the address. She had worked here for five years and now she could not even think of the address. Then, she got it. "Seven hundred Massachusetts, suite five-ten."

The elevator stopped at the fifth floor and she threw open the cage and the outer door. She figured a man that size would take a little time getting up the stairs.

"Can you run into some public place?" the operator asked.

Kate looked back at the elevator. The barbeque place across the street would be busy right now. But she'd have to cross the lobby to get out the door. Maybe the big guy didn't want to climb stairs and decided to wait in the lobby in case she made a break for it. Better to make him find her than run right to him.

"No," she said as she ran down the hall toward the main office. She got out her keys as she ran down the hall. "But I think I can hide until you guys get here. Tell them to hurry."

Kate fumbled with the keys. She finally found the right key but her hands were shaking so badly she had trouble fitting it in the lock. She listened for the thundering steps on the metal staircase. Nothing so far. Finally, she slid the key in and flung open the door. Slamming the door behind her, she ran down the hall toward Dr. Greene's office. As she passed Townsend's office, she ducked in. If she heard the Hawaiian pass by she could run to the door. Plus, Townsend's desk was sturdier.

As she crawled under the desk, the 911 operator said, "I'll stay right here with you until the officers get there."

"Ssssh!" Kate hissed. "I'm hiding."

"Sorry," the operator whispered. Kate stared at the phone in disbelief.

Crouched under the desk waiting, Kate didn't think the old building seemed so comfortable and homey. She longed for a newer, shiny building that did not creak. And had a modern security system.

After what seemed like two days, but was probably more like ten minutes, she heard the old elevator start up. It rumbled for almost a minute before it stopped, then started again. So, Kate thought, he had been waiting in the lobby. Now he's riding the elevator up. Could she make it to the stairs before the elevator opened? What if he sent just the elevator up and was still in the lobby? *Wait it out Kate,* she told herself. *Keep hiding. The cops are on their way.*

She heard the elevator stop. The metal cage doors rattled open. Then nothing. Kate listened, imagining the big man making thunderous booms down the hall with every step. Someone at the front door rattled the doorknob. After a moment, it opened. Did he have a key? More likely, the ancient locks in this piece of crap building were an open invitation to any crook in the area. They were moving out of this rickety old death trap on Monday or she was quitting.

In the distance, she heard a police siren. Great. They would get here just in time to find her mangled, lifeless body. The building itself was quiet. Even the ordinary creaks and groans had stopped. Then she heard it. *Snik. Snik.* Either the big man bit his nails or Jo was in da house.

"Jo?" Kate called out.

"Aaah," Jo screamed. "Kate, is that you? God, you scared me to death. Where are you?"

Kate scurried out from under the desk and ran out into the hall.

"Aaah," Jo screamed again. "Sweet Jesus on a stick, you have to stop doing that. Hey, what's wrong?"

"Did you see the Hawaiian?"

"Hawaiian? Did I see a Hawaiian?"

"Yeah. A giant Hawaiian man hiding behind my fake ficus. Did you see him?"

Jo blinked several times. "No, Kate. I did not see a giant Hawaiian man hiding behind your fake ficus. I didn't really look though." Jo put her hand on Kate's shoulder. "Why don't you sit down? It's been a pretty long day." Outside, sirens got louder until the police pulled up. Jo went over to the window and peered down. "Are they here for you?"

Kate tried to figure out what she was going to say. "Yeah. Listen, when they come up, don't say anything about Boris, Townsend or my dad or any of that. Okay?"

"What happened to your dad?"

"I'll explain it all later, okay?"

"Yeah, sure Kate, anything. Just sit down for a minute."

They heard the police come up the stairs and walked out into the hall to meet them. Kate described what had happened and that she had seen the man outside her apartment the day before. She did not mention seeing him at the casino. After the interview, Kate and Jo followed the police down to the street. Kate stood close to Jo as the police drove off.

"Man, I'm still a little jittery," Kate said, shaking her hands. "Do you feel like getting something to eat?" Jo hesitated. Kate backed off. "Or do you have plans? I mean, it's Saturday night, of course you have plans."

Jo shook her head. "It's not what you think." A smile broke across Jo's face. "Hey, why don't you come with me? I'm going speed dating."

"Oh, I don't think I'm up for any dating thing tonight."

"Sure, it will be perfect. Get your mind off all this. I'm telling you, I've done this before and the guys will gush over you. You won't hardly have to talk at all. Plus, for the ladies, it's ten bucks, all you can drink."

"I'm there. What do I have to do?" Kate asked.

"You sit there and talk to the guy in front of you. Every five minutes or so they ring a bell, and the guys move to the next table. There are always tons of guys at these things. I think they think it'll all be a bunch of lonely, desperate women."

"Isn't that why guys showed up at your self-defense classes?"

"Yeah, it's a pretty common theme. Guys don't want to do any work at building a relationship so they just look for the easy score. You should see the pack of scavengers who come in after a Chippendale's show." Jo ignored Kate's shocked expression. "They think we're going to be all hornied up and not notice they're balding and overweight. You take one look at them after seeing the studs on the stage and you realize the women aren't the lonely, desperate ones."

Kate grimaced. "Wow, Jo, you really know how to sell it."

Jo laughed. "You'll have fun. I promise. Ten dollars. All you can drink."

"I'm there."

In the late seventies, the Westermin Piano Company closed down its Lawrence factory. The large structure sat empty until 2003 when a local developer, George Canton, turned it into a night club. Gorgeous George's Piano Bar frequently hosted speed-dating events to get young singles into the bar early in the evening.

As they walked the three blocks over to Gorgeous George's, Kate filled Jo in on the ordeal at the office as well as what happened to her father the night before.

"So do you think he was working for Boris?"

"I certainly hope so. Otherwise, I have two crazed maniacs after me. But I laid into Boris pretty good this afternoon about Dad. He really seemed like he had no idea what I was talking about. And tonight, looking in the Hawaiian's eyes, he wanted to hurt me. Bad. And if I'm in a hospital or dead, I can't pick Boris's jury. So I don't know."

When they walked into the bar, the speed dating had already started. Twenty men and only fifteen women had shown up, so Jo and Kate were seated immediately. The guys not involved in that five-minute round stood around the bar looking longingly at the tables where the women sat. Kate thought they looked like strays at the pound begging with their sad little puppy dog eyes to be taken home. They brightened up when Kate and Jo walked in. Two more in the rotation.

A bell sounded and the men moved to the next woman. Kate assessed her momentary date. In his early thirties, he dressed well. A light blue shirt over dark blue slacks with a beige herringbone jacket. Close-cropped hair and well-manicured nails. His name tag said Kurt. It looked like some woman had put a lot of time into cleaning him up. Probably the same woman who gave him the wedding ring on his left hand.

He smiled at her as he sat down. "Hi, I'm Kurt," he said, pointing at his name tag. "You're probably wondering about the wedding ring."

"It's very pretty. Is she here tonight?" Kate raised her head up and made a big show of looking around the room. Jo stared over at the ring while her date, Perry, described the difference between financial advisers (who rule) and stockbrokers (who drool).

Kurt laughed. "No, she died about a year ago." Jo immediately focused her attention back on Perry. Kate's face flushed with embarrassment as she slowly slid down into her chair.

"I'm so sorry."

"It's totally cool. I've been getting a lot of that kind of thing tonight. I mean, you wear a wedding ring on a first date, you have to expect to catch some grief."

Jo leaned over. "Why don't you wear it on a different finger?"

"Jo," Kate said sharply, "stick to your own date." Jo glanced at Perry.

He had stopped talking for a moment. When Jo looked back at him, he continued saying something about "small caps" and "loads." Kate shot Jo a dirty look and turned back to Kurt.

"I wasn't going to wear it at all. I haven't taken it off since Donna died, but I thought tonight was the night to move on. But when I took it off . . ." He slid the ring off. A stark white band of skin stood out next to his brown skin. "I've got the mother of all tan lines here."

"Wow," Jo said, "is your ass that white?" Perry stopped talking and glanced over at Kurt's finger.

"Jo!" Kate turned to Kurt. "I'm sorry about my friend. She has a brain tumor."

"I don't have a brain tumor. The tumor was Josepherta and she is long gone." Jo finished off her drink and raised her glass in the air, shaking it for the waitress.

Kurt laughed. "You know, I had an Aunt Josepherta." Kate and Jo stared at him in disbelief. Perry, who had figured out things were not going well on his date, stared at Kate's chest.

"Really? Was she happy?" Jo asked.

Kurt smiled at her. "Okay, I lied. I never really had an Aunt Josepherta. I knew a woman named Berta though. Miserable woman. Maybe miserable is too strong. Just beat down by life, you know."

Jo nodded. "I know exactly what you mean. I just found out . . ."

"Hey, hey," Kate said. A few heads turned. Finally, Kate had an attractive, well-dressed, intelligent guy sitting in front of her and she could not get a word in edgewise. "This is my date. You have your date. Leave my date alone and wait your turn."

A bell sounded and all the men got up and moved one spot over, Kurt moving in front of Jo. Kate fell back in her chair. "Oh, that's just great."

Jo smirked at her then turned to Kurt. "So, like I was saying, I just found out . . ."

Kate turned and looked at the guy now sitting in front of her. The name tag read Austin in a fancy scroll. He was a little older than Kurt with a little more middle and a lot less hair. Kate could not help but stare at his lips. Large and flat, they reminded her of a caricature of a fish. When the lips moved, Kate looked up to eyes slightly less brown than Kurt's.

"Studies show that any successful relationship must be based on common interest." His voice was slightly higher and quite a bit more nasally than Kurt's. "So, accepting that premise as true, and without telling you my position to avoid bias, what is your opinion on J.R.R. Tolkien's *Lord of the Rings* trilogy?"

God. "I haven't read those. But I did really enjoy the Harry Potter books."

"Potter," Austin spat out in Snape-like fashion. "The Harry Potter books are an above-average children's book." Austin clearly felt he was contributing greatly to the relationship by giving her that much. "The Tolkien trilogy, plus *The Hobbit,* are literature. He created his own language for those books. I'd like to see J.K. Rowling do that."

Kate stared down the row at her next few dates. Most of the women were looking down the row at their next few dates. Turning back, she glanced over at Kurt. He had been looking at her but quickly moved his eyes back to Jo. She thought his face reddened a little.

What did that mean? Was he interested in her? She kept staring at him, but he would not look back.

"Kate?" Austin looked at her with sad eyes. Ah, jeez.

"Sorry, Austin, you were saying something about dwarves?"

Austin stared down at his thumbs, which he intently pushed together. "Look, I know this probably isn't going anywhere, but do you think you could put me down as a match anyway?"

"I don't think we're supposed to talk about who our matches are."

"I know. It's just that Mom is going to want to see my sheet when I get home. I want to have at least one match. It was her idea for me to come out here and I think she would feel bad if I didn't get any matches. I would not expect you to see me again or anything." He looked up. "Unless you wanted to."

"I'll put you down as a match, Austin." The bell rang and the men got up to move. Kate looked over to Kurt just before he looked back at her. Again, he quickly looked away.

Kate spent most of the rest of the night thinking about Kurt. The bar had seated the women on the inside of a circle with the men rotating around the outside. Kurt disappeared over the horizon one girl after Jo, so Kate could not sneak any more looks. She met a couple of nice guys and couple of good-looking guys, but only one nice, good-looking guy.

After the event, people mingled. Kate could see the hook-ups forming even now. Kurt was nowhere to be seen.

"How many matches did you put down?" Jo asked.

"Just two. Kurt and Austin."

"Austin? Which one was Austin? Wait, *Lord of the Rings* guy? Don't tell me you fell for his dear old mom bit?" She let out a hearty laugh. "Oh, you are in for it. Those sci-fi fantasy guys are one step away from stalker town. You're going to need a ring of repulsion to get rid of him. I matched eight."

"Eight? You want to be with eight of those guys?"

"I don't want to *be* with them. But I'll let eight of them take me out to dinner and see what happens. It's tough to tell what someone's like in five minutes." She took a sip of her drink. "Especially if someone talks over you the whole time. Sorry about the Kurt thing."

"Don't worry about it."

"Oh, I'm not." Jo said with a smile. Kate hit her with her purse. "Not anymore anyway. When the bell rang I felt terrible. I mean, you were right. I moved in on your date because the Finance Guy bored the hell out of me. But then, all through my fascinating Josepherta story, he kept looking over at you. I figured I owed you one, so I talked you up."

"What? You did what?"

"I pretended to be talking about my job, but I told him how wonderful you were and how much fun it was to work with you and how lonely you are right now."

"Jo!"

"I'm kidding. Well, about the lonely thing, anyway. I bet you get a match from him."

"From your lips to God's ears," Kate said as the two women clinked glasses. She looked around the room to see if Kurt had reappeared. Over in the corner, she noticed a sharply dressed couple enjoying an intimate conversation.

"Say, do you recognize that guy over there?"

Jo turned and looked. "No, but the woman looks familiar. But like famous familiar, not like I know her familiar."

"I think that's Ron Tittleton, the defense attorney on the Stiltson case."

"Sure, that's it," Jo said, snapping her fingers. "That's Elsie Stiltson. I saw her picture a few months back at some society wedding. Wow. That doesn't look like any business meeting I've been in. They look pretty friendly."

"You think they followed me here?"

"Um, no. It's a big bar, Kate. It's probably a coincidence."

"Right now, I'm not a big believer in coincidence. Do you think if we sneak over by that plant, we can hear what they're saying?" Before Jo could say anything, Kate got up and crept toward the plant.

Chapter 23

"I never figured you for a quitter," Elsie said, folding her arms and pouting.

"I'm not a quitter," Ron said a little more harshly than he meant to. "But sometimes you have to face reality. And the reality here is that we're probably going to lose."

The pair sat at a table in the back corner of Gorgeous George's. What had started as a nice romantic evening had turned sour once they started talking about her case.

"But I didn't do anything wrong. It's not like I'm the one who shot him."

"It doesn't matter what you did, it matters what they can prove you did."

"But I didn't do *anything.*"

"Yeah, you did. You publicly displayed a private citizen's image without his permission. We have to admit to that. The trial is about whether you doing that caused the injuries to Officer Beckwith."

Elsie stared at him. He had explained this to her several times, but she kept insisting she had done nothing wrong. He agreed with her but was not sure a jury would.

"Beckwith hired Olaf Gustavessen, a photography professor at the University of Cheyenne. He's going to say a reasonably responsible photographer would get a waiver from the subject of the photo. Without that waiver, a photographer is responsible for the repercussions of publishing the photo."

"That's idiotic. How am I supposed to know some drug lord is going to shoot him? Beckwith didn't get shot because of my photo. He got shot because he was an undercover cop."

Ron shook his head. "For five hundred dollars an hour, my guess is you would find plenty of photographers who would agree with him. And even if he's the only photography professor who believes that, he's the only photography professor the jury gets to hear."

"But you said you found someone, an expert who would work for free."

"Pantaine isn't technically an expert. He's an attorney I went to law school with who works in patents. He'll be able to explain some legal concepts that work for us. But he's no photography professor. And he's not working for free. You've got to do his kids' portraits for four years."

"Yeah, but that's a lot cheaper than their five-hundred-dollars-an-hour guy. Doesn't that make our guy more believable?"

"Who knows? The jury could see it as Beckwith has a high-price whore who'll say anything for a buck and we have a low-price whore who'll say anything for less than a buck. A high-price whore is always better than a cheap whore."

Elsie raised an eyebrow. "Really?"

"Figuratively speaking, of course. Plus, Pantaine's a lawyer, which makes him a cheap lawyer-whore. That's down there on the ol' believability scale with brothers-in-law, used-car salesmen, and dentists."

"I still don't think we should quit."

"Look, if we settle, we can control how much you pay and how you pay. If we lose, you're going to have to go to your father for the money. He'll lord that over you for years."

"You don't think I know that? I know exactly what he'll do. He'll make me work it off in the mustard plant." She sat there silent for a moment. "Did you know that when I got out of college, he made me Vice President in charge of South America?"

"South America? Do they eat a lot of brats in Bolivia?"

"Don't laugh. South Americans eat a ton of mustard. They think it increases sexual vigor."

"Where do you put the mustard to get the best vigor?" Ron said.

Elsie ignored him. "I walked in the first day as Vice President. Big office, secretary, and thirty people, every one of whom had been there for at least five years. All of them reported to me. One of them, I had taken his office. They looked at me like I was totally underqualified and totally undereducated. They thought I got the job because of who my father was. And they were right. I walked out after lunch."

"And Daddy didn't like that?" Ron reached out to hold her hand. She pulled it away.

"You have to understand Maynard. It wasn't just that I didn't want to carry on the family business. I had dared to defy his wishes. He commanded I be the Dijon Queen of the Southern Hemisphere and I refused. And there was nothing he could do about it."

"But if we lose . . ."

"If we lose, I suddenly need a million dollars."

"Or fifty."

Elsie laughed but saw Ron's serious expression. "Fifty? I thought you said they were only asking for ten million and that was a pipe dream."

"That's what I thought. But there was this weird package taped to the front of the building tonight. One of the new associates found it as he was leaving and brought it up. It looks like Beckwith did a mock trial."

"What does that mean?"

"He hired someone to bring in people off the street and act

like jurors for our case. The package has all their responses and verdicts. The mock jury awarded fifty million dollars."

"Fifty million dollars? Can that be right? Is it because Beckwith is a cop?"

Ron shook his head. "I don't think so. When jurors give that kind of money, it's usually because they're angry at the defendant, not because they're sympathetic toward the plaintiff. And, even if they believe you were wrong, it's not like you intended to hurt Beckwith. There's not that kind of heat in this case." He rubbed the back of his neck. "It could be Beckwith's attorney's trying to scare us into settling. But, honestly, I know Jerry Bingham and that's not his style. He's a total asshole, but he's a straight-shooting asshole."

Elsie sat quiet for a minute and then started to smile. "You know, this could be great news."

"What, that it's not a hundred million dollars?"

"No, I'm serious. Look, either Daddy put that mock thing together and rigged it so we lost really big or it's a real thing and we may lose really big. Right?"

"Okay," Ron said, not sure where she was going.

"If Daddy did it, then your boss showed him the file and they think we're going to win."

"That makes two of them."

"No, think about it. If we win, Daddy loses his big hold on me. So they put together something that says we're going to lose big. Tonetti tells you to settle big. We get scared and I have to go begging Daddy for the settlement money."

"I suppose that's possible."

"It's exactly what he would do. We can't settle."

"What about option B? What if it was a real mock and we get hit for fifty million?"

"I know my father. He's very rich and for some reason it's worth a couple million dollars to have something to lord over me for the rest of my life. But fifty million? Maynard would slather me with mustard and personally feed me to sharks before he would shell out fifty million dollars."

"Do sharks eat mustard?" Ron asked with a smile.

Elsie continued. "If the jury says I owe Beckwith fifty million, it's as good as saying I owe him nothing. Either way, I'm on my own."

"There's still the little part about you owing Beckwith fifty million dollars. So it wouldn't be quite as good as them saying you owe him nothing."

"I'll risk it. We're going to trial. If they think you can win, who am I to doubt you?" Elsie's eyes narrowed. "Why didn't you tell me about the package earlier? We've been sitting here talking about the case all night and you didn't say anything."

"Well," Ron said, staring into his drink, "I didn't see it as the wonderful news that apparently it is." He smiled up at Elsie and she nodded at him. "I thought it might upset you and I didn't want to ruin our evening."

"Oh," Elsie said, batting her eyes. "Are we having an evening?"

Ron squirmed in his chair. "Well, yeah, I mean, I'm enjoying myself."

"I thought you said it had to be all business because attorneys and clients couldn't mix." Elsie snapped her fingers. "That's why we came to Lawrence. So none of your lawyer friends would see you wooing a client."

"Is that what I'm doing, wooing? How's my wooing doing?"

Ron thought the question was a softball. The evening had been going great, but Elsie did not answer. She just stared over Ron's shoulder. "Elsie, that's not a question you really leave a guy hanging with."

"Sorry," she said, still looking over his shoulder. "You're not married, are you?"

"What? No, I'm not married. Why?"

"There's a redhead creeping around the dance floor out there. She keeps looking over here and then hiding behind people."

Ron turned in his seat. "Where?"

"You can't see her now. See that guy in the blue shirt dancing with the girl in the mini-skirt? Ugh. Boy, he's really happy to be dancing with her, isn't he?"

Ron saw the couple. As they moved in a circle, Ron noticed the guy's khaki pants stretching out just below the belt. The girl kept her hands on his shoulders, but moved her hips back to avoid the increasingly noticeable bulge. "Yes, he is. Ah, to be twenty-one again." The girl moved back farther, her arms now fully extended. "But she doesn't seem to be enjoying it as much."

Elsie laughed. "No. she doesn't. There. See the woman?"

Sure enough, in the ever-increasing space between the two dancers, Ron saw Kate staring directly at them.

Kate quickly looked down—right at the khaki pup tent. She stepped back and squeaked in horror. Unable to pretend any longer that anyone in the bar was unaware of his erection, the guy stormed off the dance floor, much to the relief of his partner who returned to her table.

Kate, however, stood still as a statue all by herself in the middle of the floor. Ron rose in his chair to confront her when Jo strode up, grabbed Kate by the collar and pulled her out the door.

"Should I follow them?" Ron asked.

"No. So, that wasn't your wife, following you around?"

Ron laughed. "No. In fact, how do we know that she was looking at me? Lawrence is known to have quite a large lesbian community."

"Oh, really?"

"Oh, yeah," Ron said. "She was probably trying to check you out when her girlfriend hauled her outside."

"Why, Mr. Tittleton," Elsie said in a bad Southern accent, "you do know how to flatter a girl."

CHAPTER 24

The key to preparing a witness for a tough deposition is convincing him that less is more.

Greene, F. (2003). *The Trial Consultant's Field Manual* (p. 366). New York: Pullman.

Sunday night, Kate rode in the elevator up to Bernie Timlin's office. From the strong smell of cabbage hovering in the air, she guessed his clients had already arrived.

Bernie's practice consisted almost exclusively of the homeless who roamed the streets downtown. In spite of this, or maybe because of it, he kept his office in a suburban office park in southern Kansas City. He often bragged about his penthouse suite, but nineteen other people had the same set-up on the top floor of the three-story building.

Kate stood outside the door to Bernie's office and tried to collect her thoughts. It had been a rough day. Maria had somehow gotten her cell phone number and had been regularly calling looking for Townsend. From the increasingly slurred words, Kate guessed she had started drinking around noon.

The last call had come in the parking lot. "Let me talk to him, Kate. Please, let me talk to him for just a minute and then I'll leave you alone."

"He's not here, Maria. I'm about to go into a meeting."

"Fuck you. You stole the wrong girl's man. You better watch out, 'cause I'm gonna fuck you up."

"Yeah, well good luck because that line is all the way out the door." She hung up.

As Kate stood in the hallway, making sure her phone was turned off, she caught a whiff of the odd smells from the casino. That brought her around.

She pushed her way into the office. Although she had been here a couple times before, she was once again struck by the starkness of the décor. Probably out of necessity, none of the furniture was upholstered. Silver steel benches, bolted into the wall, ran the interior of a nook behind the door. Two fake plants placed in each corner of the alcove did nothing to soften the harshness of the waiting area. On the benches, hands placed in their laps, sat the motley crew from the casino.

Maybe this won't be so bad, Kate thought. As she took in the rest of the room, she realized the reason for their good behavior: Mrs. Pendleton. Mrs. Pendleton had been Bernie's secretary for fifteen years and Kate had never heard him refer to her as anything but Mrs. Pendleton. Only in her mid-forties, Mrs. Pendleton exuded a matronly, school-disciplinarian aura that kept everyone in her presence in check.

"Close the door, you're letting all the air out," Mrs. Pendleton snapped at Kate.

Kate immediately did as she was told, although the air in the hall was the same antiseptically circulated air as in the office. And, once inside, Kate could not believe anyone would be opposed to letting a little of that air out.

"What do you want?" Mrs. Pendleton asked.

What Kate wanted was to know how much the hair on Mrs. Pendleton's head weighed. She had more hair on her head than anyone Kate had ever seen. Some women grow their hair down to their waist or longer. Mrs. Pendleton had about that much hair, but it was all lacquered above her neck line into a hair helmet extending a good six inches beyond each shoulder. Kate wanted to know how, but was not about to ask.

"She wants to know how much your hair weighs." Kate spun around and saw the old woman who had interrupted the mock trial pointing a dirty finger at Mrs. Pendleton.

"No, no, I don't care about your hair, Mrs. Pendleton," Kate stammered. Mrs. Pendleton narrowed her stare. "Bernie asked me to come tonight and get them ready for their depositions."

Mrs. Pendleton glared at the homeless group. When she looked up at Kate, her eyes blazed. "Bernie's waiting for you in his office," she said. *"That cowardly bastard"* hung unsaid in the air.

"Great," Kate said. "Could you take them down to the conference room?" The young one was standing with his back to Kate, legs spread and hands on his hips, facing a plant. It looked as if he was urinating in the plant but Kate could see no stream coming from his waist-area. Mrs. Pendleton took this image in for a moment before looking up at Kate, daring her to ask the question again.

Kate smiled and said, "Or maybe we should wait and see what Bernie wants to do." Mrs. Pendleton forced a smile and turned around to face her computer.

Bernie stood as Kate walked in. The office was small enough that he would have heard her out in the lobby, but he had not come out to meet her. "Kate, good to see you. Are any of the gang here?"

Unless Bernie regularly cooked sauerkraut in his office, he had to know the whole clan had arrived long before Kate.

"Yeah," Kate said, "looks like they got here just before I did." Although Bernie moved toward the door, Kate walked over to one of the leather chairs in front of his desk and sat down. "Before we go out there, let's talk about how we want to do this. Tell me a little bit about each of them. Especially the African-American woman."

Bernie went through each of the five people. Their stories were all different, but with common themes of untreated mental illnesses, bad luck and, for the women, abusive fathers and husbands. Kate felt drained when he finished, the load of their collective despair weighing down on her.

"Look, Bernie, I know you love these guys, but you know as well as I do these depositions are going to be a disaster."

"That's why we got you. You've gotta have the best to beat the best." He stood up to go out to the lobby.

"That's sweet, thanks. Sit down. I can't change who they are." Bernie's shoulders slumped a bit, but Kate kept talking. "The way I see it, the strength of your case is the David versus Goliath nature of fight."

"Exactly. 'And David smote the Philistine with a rock.' "

"Right. The poor and dim-witted homeless facing the rich and mighty party boy. You can argue Te, like society, didn't view Reggie the Mumbler as a person, let alone a person who had friends who loved him. Instead, Te saw him as a bum—someone who did not matter in society. To Te, Reggie's value came only as entertainment." Bernie scribbled notes on a pad. "That kind of argument resonates with juries because it reflects society's own disregard for the homeless and their wants and desires."

Bernie looked up from his pad, his eyes blazing. "Hell, yeah. We're going to smite that giant Philistine with the Rock of Justice."

"You know, David had the same faith as Job. Anyway, that story works great at trial, when the jury feels bad because nobody notices the poor homeless. The problem is the deposition. Because nobody ever notices them, they have to scream and shout and get in everyone's face just to get noticed. Now they're going to be in a room with a bunch of suits, everyone hanging on their every word. Christ, Bernie, a court reporter is going to be in there writing down every word they say. For the first time in years, maybe ever, their thoughts, their ideas are going to be important. They're going to talk for days."

"I've talked to them about that. I told them this is about Reggie and only Reggie. I told them there's no need to get into their own . . ." He paused and looked up to the ceiling. "Their own individual situations."

"That's great, but Te is going to have a big-money attorney in there. He knows their weaknesses as well as we do. He'll drag it out of them and it's not like it would take a lot to get them to start rambling about their own issues. Who's Te's attorney?"

"Dave Rushton."

"Rushton. Okay that's not bad. He's kind of a hot head. A yeller and a screamer. But he runs out of steam pretty fast. Someone like Dave Roberts, a slow, methodical, calm guy, would be much worse."

"Oh, wait. Yeah, it *is* Dave Roberts. Sorry, I get them confused."

Kate rolled her eyes. Before she could respond, laughter erupted from the lobby. Kate smiled, thinking it amazing that no matter how down a person gets, there is always the capacity for laughter. Bernie, however, became alarmed. He jumped up and walked to the door. "Usually, it's not a good thing when they all laugh like that."

In the lobby, Mrs. Pendleton and Cabbage Lady stood face to face. Mrs. Pendleton's makeup oozed down her cheeks like a California mudslide. Her hair, however, remained the same impenetrably coifed fortress as before the attack.

Cabbage Lady stood in front of her holding a large cup. Bernie rushed in and stood between them. "Now Danielle, we've talked about this. You cannot be throwing water on people."

Danielle stood her ground. "She said I smelled like feet." She glared at Bernie, pointing down toward her feet, just to be sure he understood what she was talking about. "Feet."

Mrs. Pendleton peered over Bernie's shoulder. "You do smell like feet."

Danielle lurched forward into Bernie. His eyes bulged, but he was able to hold his ground. Kate was impressed. Holding Danielle back, he grunted, "Mrs. Pendleton, please wait in my office." Danielle took a step back. Bernie followed Mrs. Pendleton into his office and closed the door.

The group stood looking at each other as they heard heated mutterings coming from Bernie's office. Kate moved toward the conference room and said, "Why don't we go in here and get started?"

The key to getting them through their depositions lay in the one aspect of their psychological makeup more important than their need to be noticed. As much as they wanted to be important and wanted people to listen to what they had to say, more than that, they did not want to be suckers. A sucker on the street is a dead sucker.

"Here's the thing you have to remember when you get in your deposition." Kate feared they might have short attention spans and wanted to dive right in. "Bronson Te thinks you're stupid. And he thinks you're crazy."

Danielle sat forward in her chair. "I think Mrs. Pendleton thinks so, too." The group broke into laughter. Kate picked up a large, hardback dictionary sitting on the table and slammed it down. BAM!! Everyone stopped laughing. She had their attention.

Kate glared at Danielle. "You think it's a joke?" She was yelling now, not sure whether she was actually angry or just doing it for effect. "You think Bronson Te's lawyers are going to be joking around? You think you can waltz into the deposition and they're going to hand you five million dollars because Reggie was a great guy? Well, they're not. Those lawyers are going to chew you up and spit you out unless you get it together."

The conference room door flew open. Bernie rushed in, looking wildly about the room. "Is everyone okay? I thought I heard a gun."

The thin black man looked up at Bernie. "No, it was a dictionary." He sat back in his chair, confident he had explained the situation fully. Bernie looked at the book and then up at Kate.

Kate took a deep breath. "The lawyers want to make you look like you're crazy and that you only care about your own crazy theories." She looked around. They stared at her intently, each a little angry now. Good, she thought, anger focuses. "They'll want the jury to make this case about *you,* about *your* issues. We want it to be about Reggie."

Danielle leaned forward but did not speak. Kate stared at her until she leaned back in retreat. "We want this trial to be about what Bronson Te did to Reggie," she continued. "We don't want the jury thinking about Danielle's story or Pajam . . . Larry's story. We want that jury focused. So *you* have to be focused. During the deposition, you can't start rambling. Answer their questions and *only* answer their questions. Bernie, did you work up some questions you think Te's lawyers may ask?"

Bernie stood there, enthralled by the collective attentiveness of the group. Realizing Kate had asked him a question, he looked up. "Yeah. Yes, I have several questions for each of them."

"Great," Kate said. "Danielle, why don't we start with you. The rest of you can wait out with Mrs. Pendleton."

For the next four and a half hours, Kate and Bernie asked questions and chastised and encouraged. In the end, they sat alone in the conference room.

Bernie rubbed his hands together. "Do you think they can do it?"

"I think they're as ready as they'll ever be."

"That's not really an answer."

"No, it's really not. I think they'll each be fine for a half-hour. Then it gets kind of shaky. After an hour, they'll be totally out of control. But for a half-hour, they're good."

Everyone took the elevator down to the lobby. Bernie turned to go to the back parking lot as Kate walked toward the front lot where she had parked. Bernie stopped. "Would you like me to walk you to your car?"

Kate looked over at him. Although Bernie was known as a "street fighter" lawyer, no one would confuse him with an actual street fighter. He conveyed the image of being soft and skinny at the same time. But what could she say? "Uh, sure. Thanks, Bernie."

He turned to the thin, black man. "Murder, you guys go on back, I'll be there in just a minute."

"Murder? You said his name was John."

Murder smiled. "It's just a nickname."

"No, Johnny is a nickname. Tiny is a nickname. Murder is a violent felony. Try not to mention that in the deposition. And everyone else," Kate said, raising her voice and stepping back, "this is John. Not Murder. John."

Kate glanced out the front door and saw her little car, three rows back from the front door. A large Suburban sat in the row behind hers, but otherwise the lot was empty. Why couldn't Murder walk her to her car? Because there was no sense in hurting Bernie's feelings over two hundred yards of empty parking lot.

The group shuffled toward the back lot as Bernie and Kate walked out the front.

"Thanks for helping us tonight," Bernie said. "I think everything is going to be just fine." As he uttered those words, Kate saw the door to the Suburban open. A wave of relief hit her—someone else to help if something happened. In an instant, however, fear washed away the momentary relief. The Hawaiian. Slowly, he walked toward them.

"Wow, that's a big guy," Bernie said.

Kate grabbed Bernie by the arm and took a step backward. "We need to get out of here." She looked over at Bernie who stared back, confused.

When she turned back around, the Hawaiian had moved more quickly than she expected and was right in front of them.

The man rotated his chest and cocked back his fist. Kate put up her arms and looked up at him, hoping, she knew vainly, to deflect the blow. His eyes widened in anticipation of the violence. Then, they shifted off to his right. Kate instinctively turned to follow his gaze. T.J. stood six feet behind them. He had appeared out of nowhere. They were now in between the two. Trapped.

CHAPTER 25

"Kate," T.J. said slowly, "get behind me." He didn't care about the guy with her. Clearly, he wasn't going to do anything. The Hawaiian was twice his size, but T.J. sensed the man had come to fight a woman. His sudden appearance from the night seemed to have temporarily confused the big man, but T.J. knew that edge would not last long. Kate, however, stood there looking at him with her mouth slightly agape.

"I said get your ass over here," he yelled. Kate blinked twice and then scurried over behind him, dragging the other guy along with her. The huge man began to follow but T.J. took an aggressive step forward. The man stopped and reached his hand into the coat of his pocket. T.J. put his hands up in front of his chest. "Whoa there, big man. No need to be reaching for anything."

The man kept his hand in his pocket. T.J. felt the butterflies fluttering in his stomach. He had fought plenty of guys, but this one was huge. And probably armed. He had stopped the initial attack, but now did not know how to get away. The man seemed to be facing the same dilemma. As the two stood staring at each other, Randy crept out from behind the Suburban, grossly exaggerating his steps by picking his feet up high above the ground before lightly setting them down. T.J. fought the urge to roll his eyes.

Randy was about two feet from the man when tires squealed from the far side of the parking lot. Everyone turned to look.

Randy recovered quickest. He dove into the back of the Hawaiian's knees. As the man went down, Randy stuck his hands in the coat pockets. He pulled out a Tootsie Roll pop.

The two floundered on the ground as a dark green minivan roared up to the group. T.J. stood mesmerized as the side door flew open and a menagerie of vagrants spilled out. A young white guy, wearing oversized overalls, yelled, *"Assholes!!"* and took T.J. down with a textbook shoulder-high tackle. The force of the blow knocked him into the Hawaiian, who had almost dragged himself away from Randy. The four men wrestled on the ground to the hoots and hollers of the surrounding homeless mob.

T.J. lay on his back, underneath the pile, biting on a leg so unwashed he figured it had to be his attacker's. T.J. had read books on wars in which veterans described small parts of large battles slowing down. The live action became almost a frame-by-frame re-enactment. T.J. experienced a similar sensation as he looked up and saw a large silhouette appear against the three-quarter full moon. Later, he said it reminded him of the killer whale commercials for Sea World.

Danielle, seeing her friend locked in what she thought was a three-on-one scrum, had jumped into the pile. Or rather onto the pile. She moved somewhat gracefully during the run up and left her feet about half a yard before the pile. As she rose up, she spread her arms and legs apart. Her head held high gazing out into the empty parking lot, Danielle belly-flopped on the group. The melee had been tightly packed and Danielle covered a lot of real estate. She landed on at least some part of each of them.

The Hawaiian, having almost crawled away from the group, fared the best. Only his right ankle had been caught under one of Danielle's prodigious thighs, although the guy in the overalls swore he heard a snap come from that direction. No one else had anything broken, although all had the wind knocked out of them. Danielle had taken it the worst and was unable to move for several minutes after her heroic dive. With everyone else underneath her, it took a group effort to roll her off to the side.

Danielle let out a groan as she hit the pavement. At the same time, they heard the Suburban start up and peal out of the lot. "Oh, crap," T.J. said.

A slender, black man moved over T.J. who was still sitting on the ground. "Lose your ride?"

T.J. crab-walked back a couple feet and then sprang to his feet. The day he could not take a homeless guy was the day he stopped fighting for good, he was thinking, but Kate stepped between them.

"No, John, this is T.J. He's a friend of mine. He saved me. That guy would have hurt me bad if T.J. hadn't been here." She turned and glared at T.J. "And T.J., I'm sure you want to thank Murder and his friends for showing up when they did." T.J. looked up at the man she called Murder and thought maybe he should stop fighting for good.

Randy groaned from the ground. "Oh, yeah. Sure glad Shamu decided to do her WWE imitation right on my back. Thanks for that, Grace. That was fantastic." Danielle made a "hmmmph" sound but did not move off her back.

"That was Duke Kahiluha," Bernie said. "He works for Bronson Te."

Randy, still on his back, lifted his head. "The party guy?" He looked over at Kate. "Why'd you piss off the party guy?"

"Devil spawn," Esmeralda shouted. Randy and T.J. looked up startled, recognizing her as the woman who had called them out at the mock trial.

Bernie saw their expression and moved up beside them. In a whisper he said, "That's nothing personal. She says that about everyone."

T.J. stared over at Randy, who'd suddenly became very interested in the pile of homeless people. Over the past week, T.J. had shared his increasing doubts that Boris was really the Devil. Randy had remained steadfast. One of his most compelling arguments had been that the wild-eyed stranger had singled them out as being on the side of Satan. Now that she was just a crazy lady, Randy had only the church miracle, as he called it.

T.J. helped Randy up. "We need to talk."

"Later," Randy replied, "not in front of her."

T.J. walked over to Kate, "Can I talk to you a minute? Alone." Kate narrowed her eyes as she stared up at him. Murder saw the tension and stepped toward them. T.J. glanced over at him and then leaned into Kate. "I think you owe me one. Please?"

Kate looked over at the tall guy. "It's all right, John. I'll just be over here."

They walked off to the side as Randy and the overalls guy helped Danielle up. Once they got away from the group, T.J. turned to face Kate but could not look her in the eye. He wanted to tell her about Boris being the Devil, but he could not. He felt like an idiot.

Kate spoke first. "Thanks for saving me. How did you know the Hawaiian was going to be here?"

"We didn't. Boris told us to follow you, in case you decided to go to the cops. We've been following you since the mock trial."

"What?"

T.J. smiled. "Don't worry. We didn't see anything we . . . shouldn't have. We tried to stay two or three car-lengths back, so you wouldn't notice us. Yesterday, we noticed this big brown Suburban was always one of the cars we were behind. License plate said 'Te-Bag.' So, we figured someone else was following you."

"So, you both were following me?"

"Yeah. It was like a conga line at a wedding." They both laughed. "Can I ask you something?"

"Sure."

"Do you know who Boris is? I mean, who he really is?"

Kate stared up at him quizzically. "No. I don't." He could tell she expected him to say something but he did not know what to say. Her eyes flared open and her head moved back slightly. "You're saying *you* don't know him?" T.J.'s silence answered her question. Her face flushed with anger.

"What? You kidnapped someone for a guy you don't even know?"

T.J. could not hold her gaze and looked over toward the homeless crowd, now staring at them. "Easy, now. We don't want to upset the crazies. Look, when Randy and I got into this, it seemed like kind of a stupid prank. Just something kind of crazy and out of control."

"You got that right."

"Yeah, but not this kind of crazy and out of control. We thought Boris was someone who would be able to give us really cool things. He's not. And, even if he was, I don't think we could help him anymore. It's all way out of hand."

"No shit."

"But as bad as this thing with Boris is, you don't want to get mixed up with Bronson Te."

"What do you mean? After this week, I think I can handle some prepster doofus daddy's boy."

T.J. shook his head. "No way, ma'am, you've got it wrong. Boris is a kitty cat compared with Bronson Te. Te is straight whack from what I hear."

"What do you mean?"

"I heard this story where some dude brought some bad acid into one of Te's raves. Te had his goons cut off one of the guy's toes with a cigar clipper."

"Yikes." Kate's toes curled up in her shoes. "Which toe?"

T.J. thought for a moment. "The pointer toe."

"I've never heard of the pointer toe."

"It's the little piggy that stayed home from the market. Right next to the big toe."

Kate shuddered. "That's one of my favorites."

T.J. nodded. "So, anyway, be careful with him. And as far as Boris goes, we're on your side now. What do we need to do?"

"There's no *we,* T.J. It's me. I have to fix the jury. I don't even know who the jurors are and I have to figure out which of them will screw over a cop."

Bernie walked up to them. "Is everything okay, Kate?"

"Sure, Bernie. I'm just a little on edge after all this." She waved her arms at the empty parking lot.

"We should get you home," he said, looking over at T.J. with narrowed eyes. Keeping his gaze, he said, "We'll follow you home, just to make sure you get inside all right."

As the group dispersed, T.J. saw Randy talking to Murder. He was trying to hear what they were saying when a large hand grabbed his shoulder and spun him around. Danielle stood in front him, trying to have a pouty look on her large, jowled face. "I'm sorry I squished you," she said. Before he could stop her she pulled him to her. He slowly slid into her as if she was a kind of vertical quicksand. "I was just trying to save my friend."

"It's all right," T.J. replied, although no one heard him. His face was smushed into Danielle's fleshy shoulder. He tried to pair the words with a graceful exit, but Danielle had both her arms around his and he could not get any kind of push. He felt her hands slide down, each grabbing a butt cheek. Looking around for help, he saw Randy and Murder watching them and smiling. Randy gave him two thumbs-up and silently laughed with his tongue hanging out.

"C'mon Danielle, they're waiting," Murder said. Danielle

released T.J. and said, "Let me know if there's anything I can do to make it up to you."

T.J., still embarrassed by Randy making fun of him, tried to turn the tables. "You know, you really landed on Randy more than me."

Danielle turned and gave Randy the onceover. Turning back to T.J., she said, "I guess I'll have to make up for that, too." She winked at him, then turned and got into the van.

The boys watched the van follow Kate out of the parking lot. Once the lot was empty, they walked to their car without talking. T.J. knew Randy would razz him about Danielle and was not in the mood for it. They drove in silence for a couple of minutes. T.J. could feel Randy smirking in the darkness next to him. Randy turned on the radio to an oldies station. When he started slapping the dashboard spasmodically, T.J. knew he was trying to bait a snide remark. T.J. let it go.

"Hmm," Randy said. T.J. drove on. Randy changed the station to country and again vainly tried to keep the beat, this time on his knee. "Hmm," he repeated.

T.J., knowing he should let it go, could not resist. "What?"

Randy finally looked over at him with innocent eyes. "What?"

"What's with all the 'hmm's'?"

Randy smiled. "I thought maybe Boris had given me some rhythm." He waited a moment for the perfect delivery. "He seemed to have come through with a girl for you." Randy gave out a deep, hearty laugh. T.J., not having heard that laugh in a while, had to smile at himself.

"I said a hot girl," he said, laughing.

Randy changed the station to alternative. "Oh, she was hot, man. She had to be the way she was sweating. Christ, it's thirty degrees out there and the water's pouring off her like she's in the shower."

The conversation was steady and light for most of the way

back to their house. A block away from home, T.J. said, "So, what were you talking to that black guy about? Why he was too much of a pussy to get in the fight?"

"No," Randy said, reaching into his coat pocket, "I scored a bag off him." He wiggled a cigar-sized baggie of pot between his fingers. "He's cool. He's got a couple of felonies and wasn't going to get involved unless it got nasty. Once your girlfriend took the dive, he said he knew that was the end of it."

T.J. drove past their house and down to the grade school to smoke on the playground. The swings swayed in the evening breeze, one a couple feet off the ground, the other a couple feet higher. Randy jumped into the higher one and told T.J. to push him.

"We've got to get out of this, Randy," T.J. said, giving the swing one push and then sitting down in the lower swing and rocking back and forth. "Boris isn't the Devil."

Randy swung in silence while T.J. rolled the joint. When T.J. lit up, Randy jumped off, sticking the landing. He turned with his hands up in the air like a gymnast, but T.J. did not smile. He offered Randy a hit.

Randy took the cigarette and leaned up against the metal frame. "Yeah, I know."

T.J. had been staring down at the ground, but his head jerked up. Admitting Boris was not the Devil was a first for Randy. "You know?"

"Yeah. Why would the Devil need us to watch the jury lady? He's just some ass-clown who's been using us." He took a long drag off the joint.

T.J. breathed a sigh of relief. "So, what now? We can't just leave it, can we?"

Randy still held in the smoke but shook his head. When he finally released the smoke, he looked at T.J. with sad eyes. "We're in this, man. If he's just some old dude, he couldn't have taken the doctor guy or made Kate fix that trial. He needed us for that. We can't leave them."

"So, you got a plan?"

"I got nothing. I guess we hang around and jump in when we can. Like tonight." Randy sat back down on the swing and pushed himself back and forth.

"I might have something. I was talking to Kate."

"Whoa, you're quite the ladies' man."

"Funny. No, we were talking about how to throw the case. She said she needed to throw the jury but she didn't know who the jurors were." T.J. took a long drag off the joint and looked over at Randy, his eyebrows raised.

"What?" Randy asked. "We don't know who the jurors are." T.J. held in the smoke until Randy's eyes widened. "But somebody does. Who knows who the jurors are?"

"The judge would know."

"So, we kidnap the judge?"

T.J. stared back at his brother. "Nope. We sell him some magazines."

Chapter 26

Sitting outside Bronson Te's latest rave, Boris considered the increasingly sticky problem he had with the boys. One of the unfortunate aspects of being a criminal is you frequently have to work with criminals. Trust was an unattainable luxury.

Two possible outcomes loomed in his future, neither desirable. First, the boys could get arrested on one of his errands or during some illegal monkeyshine of their own. They would, of course, tell the police everything, probably without even being asked. He would go to jail. At his age, any significant time would effectively be a death sentence.

Even if the boys avoided the police, a small possibility still existed that his plan would actually work. Somehow, someway, Stiltson could win the case. He had not allowed himself the opportunity to think about that much. All these years. Could it really be happening? But then, of course, the boys would want their reward. A girl he could get. But the other one, the violent one, he would not react well.

Boris suspected, however, that news of his lack of evil omnipotence would not come as a great shock. Lately, they had been eyeballing him suspiciously. Soon he would lose whatever tenuous hold he had over them. Most likely, they would beat him. Less than a week until trial, he could not let it fall apart now.

His main concern was Kate. He had ordered the boys to follow her, but he could not count on them any longer. As they say, if you want a job done right . . . Boris began to tail the boys tailing Kate. He envisioned himself in an old thirties' noir film. A private dick tailing a couple of no-goodniks. In his fantasy, he was trying to save the girl rather than terrorize her, but that was beside the point. Truth seldom makes good fantasy.

In this role, from behind a suburban office building, Boris had witnessed Kate being confronted by an extremely large man in a trench coat. Boris thought to himself that either trial consulting was a rougher business than he thought, or Kate was having an extremely bad week.

After the large black woman dove into the pile, he watched the big man slink away to his Suburban. A plan sprung up, fully formed, in Boris's mind. If the giant had a beef with Kate, maybe he would do for Boris what the boys could not.

Boris jumped up and ran over to his car. He got lucky when the Suburban turned onto the adjacent street in Boris's direction. Boris followed the Suburban into midtown. Formerly a warehouse district, the large open spaces had been refurbished into galleries and late-night clubs. The giant pulled in front of a two-story building with an all-glass front. Lights flashed out into the midnight sky, illuminating a makeshift banner across the top of the doorway. *Te's House of Pleasure.* Inside, a mass of young bodies writhed against one another to a rhythmic bass line Boris felt in his chest. Fascinated, he glided to a stop immediately behind the Suburban and ogled the revelers.

Fully enthralled by the partiers, he did not notice the giant get out of the truck and limp back to the car. Boris jumped at a soft rapping on the glass. The big man leaned over and made the universal roll-down-your-window-gesture with his hand. Boris stared back with the universal I-really-do-not-want-to-do-that expression. The big man's persistence won out. Boris inched the window down a quarter of the way.

"Hello. Can I help you?"

"Funny, I was going to ask you the same question. You've been following me since I left 95th Street."

"Me? Oh, no, I was just, uh, just going into the party here."

"Really?" The Hawaiian chuckled. "Okay, let's go in then." The big man smiled as he opened the door. Boris sat in the car mesmerized by the perfect, brilliant white teeth. They almost glowed in the light from the building.

"Nice teeth," Boris said, looking up.

The man nodded. "Thanks." He took Boris gently but firmly by the arm and lifted him out of the car. They walked side-by-side toward the line of about forty people standing in front of the door. Boris stopped at the back of the line. Looking ahead at those waiting, Boris marveled at how young they looked. He guessed all were over twenty-one, but he would have put most of them in high school. The giant walked a few feet before noticing Boris had stopped. His smile faded.

"We don't have to wait." Several of the high schoolers scowled at them, but none made any type of protest as they walked toward the front of the line.

At the door, another man in a trench coat stood at the end of a velvet rope. The doorman was large, although still probably only three-fourths the size of Boris's escort. As they walked up, three young couples stumbled out, laughing. The doorman looked down the line and pointed to four girls in mini-skirts waiting about twenty people back from the front of the line. His eyes moved up and singled out two hipster dudes near the front. The dudes sidled up to the women as the six went in the club.

Boris thought back to his twenties when he would stand outside the discos in such a line. The doorman had rarely picked him. At the time, he had been baffled and angry about the inequity of the seemingly random selection of who got in and who froze outside. Looking back at this line, however, even he could readily see who would make it into the party and who would stand out here all night. He saw his modern counterpart. Not ugly, but not attractive. Not a geek, but not cool. Just average. Average in a line of extraordinary.

Joe Average stood three back from the front of the line. He had been there a while. As the doorman had scanned the crowd after the couples exited, the young man had looked on hopefully, his desperation to get in the final straw keeping him out.

Boris felt his face flush. He remembered that sense of anticipation, the sense of hope that his turn had come. Surely the disco doorman had realized, as Boris realized now, that he had had no chance of being selected.

"Hey Duke," the doorman said to the giant. "The Man said to see him as soon as you got back."

"Thanks," Duke replied and walked through the door. Boris attempted to slide in behind him, but the doorman grabbed his arm.

"Hold on there, Grandpa."

"He's with me," Duke said. The doorman slid his eyes suspiciously between the Hawaiian and Boris, but let go of the arm.

Stepping inside the door, Boris's eardrums exploded. Outside he had felt a bit of a bass tremor in his chest and had been able to hear music playing. Inside, however, the sound surrounded him, thick and weighty, as if he had stepped into noise Jell-O. Colored lights strobed onto the dance floor as the crowd, dancing shoulder to shoulder, wriggled and swayed to the beat. Pushing through the crowd, Boris's nose filled with the mixed odors of sweat, marijuana, and a strong pungent smell he could not identify. Only his taste buds remained unattacked by the crowd.

They made their way through the club to the back. A wide spiral staircase led up to an office. Inside, the smell dissipated and the noise dropped to a conversational level. The room was divided between an office area and a living room area. The office area was modernly stark. A silver desk flanked by two silver chairs sat in the corner. The living room area was warmer, with two leather chairs across a mahogany coffee table from a low, four-cushion couch.

When Duke and Boris walked in, a thin Chinese man in his mid-twenties sat in a chair facing the door. A young woman's auburn-haired head bobbed in between the man's legs.

Te opened his eyes and saw Boris with Duke. He made eye contact with Duke for a moment, then re-closed his eyes and leaned his head back. Boris turned to leave but Duke caught his arm. Startled, he looked up, but the giant stood still, looking at the closed blinds behind the desk. Boris tried to concentrate on the music outside in the club to distract him from the wet noises coming from the leather chair.

A couple of minutes later, Te made a sound like he was clearing his throat and then opened his eyes. He kissed the girl on the top of the head. "Thanks, Cindy. Why don't you wait downstairs? I'll be right down." As she left, Boris saw in her face the same hopeful expression he had seen in the line outside.

Te stood up, zipped his fly, and walked over next to Duke. For most people, standing next to such a large man would make them look smaller, weaker. Te, though, looked stronger, physically larger than when he sat in the chair. "Friend of yours?" Te never looked at Boris. The question was the first indication Te had even noticed him.

"He followed me back from the job."

Te paused for a moment, still not making eye contact with Boris. "Is that a problem?"

"No. She was all alone in the parking lot. I mean the whole fucking lot was empty except me and her. I step out to talk to her and next thing I know there are like ten people jumping on me. Two kids I'd never seen before and the whole fucking homeless clan. I didn't get a chance to tell her anything."

Duke blurted this out quickly. Although the giant had no fear in his voice, Boris noticed an edge that had not been there earlier.

"When I left the lot, I saw him pull in behind me. Then I saw him again when I pulled up here. I asked him what he was doing here, and he said he was coming to the party."

Te looked over at Boris for the first time. His eyes darted up and down the old man, but his expression remained blank. "Can I get you something to drink, Methuselah? Or something else?" he asked, gesturing to a small bowl Boris had originally thought contained little pink candies. Now, looking closer, he saw they looked like the baby aspirins he took every night for his heart. He guessed they were neither and shook his head.

"I was hoping to ask you if I could borrow your man here," Boris asked, rapping his knuckles on Duke's bicep. It was granite. Te stood silent, looking at Boris with indifference. Boris let out a nervous laugh. "It seems like you have a problem with Ms. Summerlin and I have a little problem with Ms. Summerlin. Maybe we could pool our resources."

"Duke's his own man. He is not some sort of pick-up truck I loan out to friends." Te's tone made it clear that Duke was not his own man and that Te, in fact, would loan him out to anyone, friend or stranger, for the right price. "What resources are you throwing into the pool?"

The question threw Boris. "I . . . I know where Ms. Summerlin is, or I mean, I know where she will be. You seem to have some difficulty speaking with her. I can guarantee your man here could talk with her completely uninterrupted."

Te stared at Boris passively for a moment. He breathed heavily through his nose and waved his hand in front of his face as if he was shooing away a fly. "This is getting too weird. You know what, screw it. I'm just going to pay those homeless fucks twenty grand a piece. That's more money than they had in probably their whole stinking lives. I've got attorneys calling me. I think every homeless bum in the city is using our alley as a bathroom. And you." He pointed at Boris. "Weird old guys coming in here. Creeping. Me. Out."

Boris stood there, mouth agape. How had he creeped out the King of Creep?

Te looked up at the Hawaiian. "I'm done with this thing. You want to make a deal with the old man, it's your deal. But I'm out. Got it?"

Duke nodded once and turned to Boris. "Five hundred bucks an hour."

Boris smiled. "Do you know where the Tomb of Doom is?"

Chapter 27

A good closing argument does not win the case. A good closing argument gives your jurors the words to use in the jury room to win the case.

Greene, F. (2003). *The Trial Consultant's Field Manual* (p. 403). New York: Pullman.

Kate lay in bed as the Captain slept between her ankles. Rolling over she caught a glimpse of the clock. The red light shone out 4:25. Arnie was giving closings in Wrenshaw today. She had planned to get up at 4:30 and her mind told her she needed those extra five minutes to be totally fresh for the day.

She had not slept well. The large Hawaiian had almost gotten her. If the boys had not shown up . . . She could not believe they had been following her. It gave her the willies. She traced back through her steps, cringing at the Baskin Robbins stop where she had eaten a pint of Chocolate Peppermint in the parking lot.

The alarm rang. She hit the snooze and rolled onto her back. The Captain yawned and crawled up onto her chest. He circled once and then plopped down, sitting on her shoulder like a prone, furry parrot. He resumed his purring. According to the ancient Egyptians, cats absorbed anxiety and stress. Kate only knew the world disappeared while the fat cat purred against her.

The alarm clock rang again and Kate rolled over, spilling the

Captain on the bed beside her. He looked up and gave her a small squeak before starting a rigorous licking regiment. Not wanting to stick around for the end of that show, Kate went into the bathroom and took a shower. Twenty minutes and an empty hot water heater later she got out and heard the phone ringing.

Rushing into the kitchen to her cell phone, Kate's arms filled with goose bumps at the cold air outside the steamy bathroom. She picked up the phone, noticing she was standing naked in front of the kitchen window. The window sat above the sink and, up on the third floor, only the birds could see in. Nonetheless, mindful of the boys' surveillance the night before, she backed into the hall.

"Hello?" she said.

"Hello, Kate."

Boris. She immediately recognized the voice. Having just thought about the boys cushioned her shock at hearing the voice in her apartment. "I understand you had a little bit of trouble last night."

Kate remained silent. The man seemed to thrive on her fear. She was in no mood to play along this morning. Not before she had her coffee.

"Good thing I sent the boys to watch over you." Pause. "Had to protect my investment, you know."

Kate had heard enough. "Did you want something or were you just calling to pat yourself on the back?"

His voice tightened and Kate was secretly pleased her barb had hit its mark. "The trial is tomorrow. I was calling to make sure you had some sort of plan. I hear you're working on some homeless people's case. And I hear you're going to Warrensburg. But I don't hear anything about how you're going to save poor Dr. Townsend's life. You do have something, don't you?"

Fear welled up in Kate's chest. She hated that he had

regained the upper hand in the conversation so easily. Then she caught it.

"Who did you say? You mean Dr. Greene."

"No. I discovered I actually have Dr. Townsend, as you well know. I understand you're not too keen on him."

"We've had our disagreements, but I still consider him a friend."

"That's good to hear. Because if I think you're slacking off, I'm sure I can get to someone who will properly motivate you."

"I'll be fine." Kate said, although she kicked herself for making a stink about the attack on her father. She wanted to get back in control of the conversation and still had not figured out what Boris's angle was. "Maybe if you told me what you want to get out of the case, we could think of another settlement proposal and avoid trial."

Boris erupted. "I want to win! That's what I want out of the case. I want to win the fucking case. Whatever it takes so at the end of the case the defense attorney says 'I won the hell out of that case,' that's what I want."

Kate had never heard it put like that before, but she certainly understood the sentiment. "All right, all right," she said, "I just thought there might be some other way."

"Tomorrow, Kate." His voice had regained its calmness and had a mocking quality. "Tomorrow." He hung up.

An hour later Kate walked out to her car with no memory of getting dressed. She looked down and saw her beige suit. It matched the day and her mood. The clouds were low and heavy though it did not feel like rain. The clouds served no purpose except to sit over her, glooming up her day.

The gray clouds stayed with her as she drove to Warrensburg. Once, she had made the drive in the spring. She had been taken aback by the beauty of western Missouri—the thick, rich foliage contrasting with the dark, distant bluffs. Now, late in the fall, the foliage had dropped. Everything blended into a nondescript brown. Not even an interesting chocolaty brown or variegated browns. It was simply brown—the brown of death.

Kate tried to focus on the Wrenshaw trial. There would not be time to change Arnie's closing, but it might keep her mind off Boris. As she made her way into Warrensburg, though, he filled her thoughts. If she only knew his angle. Why did he need Stiltson to win?

She made her way into the courthouse and saw Arnie standing in the hallway. Several years earlier, the County had erected a bronze statue of Lady Justice on a bronze bench huddled next to a young boy, pulling him close to her side. The plaque on the wall next to it read "Protecting the Victims." The local defense bar had raised a stink but no sane politician would vote to remove a statue celebrating justice for the child victims.

Arnie stood in front of the piece, using the metal pair as mock jurors for his argument. When Kate walked up, he had reached a climactic point. Muttering unintelligibly under his breath, he lifted up his right hand, index finger extended and began jabbing it, sharply and repeatedly, at the small boy.

Kate spun her head around to see if any jurors saw the bizarre scene: Lady Justice protecting the cowering child from the maniacal ranting of the defense attorney. Not the final image Kate wanted in the jurors' minds before deliberations.

She raced over and slapped the back of his hand, hissing at him, "Stop that." The hand slap had not been purely instinctive. Having treated him like a naughty schoolboy, she expected he would react as such, remorseful and contrite. Instead, the intensity of the argument, having been stopped in full flow, piled up behind his eyes and bore down on Kate.

Taken back a bit, she still held her ground, trying to match his intensity as she met his eyes. "Don't yell at Lady Justice. Someone might see you." Arnie's eyes cooled and he looked around, as if coming out of a trance.

He let out a sharp breath and smiled, "She had it coming." Kate rolled her eyes at him and they walked toward the courtroom.

Although Kate specialized in jury selections, she regularly helped attorneys write their closing arguments. With attorneys like Arnie, it was easy. His Latin passion gave him energy and purpose to thunder around the courtroom, emotionally dragging the jurors over to his side. Less passionate clients proved more difficult. Some attorneys, despite being brilliant and ruthless trial attorneys, simply lacked the temperament to give a fire and brimstone closing. That, of course, did not stop them from trying, usually with disastrous results.

Kate had pegged Zuckerman as one who lacked the ability to play to the jury's emotions. Where jurors saw inept male attorneys as fake, they viewed female attorneys who overplayed the emotion in the case as "hysterical" or, as one particularly cretinous juror put it, "on the rag." It was an unfair hurdle only the most skilled or innately hot-tempered female attorneys could clear. Zuckerman fit in neither category.

From the beginning of her argument, though, it was clear Zuckerman understood what style best suited her. Calm and logical, she laid out the facts against Rick and explained how each fit into the elements of the crime instruction the judge had given. The brutality of the crimes and the innocence of the victim would provide the emotion to impel the jurors to find Rick guilty and carry the jury to death in the sentencing phase. Several jurors nodded as Zuckerman uttered her final line imploring them to find Rick guilty of capital murder.

Judge Mays nodded at Zuckerman and looked over to the defense table. "Mr. Montoy."

Arnie stayed erect in his chair, his hands resting on each knee. "Ms. Zuckerman did a fine job explaining to you the reasons why it is possible Rick killed Harold Pike. It's certainly possible. But that's not why we're here today." Montoy always started his closing giving some ground to the government and he always did it sitting down. Jurors liked the seemingly fair admissions. Subconsciously though, they would disassociate the statement with the arguments he made standing up a few feet in front of them.

Arnie stood up quickly, placing his right hand lightly on the defendant's shoulder. "We're here because you have to decide, not whether it's possible Rick killed someone, but whether the State proved beyond a reasonable doubt Rick *did* kill someone." He gave Rick a pat and then stepped over to the juror box. "That's why we're here.

"You know I'm a public defender. I get paid by you the taxpayers to come in here and defend people like Rick because they can't afford an attorney." Arnie slid his hands into his pockets. As he talked, he moved his eyes from the juror in the front row on the right to the back row on the left. Although he looked at no particular juror, everyone would think he spent a lot of time talking directly to him.

"I often read criticism of public defenders. Actually, the way they usually say it is that the rich get 'a better justice system.' But what they mean is public defenders like me are too incompetent to properly defend our clients. And that offends me.

"It offends me not so much because it's an unfair criticism of me." Arnie stopped pacing and gave the jurors a conspiratorial smile, "Although it's sometimes true." He turned and faced the jurors, bringing his hands up out of his pockets. The sudden change in motion would focus their attention on his next words. "It offends me because it is an unfair criticism of you, the jurors.

"Such criticism assumes you are nothing but cattle to be led around by this attorney or that attorney. That you're unable to decide for yourselves what witness to believe or how shoddy police work has tainted an investigation without some brilliant attorney's explanation. These critics believe justice for the innocent and overcharged comes only dressed in a Brooks Brothers suit.

"They're wrong. Justice comes dressed in a blue plaid shirt." With this he pointed to the Magic Eight Ball, who was wearing a blue plaid shirt. "It comes dressed in a pink sweater," pointing at the Grammar Lady. "I can't control you. Ms. Zuckerman can't control you. Not even Judge Mays can sway you to finding the verdict he thinks is the proper one."

Arnie put his hands back in his pockets and resumed pacing. "I've watched these past two weeks. You've listened to every witness, you watched all the videos and examined every piece of evidence that came in. You understand your duty here. And you realize whether Ms. Zuckerman or I am the best attorney doesn't matter. What matters is whether the State has proven beyond a reasonable doubt Rick is a killer. But let's look at what they told you . . ."

With that, Arnie launched into a detailed critique of the State's witnesses and evidence. Everyone on the trial team realized a guilty verdict was coming. But by ripping apart the evidence, Arnie tried to create a small measure of residual doubt that might carry over and cause one of the jurors to vote for life.

After the closings, the jury went into the deliberation room. Now, all the attorneys could do was wait. Zuckerman went back to her office. The defense team, though, had nowhere to go so they waited with Rick. More than likely, a verdict would come that day.

The jury had retired to their room just before eleven. Kate decided to hang around until after lunch. She tried to keep everyone's spirits up. Despite her best efforts the mood stayed low. It was a tough time, sitting around waiting for a guilty verdict.

"Arnie," Rick asked, "could I talk with Kate?"

Arnie looked over at Kate then back to Rick. "She's sitting right there, Rick, ask her yourself."

"I meant alone. Can we be alone?" He looked back toward the two prison guards in the back of the room.

Arnie looked over to Kate, who nodded. He stood up and walked to the back. After a few minutes he waved to Rick. "They'll let us use the conference room outside the door here."

Kate felt a little anxious. She was not worried Rick would try anything. Arnie and the guards would be right outside the door. She just did not know what he wanted to talk to her about.

Inside the room, Rick sat down and stared at the table. Kate sat down and gave him time to get his thoughts together. "I suppose you're wondering why I called you here," he said, chuckling. Kate gave out a little nervous laugh.

"What we say in here is confidential, right?"

"Sure, Rick," Kate said. "I work for Arnie and everything you tell us is privileged. We can't tell anyone."

"What about Arnie? If I tell you something, will you tell him?"

Kate paused. She did not really want to know anything Arnie did not know. "I guess not. If you don't want me to. But Arnie is your attorney. He really should know anything if it's important."

"I guess it's not that important. It won't make any difference. But you can't tell Arnie. Promise?"

"Okay, I promise."

"I wanted you to know what really happened. With Pike, I mean."

"You didn't kill him?" Kate asked.

"Oh, I killed him. I shot him dead as dead. But the why . . ."

His story had never made sense to Kate. How did he lose his cool at being called a name, get his gun, load it, send the little eight-year-old girl across the street, then lose control and shoot six bullets into Pike?

"I killed him for the girl."

Kate closed her eyes. "Oh, Rick, I really don't want to hear about that."

"No, no. Not like that. I wasn't touching the girl. He was. Pike was. That's what I saw through the window in my kitchen. Pike was . . . doing things to that little girl."

"Oh, God."

"I gave him a chance. I went over and sent Janie across the street. I told him I saw what he'd done and if he ever did it again, I was going to kill him." Rick's hand was on the table. Kate reached out for him, but he pulled it back. "He just laughed. Said she was his daughter and he could do what he wanted. Then he said he was going to have to give her something special, just for me. So, I pulled out my gun and I shot the son of a bitch until the gun ran out of bullets."

They sat there in silence for a moment. Finally, Kate leaned forward. "Rick, you have to tell Arnie. The jury needs to know this. That's called 'defense of another.' You killed Pike to protect that little girl."

"Oh, yeah?" Rick glared at her. "And how is the jury going to hear about it? Who do you think Arnie's going to bring in here to tell them I'm telling the truth?"

"The girl, probably, but . . ."

"No buts about it. Janie. First Arnie would have to talk to her, then the police would talk to her, then the Court Services people would talk to her. Then, after all that, she gets to come into court and Zuckerman gets to cross-examine her. No way."

"Rick, you could die for this. Do you understand? It's a real possibility you are going to get the death penalty and they will put you in the gas chamber. I respect that you don't want to harm the girl, but, come on, you can't die like this."

Rick leaned his head back and looked at the ceiling. "A couple weeks ago a preacher came to see me. We were talking about Heaven and Hell and believing in the Lord and all that. He said if you've done one really good thing, it can cancel out all the little bad things you've done. Do you believe that, Kate?"

"Rick, listen to me, if you live, you'll have plenty of opportunities to do good things."

Rick shook his head. "I've always had opportunities to be good, Kate. And I've always done the wrong thing. Until now. This is the one. I'm not telling you this so you can talk me into telling Arnie. My mind's made up on that. I just wanted you to know, you know. I'm not some cold-blooded killer. I wanted you to know I did something good."

His eyes watered around the edges, but he did not cry. Kate did. He stood up, walked over to the door and knocked on it. One of the guards opened the door and, seeing Kate crying, gave Rick a sharp look. His face changed seeing Rick, too, on the verge of tears. He did not say anything, but walked Rick back into the courtroom.

Driving back to Kansas City that night, Kate tried to keep from crying. Despite Arnie's repeated questioning, she kept her promise to Rick. Her mind drifted back to Townsend. Was throwing the Beckwith trial to save him her one good thing to get into Heaven? If your one good thing hurts someone good, like Beckwith, does that count?

More importantly, was she really doing anything at all? Arnie was right. Attorneys do not decide cases. Certainly consultants do not decide cases. Jurors decide cases. Even if she was able to pick the perfect jury for Boris, it did not mean anything. The jurors, in the end, made the decision. Townsend's life rested in their hands and Kate had absolutely no control.

CHAPTER 28

Most Master Gardeners in the Midwest hated the winter. Some claimed to enjoy the challenge of finding the perfect Christmas bloom or bragged about the contrasting foliage and berries of some Canadian Holly hybrid. In truth, the joys of gardening lay as dormant as the plants themselves. When the main activities were raking leaves and pushing down pine tree food, the hobby became more chore than joy.

Judge Gino Brandell loved the winter. Actually, he loved November: the crisp air, the sharp North wind and fallen leaves from the trees. Sometimes he thought he liked the brown leaves on the ground more than the yellow and red leaves on the trees. The clean-up that cursed so many homeowners made him warm inside. His purpose on earth was to be the cleaner.

Brandell waited eagerly for the last leaf to fall. Then he scoured the ground, returning his garden paradise back to its immaculate beauty.

The symbolism was not lost on him. Every week he sent the dregs of society off to prison, raking up the fallen souls and putting them in the trash with the rest of the State's debris. The difference was that sentencing defendants was picking up one leaf at a time. In his front yard, he could scoop up leaves in big handfuls, mashing them all together in a large trash bag.

This Saturday had been a good day. A couple days of strong winds had brought down the leaves a week earlier than usual. Brandell had spent the last four hours purging his yard and he could see the end. Although he enjoyed the process, it was the ending that he savored—looking over the once littered yard and seeing it returned to its pristine state.

He had about thirty minutes of raking left to do when a young man approached him.

"Excuse me, sir, could I have a minute of your time?" the young man said.

Years on the bench had left Brandell assuming everyone he met was a criminal. Nothing about this one's face dissuaded him from that assumption. He carried a clipboard, which made him more likely to be annoying than dangerous, but Brandell stared him down, saying nothing.

"Good afternoon." The man gestured around the yard with his hand. "Looks like you almost got it licked." He laughed, but the judge said nothing. "Boy, there's nothing like the enjoyment of a good hard day in the yard, is there?"

Brandell found himself nodding.

"Except," the man continued, "for maybe those first moments after the job's over, when you sit down and your arms ache a little and your legs feel a little sore in the back. But it's a good kind of pain, because you earned it and you earned that rest."

The speech made the judge want to get back to the yard so he could sit down and feel that soreness. "What can I do for you, son?"

"When you sit down at the end of that day," he said, "and you have a cool beverage in your hand, you know what makes that moment perfect? A good magazine." There it was. "I'm selling magazine subscriptions as part of a program that helps young people like myself earn points that we can use to compete for college scholarships. I've spent the last five years since high school doing drugs and wasting my life away. Now I'm trying to get my life back on track and I hope you will help me and get some fine reading material in the bargain. We offer many of the magazines you see in the top waiting rooms all around this great country of ours."

The young man pulled out a flyer and held it up in front of the judge. The abrupt switch to a sales pitch broke whatever spell had been cast.

"I don't want any magazines and I need to get this yard cleaned up before the sun goes down." The judge gave Randy his *I-told-you-to-turn-off-your-cell-phone* stare.

"I understand, sir, and I thank you for your time." Randy turned to leave but stopped, his head tilting to the right. "Sorry to bother you, sir. Is that a Manitoba Purple Hydrangea?" he asked, pointing to a withering bush next to the house.

The judge's eyes widened. "Why yes, yes it is. Not too many people around here can tell the difference."

Randy gave him a quick smile. "A couple of years ago, my dad read an article about them and has wanted one ever since. Mom won't let him spend a hundred dollars on a plant he'd probably kill so Dad keeps a picture of it by his table in the family room. I recognized the serrated leaves and variegation down the stem. That's pretty unusual for a hydrangea."

"Yes, yes, that's right. You know, I wrote an article on the Manitoba in *Master Gardener's Monthly.* Is that the one he read?" No yard work was getting done, but the judge didn't care. He could talk for hours about his prized hydrangea.

"Sure," Randy said. "Dad pores over his *MGM* every month. He says it should be a weekly."

"I don't know about that," the judge said. "Sometimes they get a little repetitive. Especially about roses." He spat out the last word.

"Dad says roses are for old ladies and the English."

The judge laughed. "You know, I think your father and I would get along just fine." He thought for a moment. "You know, the Manitoba is a fairly low-maintenance bush if you plant it correctly." He started walking toward his house. "I've got a flyer that explains exactly how to do it. Maybe your father could talk your mother into letting him have one as a spring present. I'll be right back."

"No, no," Randy said quickly. "Mom's pretty set against it. I wouldn't want to take your flyer."

"I've got plenty," the judge said. "It's certainly worth a try. Wait here." The judge hurried through the entryway and opened the door to the den. He walked around behind his desk, opened a drawer from the filing cabinet and found a copy of the Manitoba flyer. He closed the drawer and went to leave when he stopped. Something felt wrong. He looked around the top of his desk and everything appeared normal. He leaned to his right, looking in the foot well of the desk where he saw a young man staring wide-eyed back at him. Jumping back, he turned toward the door where Randy stood with a large knife from the kitchen.

"Easy there, judge. Be cool and you'll live to see that hydrangea bloom in the spring."

Chapter 29

Kate arrived back in Lawrence just after seven. As she drove to the hospital, she tried to put the Wrenshaw trial and the Boris situation out of her mind. Even if she could not spend as much time as she wanted with her dad, the time she did spend had to be all about him. That she could control.

The light half a block ahead turned red and she began to slow down. Movement in her rearview mirror caught her eye. A convertible BMW sped toward her. Did the idiot not see the red light ahead? A large truck slowed in the lane next to her. She had nowhere to go. The intersection was empty and Kate quickly looked both ways. No cars were coming. She sailed through the intersection. The BMW followed. Just past the intersection, the BMW rammed the back of the Bug. It swerved a little, but Kate regained control.

Looking again in the rearview mirror, Kate recognized Townsend's girlfriend, Maria. Great, thought Kate, I'm going to get killed in a car accident, Boris will kill Townsend and Maria will tell everyone that I was sleeping with him. Does the funeral home shave legs?

Kate shook her head to clear her thoughts. From the way Maria was weaving behind her, she'd started drinking long before four. Kate could see another intersection a little way ahead of her. The light was green now, which meant it would probably be red when she got there. She could not take another chance that the intersection would be empty.

There was still one turn before the light. Maybe she could veer off and lose Maria. She sped up and, just as she reached the street, slammed on the brakes, jerked the wheel to the left, let up on the brakes and floored it. For a moment the Bug went up on two wheels, but righted itself. As Kate breathed a sigh, she heard a crash behind her.

The BMW had hit the curb at an angle doing forty-five, then skidded to a stop in someone's yard. In her mirror, Kate saw Maria stumble out of the car. She appeared to be dazed but generally unhurt. Kate sighed in relief. That should take care of Maria until she made bail on her DUI. And with Townsend unavailable, that could be a while.

Finally, Kate made it to the hospital. As she walked into the lobby, she glanced over at the "Welcome to Lawrence Memorial Hospital" sign. Who would put the word "Memorial" in the name of a hospital? Seemed sort of like having a cemetery on the front lawn.

Bob had undergone what the doctor called minor surgery. He had suffered a slight fracture of his cheekbone and the doctor wanted to put a plastic plate inside his cheek to protect the bone and help it to heal. To Kate, minor surgery was getting stitches or lancing a boil. Pulling back part of someone's face sounded pretty major, but the doctor had assured her he had done the procedure thousands of times.

The surgery had been in the mid-morning and Bob was still heavily medicated. He probably would not remember her coming, but she had to see for herself that he was all right.

As the elevator doors opened, Kate's Spidey sense began to tingle. Actually, her sense of smell began to tingle at the aroma of cooked cabbage. Then her Spidey sense began to tingle.

"It's probably not them," Kate said under her breath. She tried to think of anything a hospital might serve that could go with sauerkraut but could not think of anything. Why would they come here?

Kate walked into the hallway, looking for Room 617. She passed a nurses' station where everyone seemed to be very agitated at something. She had a guess.

"Excuse me, can you tell me where Bob Summerlin's room is, please?" Kate asked. Several heads turned to glower at her. She smiled back sweetly. It would not help her dad for her to fight with the nurses.

A fifty-something woman dressed in blue scrub bottoms and a flowered smock walked over to Kate. She had what Kate guessed was usually described as a kind face. The features, now, were out of whack. "He's down the hall, third door on the left. But you can't go in right now."

Kate's heart skipped. It had not been a minor surgery. She knew it. Her father was dying. One hundred percent fault to that quack doctor. "What's wrong?"

The woman's eyes narrowed. "I'll tell you what's wrong. There's a maximum of three people visiting a patient at one time."

Kate let those words sink in. Her father was not in mortal danger. She let out a big sigh. "So, how many people are in there now?"

"More than three," the nurse said tersely.

"I'll take care of it," Kate said as she hurried down the hall.

Kate turned the corner and saw Bernie sitting on the floor, staring up at the ceiling.

"Bernie?"

When he saw her he stood up. "Oh, hey, Kate. How are you doing?"

"I'm good, Bern. What are you doing here?"

Bernie smiled at her sheepishly. "The gang wanted to come up and pay their respects to your father. They seem to credit him for everything," he said with a little sadness.

"They know my dad?"

"Only by reputation." Suddenly, Bernie's eyes grew wide. "Hey, you haven't heard, have you? We settled. Twenty-five grand a piece and we didn't have to do any depositions."

"Hey, congratulations. That's really great. What did you mean they credit dad with everything?"

"Word got around the street that Duke Kahiluha attacked the homeless consultant's father." Bernie tilted his head and shrugged his shoulders apologetically. "That's what they call you on the street."

"Great. I always thought my street name would be something like 'Jungle' or 'Straight Edge.' Not 'Homeless Consultant.' "

"Right after we heard about your dad, everyone felt terrible. Just terrible. But then, Dave Roberts called and offered twenty grand each. I talked him up to twenty-five and we got the deal done. But, because of the timing of everything, the gang thinks your dad beat the settlement out of Duke Kahiluha."

Kate put a hand on his shoulder. "Bernie, you know they appreciate what you do. You're the homeless person's best friend. I'm sure they know you're responsible for getting them the settlement."

"Oh, it doesn't matter who gets the credit," Bernie said, standing up a little straighter.

"Should we go in?" Kate asked.

"I think I better not. Out here, I can keep an eye on them in case they try to get into trouble. In there, they're pretty contained. Plus the Gildersons said they'd keep an eye on things."

"Gildersons?" Kate said with alarm. "The Gildersons are in there?" Kate pushed into the door to reveal a surprisingly calm scene. Sue Gilderson sat in the corner clutching her purse and listening to Danielle. Professor Whitly appeared to be flirting with Murder at the foot of the bed. Pajama Man stood at the window, staring out into the parking lot. Esmerelda stroked the unconscious Bob's hair as she talked with Roger Gilderson. No sign of the young guy.

Sue interrupted Danielle and hurried over to Kate. Wide-eyed and distraught, she whispered, "These people said they were friends of yours."

"We can all still hear you, dear," Roger said wearily. Sue did not take her eyes off of Kate.

"It's all right Sue, they're good people." Kate looked around the room and smiled. She walked over to her dad as Danielle resumed her monologue with Sue, "As I was saying, you can't just eat any animal you find . . ."

"How's he doing?" Kate asked Roger.

Before he could answer, Esmerelda said, "He's wonderful. Wonderful." Her voice had a longing to it. As she spoke, she rubbed his head with her left hand. Kate saw Esmerelda slip her right hand under the covers and move down toward the middle of the bed.

"Okay," Kate said loudly. "Esmerelda, Bernie told me to tell you he needed to see you outside." The hand stopped. "Now."

"What does he want?" Esmerelda snapped.

"I don't know, but it must be very important because he asked to see you right away." Esmerelda stood up and stomped out of the room. Kate did not know what would happen when she found out Bernie had not asked for her, but anything was better than watching her unconscious father get a hand job.

"When he wakes up, I'm going to tell Bob what you did," Roger said with a smile.

"Him I can handle." She laughed. "What did the doctor say?"

"He thought everything went great," Roger said. "The fracture looked a little better in person than on the x-ray. So that was good. But he still wanted to do the interior facial splint out of an abundance of caution."

Murder leaned forward, "So, will they have to take that thing out?"

"Apparently not," Roger replied. "It degrades after about six months. There may be some additional calcification, but on the cheekbone, it won't cause him any troubles. He has to stay in the hospital for a week or so, to make sure he doesn't have any adverse reactions to it, and then he's home. The doctor said he could be back in the classroom for the start of next semester."

"He'll be sorry to hear that," Whitly joked. Everyone laughed. "Say Kate, where have you been hiding this one?" She poked Murder in the ribs. He giggled. Generally, Kate worried more about Whitly's conquests, but the Professor might be biting off more than she could chew here.

"Sorry Professor Whitly, I just met John last week."

"John," Whitly said with disdain. "I thought you said your name was Murder."

Murder smiled. "My mom and Ms. Summerlin call me John. Everyone else calls me Murder."

"Well, I'm not your mother and I'm certainly not everyone else." Whitly lightly raked her nails across Murder's arm. "I guess I'll have to come up with my own name for you."

"Congratulations, John," Kate said, abruptly changing the subject. "Bernie told me you guys got the settlement."

"Yeah, it's great. Thank you so much."

Kate shrugged. "I didn't do anything. You guys were never even deposed."

"You live on the street, you learn nothing is really a coincidence. The day after we met with you, we get the settlement offer." He raised his hands and shrugged his shoulders.

"I thought you guys gave my dad all the credit?"

"Those guys do." He leaned in and whispered, "But they're crazy." In a normal voice he said, "Don't get me wrong, I appreciate what he did and all. But it was you and Bernie."

Kate blushed. "So, what are you guys going to do with the money?"

Murder laughed. "I'm trying to get them to pool it together and buy one of those small vacant buildings east of the crossroads. Bernie says we could probably get one for under eighty grand. Then we could have a roof over our heads. Someplace that was ours. But, like I said, they're crazy. 'Melda said she was going to buy a soul protection machine. So, I don't know if it will work. Bernie said he'd help me work on them."

"Well, good luck," Kate said. From the look Whitly was giving him, he wouldn't need any luck tonight.

Chapter 30

T.J. scrambled out from underneath the desk. Randy smiled at him apologetically, then turned back toward the judge.

"Sorry about this, Gino, I really enjoyed the gardening talk, but I think we need to get going."

The judge looked back and forth between the two boys, his mouth slightly open. He said nothing.

T.J. had the same look. Five times they had done the magazine bit and had never had any problems. Something about Randy made people trust him. He would go to the front door, pretending to be a college kid selling magazines. Once he got to talking, everyone fell right into his hands. He could pick up on the little unique thing that the mark wanted to tell someone about, then pretend it was his lifelong passion. Even people with no desire at all to buy a magazine (which was pretty much everyone) invited Randy into their homes just to talk to him.

Almost always, Randy was able to keep the homeowner occupied for at least five minutes. T.J. could get in the back door, hit the freezer, the underwear drawer, and under the master bedroom mattress on the side furthest from the door. Then, he was out. Five minutes or less, every time.

The judge's house was a little more complicated. They figured they needed more than five minutes because the judge probably would not hide the jury list in the freezer. It turned out the judge did not hide the list at all. T.J. found the den quickly and the Stiltson file was right on top. The trick turned out to be finding the list in the thick legal file.

Once he found the list, T.J. had taken photographs like a 007 agent. He wished he had one of those small 007 cameras that push together instead of the small disposable they had bought at the Walgreens. He got caught up in the intrigue of pretending to be a spy and barely heard the judge coming. The file still sat out on the desk.

"Hey partner," Randy said, "are we ready to go?"

T.J. nodded slowly, not taking his eyes off the judge.

The judge scanned the room, looking for any missing heirlooms. His eyes settled on the open file on the desk.

"Those are just copies. The originals are with the clerk. Stealing from that file is only going to inconvenience me. And get you a long sentence when you get caught. Judges don't like men who steal from judges."

"We'll keep that in mind, Gino," Randy said. He turned toward the door and walked out.

"Excuse me," T.J. said as he slid in between the desk and the judge. The judge chuckled derisively.

Two blocks away, Randy started the car as T.J. ran up and got in. Usually, the boys hooted and whooped in the car after a magazine job. Now they said nothing. The magazine bit had once been high crime. After kidnapping and whatever else they had gotten themselves into, it now seemed like a measly misdemeanor—a minor transgression in a larger endeavor.

"What the hell happened?" T.J. asked. "Could you not find the plant?" Prior to the job, Randy had Googled the judge and found his article with a picture of the hydrangea.

"There were two that looked like it up by the house. So I said the name and kind of pointed in the direction of the house. He couldn't tell which one I was pointing at. I thought it was going to work until he started into the house. He looked like the kind of old guy who would have swords and shit on his walls." They pulled up to the One-Hour Photo lab.

A plain girl sat in the kiosk behind a sliding window, her thumbs rapidly moving above her phone's keypad. Randy rapped on the window and, after a moment, she opened the window and took the camera. She handed back the claim check. "Should be ready in a couple of hours."

"A couple of hours? You're One-Hour Photo."

"It's just a name. Like at Jack-in-the-Box. They don't actually sell Jack-in-the-Boxes." From her disinterested tone, T.J. guessed she had had this conversation before.

Randy started to argue, but T.J. grabbed his arm. "Whatever, man. Besides, don't you have that thing?"

"Right." Randy gave his brother a big smile. "Yeah, I have to change."

He turned toward the girl. "Okay, we'll be back at—" he looked at his watch "—8:35 and those pictures better be ready."

The girl closed the sliding window. She turned and tossed the camera into a bin with at least four other cameras and resumed texting.

At 8:45, the boys pulled up in front of Kate's apartment.

Randy started to get out. T.J. stopped him. "Maybe we should slide it under her door."

"Why? So she doesn't see us?" Randy was in a foul mood. Leaning back in he said, "We've kidnapped her boss, ruined her fake trial and beat up her homeless friends. I don't think she's going to hold it against us for taking pictures of the jury list."

They walked up to her apartment and knocked on the door. A shadow passed in front of the light coming from under the door, but the door did not open.

"Boy," he said loudly, "one more delivery and I'm done for the night."

"Who is it?" Kate said from behind the door. There was no peephole.

"I've got some flowers here for a Kathy Summerlin."

The shadow moved away from the door and then returned. "It's kind of late for flowers, don't you think? I'm going to call the police."

"Don't call the police," T.J. said. "It's Randy and T.J."

"Go away." Kate's voice was weak and tired.

Randy stepped up to the door. "C'mon, Kate. We've got something that will win you the Stiltson trial. Let us in."

The door opened a crack and Randy shot his foot in the door. He slowly pushed the door open and walked in.

Kate sighed heavily. "Sure, come on in. And you don't even *have* any God-damn flowers, do you?"

"Geez, you're kind of cranky after dark, aren't you?"

"Yeah, I've been kind of cranky all week." As she moved into the better-lit living room, T.J. was shocked at how she looked. When they had met, he thought she was a pretty well put together, early thirty-something woman. Now her hair was mussed, her eyes had large bags under them and two of her fingers looked like they had been stepped on.

"What are you looking at?" Kate asked. T.J. realized he had been staring at her and moved his gaze down to a coffee table filled with Chinese take-out boxes. "And why is he dressed like that?"

Randy was wearing maroon velour pants with a matching vest and a wide-collar white shirt. "It's nothing," he scowled.

T.J. smiled. "Randy had an audition."

"Audition?" Kate asked. "For what? Roller disco DJ?"

"A Partridge Family tribute band," T.J. said. "He's a drummer." Randy rolled his eyes.

"Is a tribute band like a cover band?" Kate asked.

"No," Randy said. "A cover band plays a particular band's music. A tribute band actually dresses up like the band and acts like them and everything. Like an Elvis impersonator is a tribute band. If Elvis was a band."

Kate thought for a minute. "Wasn't the drummer in the Partridge Family like ten years old?"

"That's what made it perfect," Randy whined. "I may not be a great drummer, but I'm at least as good as a ten-year-old. And, like I told them, they wouldn't have to worry about any child labor laws."

"Huh. Did you get the part?" Kate asked.

"No," Randy said. "They wouldn't even let me drum. I know I would have nailed it. Besides, they let girls try out. When that kid was obviously a boy." He looked to Kate for support.

"Yeah, that's a shame, Randy." They stood for a moment in silence. "Uh, you guys said you had something that could win the Stiltson case?"

Randy perked up. "Yeah. I'm surprised you didn't open the door. Women always go for the flowers. Some women, they even have a peephole. They look out, see you standing there with no flowers and still open the door. It's crazy."

"It's been a while since someone sent me flowers. I guess I've forgotten the protocol."

"We may not have brought flowers, but we do come bearing gifts." Randy threw the package of photographs at her.

Kate pulled out the photographs and thumbed through them. "What is this?"

T.J. smiled at her. "It's the jury list for the Stiltson case. You said you could win if you knew who the jurors were. So there you go."

"I never said that."

Randy threw a hard look over at T.J. Kate looked back and forth between them.

T.J.'s eyes grew wide and he stuttered, "Yes, yes you did. We were in the parking lot, after the homeless people fight. We were talking about how to win the trial and you said 'I don't even know who the jurors are.' You said that."

"I don't know who they are," Kate said. "But that doesn't mean that if I did know I could throw the jury."

Randy fell back on the couch and began to groan. T.J. was not ready to give up.

"But . . . but . . . can't you, like, Google them, or do some sort of people search?"

"Google them? You want me to Google them?" Kate was getting worked up. She got up and walked over to her computer. "Okay sure, let's Google them," Kate said. She sat down and pulled up the Google search page. "All right, who do we have here? Thomas Rathbone." Kate typed in the name. "Okay. Hey, look at this. Tom won a banjo in an online raffle. Is that our Thomas Rathbone? Who knows, but we better strike him just to be sure." She glared over at the boys.

Randy snatched the pictures up from the table. "Look, we went to a lot of trouble to get these because we thought it would help. You don't have to be a bitch about it."

Kate's eyes narrowed. "What kind of trouble? Did you break into the clerk's office?"

"Do you really want to know?"

Kate shook her head.

"That's what I thought. So, really, you can't use them?"

"No. It's just names. I have to see the people, hear what they think." Her eyes grew wide. "Don't bring me any jurors."

The boys both laughed. T.J. sat down on the couch next to Kate. "Don't worry. Our kidnapping days are over. Is there anything we can do to help?"

"If you really want to help, make sure nothing happens to Townsend."

T.J. looked over at Randy who was staring at the floor. "If Stiltson wins, though, there's no problem, right?"

Kate shook her head. "You don't really believe that, do you?"

Chapter 31

All great trial lawyers have a routine on the night before trial. Some practice their openings until they can repeat them verbatim. Some stay up all night reading depositions. Some have a quiet night with their families and rest their minds for the grueling task ahead. Ron Tittleton did not know what his pretrial routine was. Having only tried two previous cases, he still sought that perfect combination of calm and confidence.

Whatever his routine turned out to be, he hoped it was not rifling through Clark and Tonetti's file room at four in the morning looking for a way to blackmail the person footing his bill. Yet, here he was, the night before the biggest trial of his life and, rather than getting a good night's sleep, he was digging through the Stiltson corporate files.

He was not worried about being fired if he got caught. When Tonetti heard he had tried to actually win the case, he would be gone anyway. What he did not want, though, was to get caught before he found something. He figured he had another hour before the early risers in the firm showed up.

It would have been nice to have Elsie here to give him another pair of eyes. That was impossible. For one thing, although a Stiltson, she was not legally able to view the files. Ron, although not authorized by the firm, legally represented Maynard Stiltson as much as any other member of the firm and could look at any file he wanted. More importantly, though, Ron thought Elsie would try to talk him out of looking. It was a big risk.

He may not have even been able to reach her. The idea had come to him late in the day. Kent Bradley, a new associate, had somehow gotten past Cora, and plopped down in the chair on the opposite side of Ron's desk.

"Say, Ron, you mind if I run something by you?"

Ron looked up from the expert report his friend Pantaine had given him that morning. The deposition was in a couple of hours. He saw Cora peering into the room with a worried face. Ron smiled at her. "Actually, Kent, I'm really busy."

"Thanks man, it won't take long. Ol' man Williams is on my back to do this bullshit memo. It's not even for the firm, so I can't bill for it." The only people more concerned about billable hours than the partners were new associates. "One of his crony buddies got caught with his hand in the proverbial cookie jar, if the jar was his secretary's shirt and her boobs were cookies." He laughed and sounded like a pervert.

"So the conniving bitch isn't suing, she's blackmailing him. She thought his wife would care, but those rich people all screw around, anyway. But, if it ever got out that the head of Maypole Diapers was a lecherous boob-grabber . . . let's just say the soccer moms wouldn't approve."

Ron had not really been paying attention. Whenever associates asked him for help, he always made up a case, "McAdam" or "McDaniel," which he told them was right on point. No one ever came back to complain they could not find his case. But Kent's story had sent Ron's mind racing. "She's blackmailing him? What's he going to do?"

Kent shrugged his shoulders. "I don't know. Williams told me to research whether a nondisclosure agreement can include a jail sentence for breach. I don't even know where to begin. What do you think?"

"Hmm. I'm not sure. But, you know, I had a question I needed some help with." Kent sat up in his chair. Ron knew the quickest way to get rid of an associate was with the threat of more work. "Cora, could you come in here a second?" Cora hurried in carrying her pad. "What was that question you wanted me to look up?"

Cora looked over at Ron warily. Ron smiled at her and nodded his head at Kent. "Mr. Bradley might be able to help us with the preliminary research."

Cora sighed, shrugged her shoulders and turned toward Kent. "My cousin Turlene was potty-training her youngest girl, Janteen. So Turlene put potatoes in the diaper."

Kent looked over at Cora. "Did you say she put potatoes in her diaper?"

"It's something her mamma did with Turlene. I guess it trains them right up. One of the neighbors saw Janteen playing in the yard and thought she had been pooping in her diaper for days. She called social services and they've taken Janteen away. So, I guess my question is, is putting potatoes in a diaper child abuse?"

Kent looked up at her and then over to Ron, who stood up and stuck out his hand. "We don't need an answer until next week or so." Cora started to say something, but a sharp look from Ron quieted her.

After Kent and Cora left, Ron began thinking about blackmail. Maynard Stiltson did not seem like the type of individual who would lead an exemplary life. If he had gotten into trouble, Tonetti would have been there to bail him out. If Ron could find the file with all the juicy details, Elsie could use it to get him to pay off Beckwith without the emotional baggage.

Ron had started at two in the morning. Three hours later, time was running short. A fierce competition ran between several senior associates to see who could get to the office the earliest. After the partners discovered one enterprising young woman was living full time in her office, they set the rule: no one was allowed in the office between the hours of twelve and five unless approved by a partner.

Ron's breaking of this rule was apparently worse than anything Maynard Stiltson had done in the last thirty years. There had been some minor mishaps, a bankruptcy in the Grey Poupon craze of the early eighties; some overzealous labor negotiation tactics; the simple battery of a hamburger-bun representative. None were particularly damning and, worse, all had been widely publicized. If Maynard had gotten into any big trouble, Tonetti had buried the files.

At ten 'til five, Ron carried the last of the Stiltson boxes back to the file room. He had failed. Maybe that was a good thing. Old Maynard probably would have turned him into the police and still made Elsie pay tribute for bailing her out of the Beckwith case. He should have slept.

"What are you doing here?" Ron spun around. Dixie Gruench, the firm's ancient file clerk, stood staring at him, hands on her hips. Ron's sleep-addled brain searched for a reasonable response.

"I'm Ron Tittleton," he said, blinking quickly.

"I know who you are. I want to know what you're doing in my file room."

"I'm Ron Tittleton," he repeated. Then he laughed. "I'm sorry, Ms. Gruench, I'm not used to being up this early. But I've got a trial this morning, Beckwith v. Stiltson. I needed a birth certificate." He cringed. That could have been better.

Gruench seemed to buy it. "That's the daughter's case, isn't it?"

That surprised him. He did not think anyone else in the firm noticed or cared about this trial. She smiled at his surprise and raised her eyebrows. "The Gruench knows all." She turned and walked out of the room. "You won't find any of her stuff in here. It's over in the next room." Ron followed her next door to an identical room filled with identical boxes. She climbed a large, wide stepladder and took down a box. She handed it to Ron. He figured it was about half full.

"Thanks." As he walked back to his office with the box, he looked at his watch. He had to be in court in three hours. Gruench scaring him had given him a little adrenaline burst. He would not be able to get to sleep quickly enough for it to make a difference. He may as well take a quick look through Elsie's life.

Twenty minutes later Ron sat staring at a piece of paper. He read it again for the fourth time. Could it really be this easy?

Chapter 32

All good jury selections come from a well-crafted plan.

Greene, F. (2003). *The Trial Consultant's Field Manual* (p. 139). New York: Pullman.

Kate lay in bed staring at the Captain, on his back with his hind legs splayed open—the most relaxed position known to cat or man. He snored softly. She, on the other hand, had not slept all night. She could not think of a way to fix the trial because it was impossible to fix a trial. The system had been tweaked for hundreds of years to make sure no one could fix a trial.

Plus, all she could do was pick the jury. She could not bribe or coerce or somehow influence the jury. It would be like asking the guy who makes out the lineup card to fix a baseball game.

Staring at the clock, she did a minute by minute countdown until 5:00, when she got up and showered. She stood with a towel wrapped around her staring into her closet. Lucky suit or not lucky suit? Would the suit know that lucky meant the side she was working with should lose? Maybe she needed an unlucky suit.

Eventually, she picked out a watermelon-colored suit that made her look fat. When she'd bought it, along with a lemon-yellow suit and a lime-green one, she had thought that bright happy colors would give her a fun, energetic, happy look. Townsend had called them her "fruit suits."

The cut of the jackets made her look more round than she

actually was. Round is not a good look in a fruit-colored suit. She figured whatever she wore that day would have to be burned. Why not get rid of the watermelon fat suit? The day would not be a total loss.

She walked out to the Bug and looked in the back seat before she got in. Sitting behind the wheel she thought about having to give up the Bug. She loved that car, but it was no longer her safe car. She could still smell the cheesy cologne Boris had been wearing. The Bug would have to go.

As she pulled out, she popped in the Erin McKeown CD and began to bob her head to the beat. She hated risking having to ditch the CD, but she had no choice. Listening to McKeown was not just a routine for luck. The music focused her. Her energy and spirit grew into an almost palpable force. Today, more than ever, she needed a good, focused energy.

Fifteen minutes later she was at her desk, poring over the data from the mock trial. She had no idea what she was looking for, but maybe something would jump out at her.

As she compared the answers from two sixty-two-year-old slot players, one black and one white, she heard the noise. *Snik. Snik.*

"Jo, you out there?"

A small mousey head peeked around the corner. "Hiya, Kate. I thought maybe you'd need someone to bounce some ideas off of. Are you ready?"

"No. No, I'm really not."

"Don't worry, you can do it. You're so quick on your feet. You can't really know what to do until you see the jurors. Then, it'll come to you, I'm sure. Plus, I'll be there. We can talk it out in the ladies' room." She gave Kate a big smile.

Kate felt the emotion well up in her at her friend's loyalty. "You shouldn't be here, Jo. What we're doing, what I'm doing, is certainly unethical, if not illegal. I don't want to get you caught up in it."

Jo waived her hand through the air. "Pah. Look, right now Josepherta would be curled up in bed with the covers pulled up around her neck, worried sick about what was going to happen to you. But you've got Jo on the job." She smiled and winked at Kate. The two of them burst out laughing.

Kate rolled her chair back, stood up and put on her jacket. Jo's eyes narrowed.

"Going with the watermelon today, huh?"

"Yes, I'm going with the watermelon. I figure I can burn it later."

"Good plan. The burning part, anyway."

Kate picked up a paper clip and threw at Jo. She wanted to make fun of Jo's outfit but, as she looked her over, Jo looked good. Real good. A chocolate brown suit with cream pinstriping showed off Jo's firm frame without being slutty. Kate made a mental note to sign up for one of Jo's aerobics classes.

They took the Bug into Kansas City. Jo had grown accustomed to Kate's pretrial rituals and danced in her seat to the beat of Ms. McGowan. "Where are the Red Hots?"

"No Red Hots today," Kate said flatly, keeping her eyes on the road. Jo paused for a moment then resumed dancing.

They drove downtown toward the courthouse. Normally, Kate parked in what she considered her "special spot." A couple of years earlier, she had noticed the tow-away sign above a spot in back of an abandoned business a block away from the courthouse. Since no one was using the business, no one would be calling the towing company. She had yet to be towed away. Today, she did not want to taint the spot. Shaking her head, Kate realized she had a lot of superstitions.

She pulled up behind Jo's Toyota Tercel. Jo had gone down the night before and secured a prime parking spot so Kate could get right in the courthouse. Jo parked her car at a timed lot three blocks away from the Courthouse and pushed a day's worth of dollars into the slot.

The security guards on duty at the metal detector in the courthouse lobby were part of a team that rotated throughout the courthouse. They smiled when Kate walked in. With little to no other excitement going on in the building, one or two of the four-man team would often come up to the Court floors to watch trials. Afterwards, they would come up to Kate to ask her why she kept a certain juror or how hard it was to get into trial consulting. Kate always took extra care to answer all of their questions. You never knew when you would need help from someone at the Court.

Once inside the door, Kate walked over to the metal detector, her heels clicking on the marble floor. The guards smiled.

"Hey, Katie Consultant. What you got going on today, you on the Nguyen case?" said the security guard with Jimison written on his tag. In his late twenties, he stood about six foot tall and weighed no more than 150 pounds.

The woman next to him, Salb, reached up and hit him in the chest, "Katie Consultant doesn't do robberies." Kate did not know the actual height at which one officially could be classified as a midget, but Salb was probably right at the line. "Am I right?"

"I'm here for Beckwith."

"Oooh," the two chimed in unison. Kate put her purse down on the conveyor belt and walked through the metal detector.

"You have a phone in here?" Jimison asked, squinting at the x-ray monitor. "Can't take a phone into Court. We'll keep it here for you. Just sign the sheet."

Kate groaned. Normally, she left it in the car, but today she had forgot. So much for focused. As Jimison wrote her out a receipt, Jo ran in the doors, out of breath. They walked up the stairs to try and get warm.

Kate stepped out into the hallway from the stairwell to chaos. About twenty Asian people, ranging in age from ten to one hundred, stood face to face, yelling at each other in a language Kate did not recognize. Kate and Jo moved over to the right side of the hall. There was a small gap between the screaming mass and an elderly Asian woman sitting on an old wooden pew. Dark creases lined the old woman's face and they deepened as she scowled at the angry mob. Moving single file and turning so they faced away from the bench, Kate and Jo tried to sidle through the throng without being noticed. A bony claw grabbed Kate's arm from behind. She turned with a start.

The old woman looked weak and frail, but her grip stopped Kate cold. She could not break free. The old woman looked up and moved her lips. Kate could not hear what she said above the yelling behind her. Even if she could have heard, Kate's rudimentary lip-reading skills told her this was another language. She looked around and saw a teenage girl watching them.

Kate pulled at her arm, but the hand stayed there. The girl walked over, leaned down and said something into the old woman's ear. The woman continued to stare at Kate, but her lips moved in the girl's ear. The girl looked up at Kate and said, "Gramma says there is a tiger waiting in your tall grass. The monkey must enter the mouth of the snake to defeat the tiger." Kate stood there, dumbfounded, as the old woman pulled the girl's arm down and whispered again in her ear. "And she says you should eat Moon Pie."

Kate furrowed her brow and the young girl shrugged her shoulders. "I don't know. That's what she said."

The old woman gave Kate's arm a squeeze and then let go with a small push. Kate and Jo made it through the crowd and around the corner. Jo looked over at Kate and asked, "What did she say?"

"I think she called me a monkey. And I should eat more Moon Pies."

"That's solid advice."

Kate rolled her eyes and they walked into the courtroom.

It was just after eight and the jurors were filling out the questionnaires downstairs. In the moments before a trial starts, courtrooms buzz with electricity. Kate had not participated in high school sports, but she imagined this is what the field felt like before the big game.

Although it was still an hour before the jury would come in, both attorneys and their clients were already there. Some attorneys think it gives them an advantage to be right next to the jury box. Choice of table was strictly on a first come, first serve basis. Young associates sometimes showed up when the building opened at 6:00 A.M. just to get the "right" table.

Kate and Jo walked up to Beckwith and Jerry. They were sitting at the table next to the jury box. Ron and Elsie huddled together at the other table. "Mr. Bingham, Officer Beckwith, how are you doing? Get the good table?" Jerry winked at her.

"Mike, this is Kate Summerlin. Best jury consultant in the Midwest. Going to pick us a winner today, Kate?"

Kate saw Ron look over and then lean in and whisper to Elsie. Most attorneys did not want anyone to know they used a jury consultant, partly for their own egos and partly out of worry that jurors would think the consultant was manipulating them. Either way, Kate often sat in the back of the courtroom, giving the attorneys feedback only at breaks. Jerry, on the other hand, thought a consultant intimidated the other side. He always paraded Kate around like a show horse.

Beckwith grabbed her hand and shook it. "Nice to meet you, Kate. Jerry has told me all about you. I really appreciate everything you've done for me." She had seen his photograph in the file. Now, in person, he seemed smaller, less authoritarian.

He was probably about five-nine with shaggy brown hair and a slim build. His face seemed too sweet for an undercover cop, but it should play well with the jury. Plus, he leaned against the table as they stood there, obviously favoring his hip. There was a lot of standing up and sitting down in court. A smart jury would certainly notice the pain he was in as he struggled to get to his feet.

She had been coping with the guilt of screwing this guy over by imagining him as an overbearing authority figure. With no shortage of distasteful authority figures in her background, Kate shoved him in with that lot and felt a little better about what she had to do. Here he was, though—a gentle face and a kind manner. Damn.

"Don't thank me yet," Kate replied. Jo gave her a sideways glance, which Kate ignored.

Ron stood up, buttoned his jacket and then walked over. "Hi Kate, I'm Ron Tittleton. I represent Ms. Stiltson. I've never met a real live jury consultant before." His voice took on a sing-song quality Kate did not like. She tried to think of a snappy comeback but Jo stepped in.

"Hi, I'm Jo. Now you've met two real live jury consultants," she said, her voice mimicking the mocking sound of his.

"Two consultants? What are you trying to do me, Jerr? I'm all by my lonesome over here."

"You've got Ms. Stiltson," Jo said. Ron nodded, but the rebuke appeared to have stung him.

"Of course. We better start putting our heads together then." He sat back down at his table as Kate unloaded her pads and pens. Under normal circumstances, she would have liked the acrimonious banter. She liked to dislike the other side. Some attorneys liked to joke and laugh with the opposing attorneys before court. Sometimes they would leave their clients sitting alone to do it. Kate hated that. They are them and we are us and if you want to be their buddy then buy them a drink on the weekend. When you step into court, they are the enemy and should be treated as such. But today, the line between the teams was blurry.

The morning hearing moved slowly with the attorneys arguing over motions Kate neither understood nor cared about. During the lunch break, Kate retrieved her cell phone from the guards and checked her messages. Arnie had called. He was out of breath in his message. "Kate, call me as soon as you get this." The jury had not come back yesterday, but Kate doubted he would bother her to say they had found Rick guilty. He knew she was in court. She went outside the court and dialed his number.

"Kate," he said anxiously without saying hello, "tell me what you think this means. The jury was given a menu for lunch from the Applebee's down the street. We're talking the full take-out menu. It's like four pages. They all ordered chicken Caesar salads. Every last one of them. What does that mean?"

Kate stood silent.

"Kate? You there?"

"Yeah, I'm here. That's not good, Arnie. Our whole theory was based on them hating each other. If they're all ordering the same food, that means they're not only getting along, they're all on the same page. It's not chaos. It's complete order. Who's the foreman?"

"Wigginstaff."

Kate coughed at the name. "The Farter? Oh, my God, I thought they would *hate* her. Look, Arnie, we're going back in. I'm sorry. But that's not good news at all." She hung up and shook her head. Wigginstaff? Chicken Caesar salads? She had completely misread that jury. For Beckwith, maybe she should trust her faulty instincts. The jury would naturally come back for Stiltson.

After lunch, the prospective jurors came in. Kate scanned them for her salvation. No one jumped out at her.

As the plaintiff, Jerry went first. He started with general questions before moving on to ask specifically what the jurors thought of police officers. Kate watched helplessly as one juror after another gave nondescript, perfectly acceptable and uninformative answers to Jerry's questions.

Toward the end of his questions, Jerry came to prospective juror number four, Turnley Dixon. Dixon managed a local photocopy service. Jerry asked him the standard questions about lawsuits and got all the standard answers. Jerry then began his questions about police officers.

"Now, Mr. Dixon, as I said, Officer Beckwith is a police officer. What are your opinions generally about police officers?"

"I have the utmost respect for police officers. Every day they put their lives on the line for us. I think they're heroes."

Kate froze. Dixon's words were the essentially the same as the jurors who had already talked. But he had rubbed his nose when he said it.

Jerry did not notice. "But Officer Beckwith was an undercover officer. Those officers have to lie and deceive people as part of their jobs. Would you view Officer Beckwith's credibility any differently because he was an undercover officer?"

Dixon shook his head and laughed. "Of course not." He rubbed his nose. "They couldn't exactly tell the truth to the criminals, could they?" Everyone laughed with him. Jerry decided to end on that note and came over and sat down. The judge called a fifteen-minute recess to allow the parties to figure out their strikes.

Kate's head was spinning. Jerry turned and looked at her expectantly. "Babe, what do you think?"

She looked over at him and stood up. "I need to go to the bathroom."

Jerry nodded. "That's where I do my best thinking. Don't be too long."

Kate stood up and walked out of the courtroom. As she passed Jo, her eyes widened and Jo followed her outside. They ducked into the attorney conference room just outside the courtroom.

"Dixon's a stealth juror," Kate said breathlessly.

"The photocopy guy? He's a what? A stealth juror?"

"Someone who tries to fly beneath the attorneys' radar. He appears to be a neutral, normal, ordinary kind of person no one would waste a strike on."

"That's what I was thinking."

"Really he's dying to get on the jury because he's got some sort of ax to grind with the cops."

Jo's eyes narrowed. "He's a stealth ax grinder. Ooh. That sounds bad. How do you know?"

"When Jerry was asking him how he felt about cops, he said he loved cops and rubbed his nose the whole time like some sort of neurotic cokehead. He was lying, I'm sure of it. Everyone else is trying like hell to get off the jury and he's lying to get on the jury? He's going to screw Beckwith, I just know it."

"That's fantastic," Jo said, rubbing her nose.

"What? What?" Kate screamed, pointing at Jo's hand on her nose. "Is the air in here dry or something?"

"No, I was lying. Don't get me wrong. I'm super impressed you sniffed out a stealth juror. But does it really help us? I mean, so we can sneak one double-agent juror on. We need twelve to get a verdict. All one juror can do is hang them up."

Kate froze. "What did you just say?"

"Just that one juror can't really do anything. We need Stiltson to get twelve to win."

Kate smiled. "What if we don't? I've been spending so much time trying to help Boris win, I didn't even think about trying not to lose. We use the Wrenshaw strategy and hang the jury. Beckwith wants the case to settle because he needs the money. If the trial hangs, Stiltson will push the next trial back at least six months. Maybe more. Then you figure appeals after that. Beckwith will have to settle."

"That's great for Stiltson, but will Boris hold out until then?"

"I don't know, Jo. I guess he'll have to. The important thing is, with Dixon on the jury, Boris won't lose. Right now, that's what matters."

"Let's get back in there. Maybe you'll see another one."

They dashed out into the hall. They opened the door too quickly, hitting a small man hunched in front of the courtroom doors.

Boris. His face grew red. "What the hell are you doing out here? The trial's going on in there." His fat finger jabbed toward the courtroom. Kate grabbed him by his shirt and pulled him back into the conference room.

"Shut up. They'll hear you in there. And we're on a break."

Boris shrunk his head down in his neck like a scared turtle. He glanced toward the door. "Okay. Sorry. But what are you doing out here?"

"We think we've got something."

"We? You told her about it?" He looked over at Jo. Jo leaned forward and stared at the top of his head, accentuating her height advantage.

Kate put her hands on each of their shoulders, trying to team build. "You want to win and I can't get you a win without Jo. So, Jo's in."

Boris frowned but let it go. "You said you had something?"

"Yes, we think we've got a guy on your side we can sneak onto the jury." She eyeballed Boris. "Did you pay off one of the jurors?"

Boris's mouth dropped open. "No. I didn't know you could

do that. Can we do that?"

"No. We can't do that. But there's a guy who is lying to get on the jury and we think he's going to try to throw the case your way."

Boris broke into a big smile. "A ringer. That's fantastic. So, we'll win."

"Well," Kate said, "you shouldn't lose. Maybe the guy won't be able to convince the other jurors, but we think he won't let Beckwith win."

"Okay, that's something. But what happens if he can't convince the others?"

Kate started to answer when the door opened and Jerry and Ron came in. Kate noticed a look of panic come across Boris's face.

"Sorry, Kate, I didn't know you were in here. Are you going to be here long? Ron and I might be able to settle this thing after all."

Boris had shuffled off to the other side of the small table sitting in the middle of the room. Kate looked at him, confused. Jerry followed her gaze and said, "Unless you two are in the middle of something. It's just I think this is the only quiet room on this floor."

Kate did not know what was bothering Boris, but figured it was wise to get him out of the room. "No, we were just finishing up. It's all yours. Good luck." As she turned to walk out the door, she noticed Ron staring at Boris quizzically. Boris, staring at his feet, came around the table and tried to squeeze out the door. Jerry extended his hand.

"Hi. Jerry Bingham." Boris looked at the hand as if it carried the plague.

Kate stepped over. "Jerry, this is Boris. Boris, Jerry. And this is Ron Tittleton." Boris looked up, staring straight into Ron's eyes. Sadness had replaced the panic. He looked like a cancer patient about to hear how long he had to live.

"Did you say Boris?" Ron said. He looked over at Kate and then at Boris. "Dad?"

CHAPTER 33

RUINED!!!!

All of Boris's plans lay ruined. He stared into the eyes of the son he had not seen in thirty years. Ron had his eyes. There was an awful lot of Angela in him, probably mostly Angela. But the eyes were Boris's. Maybe there would be forgiveness in those eyes.

But there was not. Confusion, anger, probably a little suspicion. But no forgiveness.

"Dad, is it really you?! What the hell are you doing here?! Are you working for Beckwith?!" Ron yelled. Boris stepped back in shock. Everything was going wrong.

Kate leaned forward between the two and asked Ron, "This is your dad?" Her eyes widened as she looked over at Boris.

Kate's voice brought her into Boris's focus. "You. You set me up." He poked her hard in the chest. "*You set me up!* The deal is off." Boris pushed past Ron and ran down the hall to the stairwell. Not being used to physical exertion, he barely made it to the bottom of the stairs. He had to stop and catch his breath. A door somewhere up above him clanged open. Boris ran out into the lobby.

Two security guards sat at the desk staring at their monitors. Boris froze, wide-eyed and open-mouthed. The guards did not notice him until the door slammed shut behind him. The short security guard turned around on her stool and glanced casually at Boris. His panicked look alerted her and she slapped Jamison on the back of the head.

"Hey, you. What's going on?" she yelled at Boris as she jumped off the stool.

Boris ran out the door. What now? That bitch Summerlin ruined everything. She had to pay. If she took his chance to save his son, he would take her chance to save Townsend. An eye for an eye.

When he got into his car, he pulled out his cell phone and dialed Duke's number. "I need you now. Everything is happening. Get to the Tomb immediately."

"Boy, now's not really a good time for me."

"What?"

"I'm just messing with you, man. You sound kind of stressed. I'm in midtown, so I'll be there in about fifteen minutes. You have the money?"

"Yeah. Just get there." Boris hung up and felt better. He found bossing others around very soothing.

Cutting through the downtown on the way to the old warehouse, he caught himself speeding. He slowed down to five miles an hour under the speed limit. A ticket now would be the final straw.

Going to the courthouse had been stupid and completely unnecessary. He had told himself Kate needed a last-minute push. In fact, he had been impatient. Now, he had nothing. Nothing except a final act of vengeance.

Pulling into the parking lot and seeing the looming warehouse, he began to doubt whether he could actually kill someone. Threats and plans were one thing—actually killing was another. "That's why I have the Hawaiian." He looked at himself in the rearview mirror and smiled.

Chapter 34

Townsend was sleeping on the table and his head jerked up when Boris rushed in. Boris could see the fear in the old consultant's eyes.

"What happened?"

"It's all over, Doctor. I'm sorry. But your Miss Summerlin fucked me over and that means she fucked you over."

Townsend kept eye contact with Boris. "I find that very hard to believe. Kate is very dependable. Wasn't she at trial?"

"Oh, she was there," Boris said. Townsend used his foot to push a chair out on the other side of the table. Boris sat down. "And she ruined it. She brought Ron into it."

"Ron? Ron Tittleton?"

"Yeah," Boris said, his voice filled with sadness, "I'm his father." He hung his head, unable to meet Townsend's eyes—his anger gone.

"So, he's the one behind all this?"

"No," Boris's tone changed to pleading. "He was never supposed to know anything. I was trying to make up for everything." Boris looked up. "I haven't been a good father. Honestly, I wasn't a father at all."

Townsend tried to comfort him and buy some time. "Oh, I'm sure you did the best you could."

"No, you don't understand. I left. I never met him before today. I was a ranger up in Yellowstone. A lot of the guys lived alone in the Park. Rangers can be kind of odd fellas."

"You don't say?" Townsend said. Boris missed the sarcasm.

"Oh, yeah. The stories I could tell you." He gave a little laugh. "Anyway, I lived in this little town called Gardiner, just inside the Montana line." Boris smiled at the memory. "It was a great little town. The people there didn't like the tourists much. But they really took to the rangers. I think because we respected the park so much. Lots of nature folk up there.

"I was there for about a year and a half and I got to where I felt like part of the community. Every day I'd go to down to breakfast at Frosty's Diner on the Fourth Street. That's what they called it. 'The Fourth Street.' "

Townsend tried to look interested. He did not know how long he could keep the conversation going, but he could guess what would happen when it stopped. He nodded at Boris.

"Pretty soon, I began to recognize people. And they began to recognize me. Have you ever had that? Where you walk around and people know you and say 'hi'? It's really quite something."

"I taught at a small college in New Hampshire for a couple of years," Townsend said. "It was sort of like that."

Boris paid no attention. His memory consumed him. "Yeah, yeah. Anyway, there was this cute little waitress working at Frosty's, Angela Tittleton. Well, cute's the wrong word. Fetching, I would say. It's not that she was unattractive. But she didn't really become beautiful until you got to know her. She was so friendly and nice and, just, pure. It was like the whole little town wrapped up in one person.

"Every morning, I'd go in and sit at the far end of the counter, near the coffee burners. I think she knew I was sitting there just for her. After a couple of months, she started flirting with me. I'd never really dated that much. Maybe she was attracted to the uniform. Chicks really dig the uniform."

Townsend smiled. "I bet you looked good in green." Again, Boris ignored him.

"It also could have been that I was a bit older than her. She was fresh out of high school and had always dated those jock lunk-heads. But mostly it was that I was a different man when I was in Gardiner. I was one of them. Even though I hadn't had a lot of success with women, the town had accepted me. So, I knew she would accept me. Confidence is a powerful aphrodisiac, Doctor.

"One night, she was closing up. I stayed to help her. We sat there talking about nothing until after midnight. Finally, Angela asked me to take out the trash. In the kitchen, I grabbed her and kissed her. I thought she might slap me, but she kissed me back. Next thing I know our clothes are off and we're down on the floor next to this metal worktable. We made love. She was on top of me. After a little while," Boris whispered as his face flushed, "I had finished my part, if you know what I mean?"

"I can guess," Townsend said.

"She hadn't finished her part. I've never really liked that face women make during their, uh, turn. It makes it look so painful. So, I turned my head. About ten feet away, next to the stove, I saw this baby rat. He was nibbling on some crumb. Suddenly, I realized where I was, on the grimy floor of this dive diner's kitchen. A diner with rats. And, you know, there's never just one rat."

Boris stared down at the table, his face contorted into a disgusted scowl. Townsend spoke softly.

"What did you do?"

"It was revolting. I tried to look away but then I saw probably twenty years' worth of grease and grime under the work table. I couldn't take it anymore."

"What did you do?" Townsend repeated.

"I ran away. I threw her off me. She hit the table and kind of collapsed on the floor. I looked back and she had a pained look on her face. I'm not sure if it was the hitting of her head or she was, uh, having her turn."

"I'm no expert," Townsend said with false modesty, "but I'm pretty sure her turn ended when you threw her into the table."

Boris looked up and met Townsend's eyes, not having heard the last remark. "I ran away," he said with finality.

Townsend had been in many similar relationships without the rats and grime but had never experienced the emotional grief Boris clearly felt. Leaving was the easy part; the inevitable post-coital meeting caused all the problems. He felt a certain kinship with his captor at this new revelation.

Genuinely interested now, he asked, "So, what happened when you ran into her again? Did her father contact you?" Townsend had never satisfactorily figured out the father dilemma.

"I never saw her again. The Park Service always has job openings somewhere. When I got home, I looked at the list, saw a posting at a fort in southwest Texas that had been open for a couple of months. I got in my car and drove. Never went back. Never saw her again."

"So, you completely abandoned your life to avoid confronting the woman you dumped?" Townsend asked, impressed with the commitment to the plan, if not the plan itself. Mostly he was disappointed. He had hoped to pick up a new strategy.

"With no Angela, I had no life. And I couldn't face her after I threw her off. How do you explain that to someone?" The two men sat in silence for a minute.

"But I kept tabs on her. I took the Gardiner weekly paper. Nine months later, there's a little article that she's given birth to a boy. Ron's name would appear there over the years. It's a pretty small town. Once he got to be about ten, I could see he had my eyes. I never saw where Angela got married. I suppose it's tough in a small town when you have a kid out of wedlock.

"About six years ago, Ron graduated from the University of

Montana. I went. Angela had done such a fine job raising him. I wanted to go up to him. Tell him who I was. I knew he'd hate me. I deserve that, I know. Growing up without a father. I can't imagine what story Angela had to tell him. I wanted to make it up to him, to help him somehow. That's what fathers do, right?" Townsend did not say anything.

"He graduated from law school and joined one of the top firms in Kansas City. Every year he did better and better and got more and more successful. I saw the window closing.

"Then one day, I was reading an e-mail he sent to one of his friends saying he had landed this big case." Townsend raised his eyebrows. Boris waved a hand in front of his face. "Everything is possible online.

"According to Ron, if he won the case, he would make partner. If he lost, they would bury him so far down he'd have to quit. This was it. If I could make sure he won, I would be helping him. Even if he never knew, I would know."

Boris's eyes blazed at the thought of his triumphant plan. Behind them, by the door, a loud clattering of metal shattered the silence. The fire in his eyes faded, but Boris smiled. "A few Coke cans tied to a string are still pretty effective, you know?"

"Ms. Summerlin," Boris yelled. "Glad you could make it." Silence. "You know, I do hate to kill the good doctor. He's been nothing but a pleasant guest. Tell you what, I'll count down from ten. If you can make it through the maze by the time I get to zero, you can take his place. One. Two."

T.J. stepped out of the shadows by the office. "You said you were going to count down from ten, not up from one."

Boris jumped at the sound. He turned and faced T.J. and Randy, who had walked up behind him. "It doesn't matter which way I count. It's still ten. She has until ten."

"I'm just saying, you said you were going to count down."

"Okay, fine. Ten. Nine. Eight." Boris heard some crinkling

and then the sound of paper being torn. The maze was made of taped-together black butcher paper. Rather than finding her way through the maze, Kate was bulling her way through the walls. Boris quickened his count. "Seven. Six. Fivefourthree."

Kate busted through the wall into the center room, covered in the butcher paper, arms windmilling forward. Boris stopped counting as Kate stripped off the paper.

"I'm here. I'm here," she yelled. She looked deranged as she shook off the panels of paper. That is when Boris saw the gun.

Boris shook his head. "Jesus. I can't catch a break today. Kate, I didn't figure you to be a gun nut. In fact, I don't think you're going to shoot anyone. Boys, get the gun."

Boris turned to look at the boys, who looked at him with a mixture of surprise and incredulity. Randy chuckled. "You know what, man? We think you're full of shit. You want that gun. You can walk over there and get it. You're immortal, right? So you don't have to worry about her shooting your ass."

Boris sighed. He looked over at Townsend with a do-you-believe-this-is-happening-to-me look. Out of the corner of his eye, Townsend saw movement behind Kate. He turned as the Hawaiian moved out of the torn maze toward Kate.

She saw them looking behind her and turned, but it was too late. Duke grabbed the gun. His other arm snaked around Kate's waist and picked her up. He turned her so she was parallel to the ground, kicking and screaming.

"Ah, our special guest has arrived. Your timing, sir, is impeccable. Why don't you put Ms. Summerlin here by the doctor." Boris slid over another chair and Duke sat Kate down hard.

"How's your dad doing?" he asked, sneering at her.

"He's fine. It was a few scratches." Kate did not want to give Duke any satisfaction. He shrugged, pulled a roll of duct tape out of his pocket and tossed it to Boris.

"Aren't you the boy scout?" Boris said as he began taping

Kate to the chair. When he finished he looked at the boys.

"Boys, I've got good news and bad news. The good news is, as I'm sure you've guessed by now, I'm not the Devil. So, there's still a chance your souls won't rot in hell for all eternity. Although, at the rate you're going, I wouldn't bet against it.

"The bad news is you quit the winning team a little too soon. If you're not with me, you're against me. Against me and my large friend with the gun." As if on cue, Duke pointed Kate's gun at them and took out another semi-automatic from his pocket.

Boris finished taping up Kate and turned to Duke. "How much to kill them all?"

"Ten grand each."

"Wow, that seems kind of high. Isn't there some sort of volume discount? I mean, is dumping four bodies any harder than dumping one body? Thirty thousand total."

Duke kept the guns trained on the boys. "Ten grand each."

"Look, you don't have to kill them all right away. Kate here is very attractive. You know what I mean? It doesn't matter to me what happens before . . ."

Snik. Snik.

Boris stopped in mid-sentence. "Did you hear that? Some sort of clicking sound."

Nobody answered. Boris waved it off and continued bartering with Duke. Townsend glanced nervously over at Kate who was staring back at him. Both had heard the clicking. Both knew what it meant. Jo was in da house.

CHAPTER 35

A consultant must be prepared for moments of chaos during a jury selection. All too often, there comes a time when everything falls apart.

Greene, F. (2003). *The Trial Consultant's Field Manual* (p. 205). New York: Pullman.

Jo shouted to herself *"Remain calm! Remain calm!"* She took a couple of deep breaths. Slowly, her mind began to focus. She peered out through a large hole in the paper wall into the center of a cavernous room. Boris had his back to her and was talking to the big Hawaiian guy.

Boris had heard her biting her nails and looked right at her. Black tape covered the windows so the only light came from lamps in the center. She guessed the darkness hid her. Still, her nail-biting had almost gotten her caught. She would have to quit. This time she meant it.

"Look, I can get you thirty grand right away. But forty, that's going to take at least a week. And I don't think you want to wait a week." Boris was still haggling with the Hawaiian. Jo figured she had a little time, but not much.

Back at the courthouse, Kate, Jo and the attorneys had been dumbstruck by Boris's outburst. Ron stared at the open door. He spoke in a soft whisper.

"I, uh, I never really knew him. My mom had this picture and she told me he was my father and his name was Boris.

That's all she ever told me." He looked at Kate for some indication that that was enough of an explanation. Kate stared blankly back at him.

Jerry looked around the group, trying to make sense out of what was happening. Finally, he turned to Kate, "Did Ron's dad say you two had a deal?"

Kate looked up at him, unable to come up with an answer. She turned to Jo and said, "Wait here. You have to pick Jerry's jury." She slowed down and spoke deliberately. "Pick Jerry a good jury." Jo understood. The fix was off. She would have to pick a real jury.

In her mind, the Josepherta voice returned. She did not have any data to base any reasonable selection on. All she could rely on was experience, of which she had exactly none. Zilch. She was no more qualified to pick a jury than the table in front of her. In fact, had Kate wanted to pick a jury so that Jerry would lose, she should have let Jo try to pick a real jury. That would have done it.

Kate turned and started down the hall.

"Wait," Jo yelled and ran down after her. "Kate, I can't pick a jury. I'm not ready. I don't . . ." Her words died off.

Kate stopped and held Jo by the shoulders. "You're ready, Jo. Trust me. Strike the nose rubber and two other people you think are bad."

"Which two? I don't know. I don't think I can do it."

Kate looked down the hall where Boris had run and then back at Jo. "Don't make me slap the Josepherta out of you. You're Jo. You can do this. You have to." Kate turned and ran down the hall and disappeared into the stairwell.

Jo took a deep breath and walked back to Jerry and Ron. "Kate had to step out for a moment." They both turned and stared at her in disbelief.

Ron stepped up in Jo's face. "She better step back in. What

the hell was she doing with my father? It's kind of funny that I don't hear shit from him for thirty years. Then, as soon as I'm defending a million-dollar case, he shows up on the plaintiff's team."

"Wait just a minute, Ron," Jerry straightened up and his voice dropped a bit to his trial voice. "I hope you're not implying there was some kind of collusion here. If anything, I should be the one upset that someone on the defense had a deal with my jury consultant. Isn't that what he said?"

Ron eyes narrowed as he took a step forward. Things were getting out of control. For a second, Jo thought it might be good if they came to blows. The judge would have to stop the trial and everything would come out. The publicity would be brutal, not only for Kate, but for Ron and Jerry, too. On the positive side, she wouldn't have to pick the jury.

Suddenly, she saw an out. "Look, guys, there's no collusion going on here. Ron, Boris apparently doesn't know anything about you and he certainly doesn't know anything about how you're going to present your case. Jerry, you're talking about Kate. How long have you two worked together? You know she wouldn't screw over her favorite client."

Both of them looked at her doubtfully, but they didn't interrupt. "So, there's no collusion or anything like that." She paused, then dove in. "The problem is that there is kind of a stink about this thing. It's the kind of thing that may cast a pall over the whole trial. Whoever wins, he can't feel that good about keeping the verdict on appeal. We may be back here doing this all again."

Jo looked at Ron. He was the one she would have to swing. Delay only helps the defense; the longer they can go without paying, the better. Ron crossed his arms in front of his chest. Classic protective position. For whatever reason, he was worried about a retrial. She pushed on.

"You know, this case always seemed as if it should have settled a long time ago. Why don't I go tell the judge that you two are engaged in serious settlement talks?" Before either one could say anything, she ran out of the room.

Jo ducked her head in the courtroom and saw the judge's clerk filling a glass of water at the witness chair. "I think it may settle," she yelled into the courtroom and then pulled her head back before anyone could ask any questions. She flew down the stairs and ran to her car.

Great, now what? Kate had gone after Boris who probably was headed to Townsend. Kate had described Boris's hideout as old and warehousey. Around downtown, there were two main areas with old warehouses. One had recently undergone a revitalization into art galleries and hip restaurants. That didn't sound like a good hideout place. She headed toward the Bottoms, where a bunch of old buildings had been turned into haunted houses.

"What am I doing?" she cried. She should have stayed at the courthouse like Kate said. If Jerry and Ron could not reach a settlement, then they would pick a jury. Jerry had not taken any notes on the jurors, figuring his two jury consultants would take care of that. Now he had no notes, no consultants and no way to pick a jury better than pulling names out of a hat. Jo tried to convince herself that she had urged the settlement because it was best for both parties. But she had been scared. She could not do the job and passed the buck. Same old Josepherta.

About two blocks from the warehouse district, a large Suburban passed her on the right. Jo glanced over at the driver—a giant Hawaiian man. She remembered Kate saying the large man who attacked her had gotten into a Suburban. Plus, that Hawaiian had tried to attack Kate at the office.

Jo slowed down and fell in about a block behind the Suburban. She looked around to see if someone was following the truck. No one seemed to be.

Ten minutes later the Suburban pulled into a parking lot of an old coffee warehouse with Tomb of Doom printed on a banner above the door. Jo pulled to the curb next to a large shed, just out of sight of the lot.

She peered around the corner of the metal shed and saw the Hawaiian walk into the building. Kate's car sat next to Dr. Greene's Camry. Jo called the police and told them there was a gang fight at the Tomb of Doom. She knew she should sit behind the building and wait for the police, but she had to know what was going on.

Now, inside, she realized she had only a few minutes before Duke the Giant Hawaiian killed Kate and Townsend. She eyeballed it to be about twenty feet from the hole to Duke. Even assuming she could do something if she reached the giant, Boris would see her as soon as she came out of the hole. The Hawaiian would have a clean shot. She needed to focus their attention on the other side of the room.

She snuck out to her car and got the boom box she used when she taught aerobics. The CD player was top of the line and had a remote. She liked to adjust the volume during the sessions, depending on what song was playing.

Sneaking back in, she held her breath as she crossed the hole. Boris did not see her, or at least did not stop talking.

"I'm just saying if you kill three and leave one alive, that's really as much of a problem for you as it is for me. You can't leave any witnesses, isn't that some sort of criminal mantra?"

Jo made it to what she judged to be the other side of the room from the maze. She put down the boom box and snuck back to the hole. Now she had to wait for the right moment. As she kneeled there, the Josepherta voice started again.

Out of the frying pan and into the fire. From a situation where she was underqualified to one where she was completely unqualified. Two men out there, one huge, both probably armed and she was going to take them out. Ha! She had not been in a fight since Wendy Barrett kicked her ass on the bus in the eighth grade. Self-defense classes are great when you are in a gym and you are fighting Chuck the inanimate attack dummy. These guys were real and mean and had guns. She was going to die and get Kate and Townsend killed in the bargain.

Jo closed her eyes and screamed in her head. I am Jo. I am not a Josepherta. I am Jo. *I am Jo. I. Am. Jo.*

She opened her eyes just as Duke and Boris reached an agreement.

"So, I do all of them and we go together, tonight, and get the thirty grand. If you fuck with me, I will make your last hours on Earth worse than you can imagine."

"Deal."

Duke turned from Boris. He aimed both guns at the boys. Jo hit the remote on the box and a reggae drum beat blared out into the room. Duke jerked the guns toward the noise and fired several rounds. He had aimed chest high and the music still roared into the room.

Jo sprinted toward the Hawaiian. Boris had also turned toward the noise and, too late, saw Jo barreling across the room.

Jo ran full speed and jumped as Duke started to turn back. In the air, she kicked out both legs, striking the big man square at the back of the knees. He grunted as legs collapsed under him. As he went down, the boys charged him, T.J. pushing Boris down as they ran past.

Duke was stunned. He got to his knees and was looking around trying to see what had hit him when T.J. kicked him in the ear. Blood splattered out of Duke's mouth onto Jo who was trying to wrench one of the guns out of his hands. Randy jumped onto the Hawaiian's back and repeatedly punched him on the back of the head. T.J.'s blow had loosened Duke's grip on the gun and Jo jerked it free. Still on his knees, Duke swung up with his other hand, pistol-whipping Jo on the side of the head. She went down in a heap.

Duke was powerful, but slow. Swinging to hit Jo had moved him off-balance. T.J. stepped up and kicked him square in the temple. He fell face first to the floor.

T.J. stepped up to kick him again, but Duke had no fight left in him. Randy, however, continued to rain down blows on his head. T.J. moved to stop him, but didn't. He noticed what could only be called a rhythm to Randy's shots. T.J. listened to the drum beat still blaring in the background and he was certain Randy was hitting Duke in perfect time to the beat.

Randy remained oblivious to his newfound ability and continued to swing even as T.J. pulled him off. He only came out of his trance when Kate yelled at them.

"Get me out of this." She strained against the tape. T.J. pulled out a pocket knife and cut her free.

Kate stood up and pointed to Duke. "Watch him." She ran over to Jo. "Are you okay?"

"Uuggh. I should have parried," Jo groaned. "I'm fine." She sat up. "Where's Boris?"

Everyone looked around. The little bastard had run away. Jo picked up the gun and shook it at T.J. "Here, go get Boris."

Kate grabbed the gun from Jo. "Call the police," she said as she ran through the door into the Haunted House.

Chapter 36

Sometimes, emotional commitment to a case may cause an attorney to lose his composure. It is the trial consultant's job to control the situation and restore calm.

Greene, F. (2003). *The Trial Consultant's Field Manual* (p. 3). New York: Pullman.

Kate stepped through the door into total darkness. She felt around the wall and found a light switch. She flicked it and groaned. Black light. And a cemetery. Headstones stood sporadically over some sort of undulating surface. The white writing on the markers shone brightly in the black light, giving some illumination. Mannequins rose out of several of the graves and into Kate's peripheral vision.

She stood perfectly still. Only the mutterings of Jo and T.J. filtered in from the other room. Then, a slight rustle from somewhere in front of her.

"I know you're here, Boris. There's only one exit and you can't get by me." Nothing. Kate aimed at a mannequin head twenty feet in front of her. When she pulled the trigger, the gun jumped in her hand. The sound crashed in her ears as dust flew up five feet to the right of the undisturbed mannequin head.

Boris jumped up from behind a tombstone to her left. He ran to the door on the other side of the room.

"Hold it," Kate screamed.

Boris opened the door and ran through it.

"Shit," Kate said under her breath.

Daylight streamed from a broken-out window near the ceiling. The room had a Dracula's lair décor. A large black coffin sat on a dais surrounded by a red carpet stamped with pentacles.

"Please don't be in the coffin. Please don't be in the coffin." Kate crept toward the coffin, holding the gun out in front of her like a protective cross.

Behind her she heard clanking. She turned and saw Boris climbing a narrow spiral staircase to a catwalk that ran high above the room. She breathed a sigh of relief as she turned away from the coffin.

She ran over to the stairs. In her limited haunted house experience, they all had a slide at the end of the tour. Whatever the theme, whatever rooms you had to go through, at the end, you slid down a slide filled with goo and grabby hands until you popped out by an exit. An exit, Kate thought, nowhere near Jo and the boys. Kate hurried up the stairs. She could not let him get to the slide.

When she reached the top, Boris hit her square in the jaw. She recoiled from the blow, reflexively pulling the trigger of the gun and shooting Boris in the foot.

"Son of a bitch!" He limped around in a small circle, then looked up at Kate. "You shot me. Right in the foot."

"I'm sorry. I'm sorry," she cried instinctively. Before she could wonder why she was apologizing to this maniac, he punched her again, this time standing away from the gun.

"You've got to be kidding me," she moaned, bending over and holding her jaw. When she looked up, Boris was scuttling down the catwalk.

"Freeze!" Kate cried, trying to sound police-womanish. She bent her knees and held the gun with two hands like she'd seen Angie Dickinson do. Boris kept on scuttling.

She closed her eyes and pulled the trigger. She heard a

window break and opened her eyes. Boris stopped and turned around. "You know you might actually hit me if you keep shooting."

"That's the idea."

"I don't think so. The only time you came close to hitting me you didn't even mean to shoot."

Boris had reached to the end of the catwalk. The slide started right behind him. A huge, green papier-mâché snake's head surrounded the entrance. Boris slowly started walking toward Kate. "I don't think you can look a man in the eye and kill him."

Kate wanted him to be wrong, but he was not. She had heard shooting a gun caused an adrenaline rush. For her, shooting Boris in the foot had caused a nausea rush. As he walked up to her, smiling his oily smile, she knew she could never shoot him with the gun.

She could, however, whack him in the head with it. As Boris reached to take the gun away from her, she pulled it back and cracked him square on the nose.

"Ugh," Boris grunted as he stumbled back and fell head first down the slide. And he was gone.

Kate ran up and peered down the slide. It curved around into darkness. By the time she ran back down the catwalk and the stairs, through the Dracula room and the cemetery, got the others and found the slide exit, Boris would be halfway to Iowa. On the plus side, she would not have to go down a curvy slide into the scary darkness.

She took a deep breath and jumped feet first on the slide. She had hoped it might be one of those sticky slides, but as she sped down the slide, Kate thought someone must have greased it. Seventy percent fault to the slide greaser.

The tight turns kept her from seeing anything more than a few feet ahead. A blockage in the middle of the slide appeared just before she hit it. At the moment she made contact she realized it was Boris. Somehow he had turned and stopped.

Kate hit him square in the crotch doing about 30 miles an hour. Boris's legs popped up and he tumbled on top of her. When Boris did not grunt or react, she figured the gun blow must have knocked him out.

For what seemed like minutes, Kate slid down the tunnel face-to-face with the man who had tormented her for the past two weeks. At last, they shot out into a pile of foam.

Someone shouted, "Freeze."

"Get him off me!" Kate screamed, pushing at Boris. With only foam beneath her, she sunk down into the pit. Boris barely moved.

Finally, a police officer pulled Boris off her and handcuffed him. Another officer stretched out a hand to help Kate out. Jo and the boys stood with two officers. As she wiggled her way off the foam pad, Boris came to.

He squinted through the blood dripping from his forehead at the cops standing over him. "What a shitty day this turned out to be."

Chapter 37

Ron sat nervously in what he guessed was a parlor. He had never lived in anything larger than a two-bedroom apartment. Stiltson Manor was a bona fide mansion. Elsie had told him to go into this little room off the foyer. Looking around, he felt like he had stumbled on the set of the *Beverly Hillbillies.*

He was still a little shaken from meeting his father. They had charged Boris with attempted murder, kidnapping and, from what Ron had heard, just about everything. All those years creating fantasies about what kind of man his father was, and it turned out he was a lunatic. Ron thought about the silly dreams he used to have. He had never picked those dreams apart as an adult and so they had stayed in his subconscious, frozen with a child's innocence intact. His father as a world traveler. His father as an ambassador to another country. Every fantasy protected him from the idea that his father chose not to be with him.

In the end, that's what pulled Ron to the jail to see him. To ask the question, "Why didn't you love us enough to stay? Why couldn't you love me?" In the years when Ron still thought about his father, and fantasized about him returning, he never had to ask the question. The answer was always apparent. Boris had just returned from outer space or a Vietnam prison camp. Now Ron had to ask.

He was shocked at the cleanliness of the jail. He had imagined it something like the monkey house at the zoo with inmates throwing feces around at each other. To the contrary, most of the inmates passed the time mopping. The jail was depressing and sad, but clean.

Ron also mistakenly believed that there would be a thick piece of bulletproof glass between him and Boris and that they would probably have to talk through a phone. When he walked into the room and saw Boris sitting at a table in the middle of the room, he stepped back. A large guard blocked his path out of the room.

Boris looked up, "Hello, Ron."

"Hello . . . Boris." Ron did not know what to call him.

They sat quiet for a moment, neither looking at the other. Boris broke the silence. "Thanks for coming down. It means a lot to me."

Ron stared out a barred window high on the wall, then looked over at Boris. "Where have you been? Did Mom do something?" Ron threw the last line in as a trap. If this son of a bitch blamed his mother for his absence, Ron could hate him with impunity.

Boris's eyes flashed and he rose up, reaching across the table and slapping Ron hard across the face. "Don't you dare blame your mother for this." The guard at the door shouted into the radio on his shoulder and ran over to Boris. Horror crept over Boris's face as he realized what he had done.

"It's all right, officer," Ron said, although his eyes watered from the sting of the blow. "I'm fine."

The guard pulled Boris's arms back. "No, it's not. It's far from all right. You can press charges or not, that's up to you, but this visitation is over." He handcuffed Boris and pulled him up out of the chair. Boris looked back apologetically as the guard hauled him toward the door.

Ron stood up. "What happened? Why didn't you come back?"

Boris met his eyes for a moment and then turned his head as the guard took him out of the room. Ron sat quiet for a moment, until another guard came to escort him out. Maybe that was for the best. It did not matter why Boris left or why he did not come back. Ron's mother had been his parents, mother and father. Nothing Boris would have said would change that. The fantasy of the perfect dad was dead. Ron decided to let it lie.

Part of the deal with Elsie was that, if he met with Boris, she would meet with Maynard. About an hour after she put him in the parlor, Elsie came into the room with her father.

"Ron, this is Maynard Stiltson. Daddy, this is Ron Tittleton."

Stiltson crossed the room, hand outstretched. "Mr. Tittleton, nice to meet you. I'm sorry you've been sitting out here for so long. My daughter didn't tell me she'd brought a guest." His voice had a strong Ozarky twang.

"Please, Mr. Stiltson, call me Ron."

"Very good, Ron. Come on back to the sitting room. It's more comfortable back there." He turned around and walked out of the room. Elsie gave Ron a hopeful half-smile.

Ron followed them down a little hallway, which opened into a huge room. The entire back wall was glass, giving a spectacular view of the meticulously landscaped back yard. A fire roared in the yellow stone fireplace on the opposite wall. Ron sat down next to Elsie on a very modern, very uncomfortable black leather couch.

"Can I get you a drink?" Stiltson asked as he sat down in a brown recliner that matched none of the high-end décor.

"No, sir, I'm fine, thank you."

"I understand you're to blame for my little girl finding out about the trust fund her mother set up for her?"

"Daddy," Elsie said, sounding very much like a whiny teenager.

"Oh, I'm just kidding him," Stiltson said, waving his hand. He did not look like he was kidding. He looked pissed.

"It was her mother's idea to keep it from her. Wendy came from old pickle money. Those pickle people are a strange breed. She said no one in the family ever got a dime of the pickle money until their thirtieth birthday. It's supposed to let the kids develop into adults before finding out they have millions. She wanted Elsie to have some sense of independence."

Ron smiled at her. "I think that part worked out pretty well, sir."

Stiltson chuckled. "Maybe a little too good, eh? What I don't get is how you got them to wait two years until Elsie gets control of the trust? When people sue me, they never want to wait a day to get their money, let alone a couple of years."

"They were pretty ready to settle. Beckwith's attorney wasn't all sold on the case. He thought they might get something, but he was worried the jurors would like Elsie. Plus, if we had gone to trial, with the appeals and everything, it still would have been a couple of years before they ever saw one dollar. Once we showed them the trust documents and drew up something ironclad, they were ready to sign."

Stiltson harrumphed. "Very clever. I hope Tonetti puts some of that cleverness to work on some of my other cases."

"Well, sir, they fired me. So I don't think I'll be working on any Stiltson stuff. At least not Stiltson Mustard work." He smiled over at Elsie. She kept her eyes on her father, but a smile crept onto her lips.

"What?" Stiltson sat up in his chair. "Tonetti fired you? Over this case?" He looked over at Elsie. "Consider yourself unfired. I'll call him tomorrow first thing."

"That's okay, sir. I probably would have left anyway. It wasn't really the place for me. At least this way I get a severance package. I do appreciate the offer, though."

Stiltson leaned back in his chair. "I owe you one. Elsie tells me you're responsible for her coming here today."

Ron shook his head. "You don't owe me a thing, sir. That was Elsie's decision. We talked about it and she wanted to come."

"If it was as easy as that, she would have been here a long time ago. At any rate, let me give you a free business lesson, son. When a man like Maynard Stiltson says he owes you a favor, even if he really doesn't, you smile, put it in your back pocket and say, 'Thank you sir, I'll be in touch.' "

Ron raised his eyebrows at Elsie. She gave him a soft, knowing smile. Ron winked at her, turned back to the elder Stiltson and said, "Thank you, sir, I'll be in touch."

CHAPTER 38

The legal world is a small one. Adversaries often become allies.

Greene, F. (2003). *The Trial Consultant's Field Manual* (p. 366). New York: Pullman.

"Do you want another drink?!" Kurt yelled into Kate's ear. Kate held up her beer and nodded rather than try to be heard over the noise. The two weeks since the speed dating had been hectic, but Kate had still managed to find time to exchange e-mails with Kurt. *A girl's got to have her priorities. Six foot and charming is always at the top of the list.*

Kurt took two steps over to the bar and held up two fingers. With only six paying customers in the place, the bartender remembered their orders. Still, the bar was small enough that everyone sat practically shoulder-to-shoulder.

The band, Noxious Worm Food, played as if they were rocking an arena. Specializing in neo-punk, they emphasized angst over ability. All except the drummer, whose rhythmic, violent beats perfectly combined the two.

After eight ear-shattering songs, the band took a break. As he stepped out from behind the drum set, Randy ripped something off his ears and walked over to the bar to order a beer with the band. It took the group at the table a few minutes to get their hearing back.

"Kate," Jo said, "what happened with the Wrenshaw trial?"

Townsend had given everyone two weeks' paid leave. While he was shackled to the table, he had run though several different coed/vacation possibilities if he made it out alive. He had settled on Betty in Bermuda. Jo and Kate had stayed in town, but away from the office.

"I told you about the chicken Caesar salad thing, right?" Kate asked. Jo nodded. "Turns out the jury chaos theory fell totally apart. They loved each other. It was all these misfits society had crapped on. They understood each other. Even the normal people, in the culture the jury created, were misfits for not being misfits."

"I'm sorry," Jo said, scrunching her face up.

"No, it turned out great. Not only did they bond with each other, they felt sorry for Rick. Being so short and picked on all his life, they figured when Pike called him out, he snapped. They understood that. They only found him guilty of voluntary manslaughter."

Jo raised her glass. "To voluntary manslaughter." Everyone raised their glasses and clinked.

"Is that good?" Kurt asked, taking a swig. "That doesn't sound good."

"He'll probably get twelve years or so. But it's certainly no death penalty."

Jo raised her glass again. "To twelve years in prison." No one clinked with her. "It's no death penalty," she added with enthusiasm, punching her glass into the air again. Reluctantly, the group clinked her glass.

Randy came over and sat down next to T.J. "So, what did you all think?"

"You were great," Kate said, still enjoying the blessed silence.

"You really kept everyone together," Jo gushed.

"Man, you guys are loud," T.J. said. "You know there's like six people in here. Do you really need amplifiers?"

Randy shrugged. "Beetle says it gives us veritas, or gravitas, or some kind of tas. I don't know." He turned to Kate. "Did it really sound good? I felt like I was really on."

"Oh, you were," Kate said.

Kurt pointed toward the stage. "What was that thing you pulled out of your ear? Is that some sort of monitor?"

"No, it's a battery cable. I need the pain to keep me focused."

Everyone but T.J. gasped. Randy laughed.

"No, it's fine. When I was pounding on that big Hawaiian dude, I got lost in my anger, man. I was so mad all I could think about was the hate, you know. But T.J. says I was in perfect rhythm." T.J. nodded. "I guess I always had a beat in me. I wanted it so bad that I kind of got in my own way. So, if I block everything out, I can really drum.

"I'm still working on it, though. I can't get really angry all the time, so I have to use the battery cables to give me pain. It's getting better though. I've got it dialed down halfway now."

"Great," Kurt said and rolled his eyes at Kate.

Randy ignored him. "Thanks for coming out tonight. It really means a lot."

T.J. put his arm around Jo. "I'm just glad we can go somewhere without me getting beat up."

"You were getting into fights?" Kate asked, raising her eyebrows at Jo.

"We weren't starting them," said T.J.

Jo smiled sheepishly. "It was my black eye. From when the Hawaiian hit me. Everyone thought T.J. was smacking me around."

T.J. nodded. "Those anti-violence folks can get pretty rough."

Kate smirked at Jo.

Jo glanced over at her and smiled. "What? You got a problem?"

"So you two are an item now?"

"I wouldn't say an item, really. I've been helping him and

Randy get ready to testify against Boris."

"Wow, when's that?" Kurt asked

Randy shrugged. "I don't know. They said they wouldn't charge us because of what Kate told them. But we have to testify about the whole thing. We're going to sound like the biggest morons in the world saying we thought he was the Devil."

"Jo's been great, though," T.J. said as he smiled over at her.

"So it's all business, huh?" Kate asked, her eyes narrowed.

Jo leaned to the side and looked T.J. up and down. He stared back at her nervously. "I suppose we've been enjoying each other's company."

"You're kind of robbing the cradle a little, don't you think?"

"Ho!" Kurt said, turning toward the stage. He glanced back over his shoulder.

"I'm twenty-one," T.J. said, although he realized how young it sounded as soon as he said it.

"At least I can dance with my date without worrying about him throwing out his back," Jo said, laughing.

"Hey," Kurt said, "what'd I do?"

"Oh, you don't want to get on my bad side, man. I'm just telling you."

Kate rolled her eyes. "Yeah, you don't want to mess with Josepherta when she gets angry."

Everyone laughed but T.J. He looked over at Jo and asked, "Is your name really Josepherta?"

Jo raised her arms above her head. "I'm Jo, baby, and I'm in da house."

ABOUT THE AUTHOR

Korey Kaul is a public defender living in Lawrence, Kansas, with his wife Lisa and their two children.